Barnyards, Barefeet and Bluejeans

A Horse's Tale

By Allen A. Mills, Jr.

SHIRES PRESS

4869 Main Street
P.O. Box 2200
Manchester Center, VT 05255
www.northshire.com

Barnyards, Barefeet and Bluejeans
A Horse's Tale

ISBN Number: 978-1-60571-431-8

Building Community, One Book at a Time
*A family-owned, independent bookstore in
Manchester Ctr., VT, since 1976 and Saratoga Springs, NY since 2013.
We are committed to excellence in bookselling.
The Northshire Bookstore's mission is to serve as a resource for
information, ideas, and entertainment while honoring the needs of
customers, staff, and community.*

Printed in the United States of America

Dedication

Courage:
Lynne Smith Washburn: *a whirl-of-mirth-girl*

Example:
Allen Austin Mills, Sr.: *as a boy I tried to walk in the huge shadow he cast and always said: " Lord, let me be like him." Now as a grown man, I walk in his valley, and when the shadow of a cloud passes over me I still say those words: "Lord, let me be like him."*

Love:
Ferne Spaulding Mills: *her love was her greatest gift and she shared her love and generosity of spirit to every being she encountered; human or animal. You never felt judged by her. She accepted you as she found you.   You could not find a better listener. She gave everyone the gift of herself. No one ever left her kitchen hungry, and never left the farm without having felt the kindness of this beautiful woman.*

* * * * * * * * * * * * * * * * *

For my daughters and Ian and Carson

Introduction

To begin, let me tell you about a very special animal whose spirit put this story all together. You can't grow up on a farm with all these animals without feeling this very special connection and here we were blessed.

We humans with our inhibitions of science and knowledge, try to reason our way through life's experiences. In doing this, I feel we truly miss what connects us to each other, the animals, plants and the earth itself.

The dictionary defines "Horse" as a solid-hoofed, herbivorous, quadruped; domesticated as a draft or riding animal. What a shallow definition for such a magnificent creature!

Have you ever stood close to a horse with your hand on his neck and heard his soft murmurs, or felt the pulse of blood being pumped through his body, or the quiver of his skin under your touch? Have you ever really looked into a horse's eyes? They seem to draw you into a very understanding and loving place. If you have, you have been blessed. If you haven't, you truly need to be and to experience this unique communication between a human and an animal.

Since ancient times, horses have carried humans on their backs in racing for sport; giving all they had. In their centuries-long history, horses have also carried our soldiers into battle, fighting and dying in our wars. Horses were essential in pulling the wagons and supplies for settlers as new territories were explored. Only in relatively recent times has the horse ceased to be an essential and daily part of human life.

Oh, Brud! Enough of this horse crap. How you can rant when you get going!

That's Dick, who was once my family's work horse. From his unique perspective, he will be telling this story. A story about a farm tucked into a beautiful valley in Vermont. And a story about one very special couple and the family they raised on the farm during roughly the years spanning 1947 to 1963. This was a time before the modern machines that we use today were widely available. So, a good working team of horses was crucial in the work of a farm.

So, let's get this magnificent horse unhitched so he can put his hooves up a bit and tell you about his life on the farm, and all the interesting animals and people who came there. To live, work, grow and play. Listen to, read and enjoy these stories as Dick, the Work-Horse tells them. Straight from the horse's mouth you might say.

Contents

Early Farming

First, let me begin by describing myself so that you will know me and who I am. In describing myself, you may think I am being boastful and self-centered; but with us animals, we think differently than you humans; we are who we are and feel self-pride is a good thing.

I was a young, handsome, intelligent, horse with huge equine muscles that rippled under my coat of pure white. My base coat sported small, blue dapples, which as I grew older, changed to a reddish-brown. At first, I wasn't sure that I liked this change in my appearance until I noticed that my dapples looked like the freckles that dotted the nose and cheeks of all the Mills children.

I was an extremely strong Work Horse. That is what the farmer that I worked with called me. He named me: Dick. He did not use the term Draft Horse as this seemed to him probably too sophisticated and not truly purposeful. Work Horse was more appropriate and less distracting.

The farmer, Allen Mills, was a very strong, practical thinking, hard-working man who always accomplished what he started and did it the right way. I feel our personalities were a lot alike and together and we accomplished great things. I could always count on him to be right behind me; with a strong hand guiding me in just the right way and making the work as easy for us as he could. Sometimes, as I would be gazing at the beauty of the valley where I worked, Allen would shout my name along with another word that his children had learned in Sunday school that they were not supposed to use in vain. I had to let them know that the way he used it was not in vain, but only to get my and their attention.

The farmer's wife and partner in the business of farming, Ferne, was a most loving and kind woman. She taught me to love and care for all people and animals who came to the farm. I can remember standing in my favorite spot under the huge oak tree that grows in my pasture just a little way behind the barn. From here, I can watch most of my beautiful valley farm and all that happens here. As I watched from my spot under the oak tree, I saw Ferne come out onto the open walkway that connected the farm house to the woodshed. The woodshed was a fairly large building, in terms of sheds. It contained all the wood needed to feed the pot-bellied stove that heated the entire house in the coldest winters and the wood needed to fuel the cook stove in the kitchen where Ferne prepared all the food needed to feed her growing family and anyone else who stopped by. No creature, human or animal, ever left the farm hungry.

As I stood watching, Ferne held out her hand. The palm of her hand contained bird seed; she stood there, patiently waiting as chickadees soon started to gather. The little birds, sensing no danger, soon started landing on her hand and began to eat the seeds.
It was then that I knew what a special lady she was and what kind of horse I had to become.

* * * * * * * * * * * * * * * *

There were many animals who lived on the farm with me. The noisy chickens with their constant cackling and the stupid rooster who would crow every morning; often waking me as I slept peacefully in my stall. There were honking geese, the worthless Billy goat, and the smelly pigs. There were also two dogs, both mongrels. One is Tippy, a little cream-colored rascal. He is mostly a House Dog, too cute for his own good and he seems to think he is lord of the whole place. Our other dog was a reddish colored dog called King, He was inappropriately named as he was a rather homely fellow and not royal looking at all. The dogs only purpose seemed to be mischief and mayhem. Unfortunately, this behavior caused Tippy to be badly injured and forever after traveled on three legs.

While chasing a cat, Tip fell off the manure chute, hanging by one leg until Ferne, hearing his cries of pain and distress rescued him and nursed him back to health.

Tippy after wading in the gully.

There were plenty of cats to be chased and, at times, there were too many of them. I had to be careful not to step on them as they lurked and prowled around hunting mice. They didn't seem to be very good "mousers "as the term goes, probably because they were too lazy and were fed regularly in the barn. So there always seemed to be a thieving little mouse scurrying around trying to steal my grain.

We also had many cows on the farm. They took a lot of my patience and understanding. These huge, bawling, glutinous creatures seemed to just awkwardly amble around in the pastures. Hanging out in the lower level of the barn, and they were constantly eating. The cows demanded more and more while giving nothing in return except a great deal of work for Allen, Ferne, the family and me. As I think of it, though, in this was the cows' real worth. The work brought us all together – Family, Farm and Animals on our Whipple Hollow Farm. Now I must tell you about the children. Oh, how I loved them! Nothing in my life did I enjoy more than their attention. They would caress my long white mane and tail, and their gentle little hands patting my powerful legs and flanks, for this is as high up on me as most of those wonderful little people could reach. The Mills children were often joined by many other children, friends, cousins and Fresh Air Kids (as they were called) and foster children. They all adored one magnificent animal creature, Me – Dick, The Work Horse! Now do you wonder why I feel a bit of justified conceit? Along with this adoration, I knew, came a lot of responsibility and that I had to always be a good example to these special children.

The Work Team
&
My Many Partners

*S*ome of the work that I did on the farm I did by myself if the equipment was light enough and could be handled better by one horse. I was always chosen to work singly when the need arose because of my great strength and ease of control. When the work was more difficult and needed more horse power (yes, a little more corn, please) a second horse was added to work beside me. We were called a Work Team and I had many different team mates over the years, but none were as strong and beautiful as I was. And none of them became a part of the family in the way that I did.

My first partner was a big, white horse named Bill. He was quite a bit older than me. I don't remember too much about his personality. I was young and quite self-involved, the way that most of us are in our youth. I was also very busy learning all the different jobs and commands along with getting used to all the equipment. I remember that Bill and I were nearly evenly matched in size, strength, and color and I must say we looked and worked well together.

My next partner was a big black mare named Dolly. Her most prominent trait was that she was extremely lazy. I can remember many times when pulling seemed unusually hard for the size of the load, Allen would suddenly holler at

11

her: "Get up there Dolly, stop walking in the traces!". This scolding usually began and ended with Allen yelling angrily one or two of those words that the kids had learned in Sunday school that they were not supposed to use. Dolly got quite overweight because she was always eating and not working any harder than she absolutely had to. Allen said that because of her huge weight, she was great at holding back the load while going downhill.

I laugh, a big horse laugh, (more corn) when I think about the time when two of the kids, Ferne Marie and Brud were allowed to ride on our backs as we were coming back from the North Meadow. As Allen drove us, the kids sat on our backs. Brud was a short, kind of pudgy, little fellow. His short legs didn't even begin to reach over the sides of Dolly's huge back. The little fellow clung desperately to hide, hair, and the leather straps of the harness. His short, little arms couldn't reach the hames. He slipped from side to side. Sometimes, Ferne Marie would give her little brother a small shove when he slipped to her side. All the rest of the family laughed, including myself, as we watched the performance.

My next partner was little Danny. He was much smaller than me. He was so much smaller that Allen had to add lengths to his trace chains so that we would pull evenly. What Danny lacked in size, he made up for it with his strength and eagerness. He was nervous and fidgety and loved to run. These characteristics don't serve very well in a work team. I can recall many times, even in our own pasture, when Danny would just take off running most likely having been spooked by a chipmunk or toad.

One cool and cloudy spring morning we were working in the South Meadow or the Flat Meadow [as the family called it] under a sky that promised rain. Allen was smooth-harrowing the field. This is the final step before seeding. Allen wanted to get all the ground seeded that he could before the rain came. A farmer must work with nature and in our part of the country we are no strangers to rain and snow.

Danny and I stood with Ferne holding the reins. She was on our left side while we waited patiently for Allen. Danny and I were hitched up to the seeder or grain drill. It was a noisy, rattling, grinding machine which made many strange sounds as it traveled over the ground doing its work. I stood, waiting patiently, as Danny fidgeted and rubbed back and forth beside me. Somehow, Danny managed to get his bridle caught on my hame strap. His bridle came off. This sudden feeling of freedom was enough to make Danny run and I felt I had no choice other than to run with him. Poor Ferne hung on desperately to the now useless reins as she was dragged on her stomach through the soft, dusty dirt. Allen saw what was happening and leaped from his little grey tractor [which I'll tell you more about later]. As Allen ran trying to cut us off and stop us, he was yelling to Ferne, "Let them go! Let them go!" He feared she would be hurt, if she wasn't already. His yelling then changed to "Whoa! Whoa!" followed by some more of those words banned at Sunday school.

Allen managed to catch us just as we were about to go over the stone wall and surely wreck the machine. He grabbed my bridle on my off side and pulled us into a circle. Seeing Allen there, I knew everything was under control again, so I stopped, along with Danny and the seeder.

Danny's nervousness brought about his tragic and abrupt death. We were in the upper end of the barn yard. Something frightened Danny. He reared high on his back legs, pawing frantically with his front legs. He could not control his loss of balance and fell right over backwards, striking his head on a large rock. Poor Danny died instantly. I miss my eager little pal, even his nervousness.

It was the busy summer haying season when Danny died. With not much time to mourn, Allen had to find another horse to work with me and we needed him. Now. Jim Harrison, a neighbor, had a big white work horse called Gus. Allen borrowed Gus until he could find a permanent replacement to work with me. Gus had been a logging horse. He was a good worker, but didn't care much about his appearance, so he never looked groomed and was always dirty. I suppose if you spent most of your time in the woods, you wouldn't much care about how you look, either. I, on the other hand, was just like Allen. Although we worked hard all day and might get a little sweaty, we wouldn't be dirty and we kept ourselves neat.

In the autumn of that same year, Allen found Roany. She was a big, Strawberry- Roan, Mare with a black mane and tail. She had one enchanting "Watch Eye". She was a little stocky but very strong. A real pretty Work Horse, mare. Roany was intelligent, strong, gentle and graceful. Though she was a horse of a different color, (sorry some more corn) we made a terrific match. Allen finally, had a great Work Team. We became great friends and truly loved each other. Roany loved me with all her heart. She would always work a little harder than she should have just trying to make it easier for me. I was a gelding, and she was a mare. It was hard for her to understand my total devotion to the farm, family and purpose of work. On our farm, Roany learned that the love of a true friendship where two horses loved, respected and cooperated with each other and shared work and purpose was the best love of all, for these are the seeds from which true love grows. Roany and I thought: What if all humans knew to start their relationships this way?

Roany and I knew that Allen and Ferne knew this way of living too. We knew this farm to be truly a place of growth and love. As I stand under my oak tree, I watch seasons change; plants sprouting from the earth; the animals

14

that come and the ones that go; and my beloved children. All flourishing here in my beautiful, secluded Whipple Hollow Farm.

Roany was my best team mate. One day, as were leaving the barn to go out into the pasture, Roany's huge loving heart just stopped. My beautiful Roany died right in the doorway of the barn. I had lost her; my best friend. I will remember her always. In life, as in farming, there are times of growth and times of loss. A time of purpose and then a time of dying...those we love live in our hearts always and are not forgotten.

As it turned out, I never worked in tandem with another horse again. I guess Allen and I knew there would never be another Work Team that was as good a fit as Roany and me. I work well singly though and was quite happy working with Allen. We were alike in many ways; kindred spirits.

VLM 2016

Oh, there was another horse that came and visited the farm often. How could I have almost forgotten Mary! She was a wise old mare. She was full of fun and had plenty of horse

15

tales (sorry but I do love corn). Mary and Harley (the man she worked with who was Allen's father) were just as much alike as Allen and I were.

Mary lived with Harley on a little farm just over the hill from our farm. I have seen the old house where Harley lived while haying the steep sidehill meadow just south of the house. I always enjoyed seeing what a great view it was from up there. The work was always good there except for the dreaded "Devil's Pocket". While we were working the meadow one day, a neighbor said to Allen, "Oh God! The Devil's Pocket is so steep there that you could tip over "even usin' a hand scythe!"

Harley had a barn that stood just north of the small orchard that was next to the house. The barn was built right on the town line between West Rutland and Pittsford. Harley only had two milk cows, but he would say that he started his milking in West Rutland and keep right on milking until he finished in Pittsford.

Harley often hitched Mary to a buggy, which is a small, light-weight, four-wheeled wagon designed to be pulled by one horse. It had one bench seat and a small space behind the seat to carry various items. Harley would hitch Mary up to the buggy and head over the hill to visit our farm. I can remember how excited the family and I would get when we saw Harley and Mary coming. The children would run to meet them because the faster they ran, the longer the ride, back to the house. They would get quite a ride as dear old Mary only had one slow gait. It would most accurately be described as a "plod". Harley would stop Mary and the buggy and the kids would climb aboard. Two kids would sit on the seat beside Harley and he usually let one of them drive Mary. It isn't as if she really needed the control of a driver anyway. The other two kids would ride on the shelf behind the seat. Often times, a couple of cousins, Ron and Lynne Smith, and the Fresh Air boy, Mike Horan, would be squeezed in the buggy somewhere, too. Allen, Ferne and I would laugh when we saw them come plodding into the yard.

16

Mary, I am very sure, was quite a looker, during the early years of her life, though, I did not know her then. To me, she was a grand old mare; full of wisdom and funny stories. Her base coat, I'm sure people would describe as a Blood Bay. She had black points: mane, tail, feet and hocks. Most times her hind feet and hocks were spattered with a brown stain. This stain would come from a strange powdery substance that Harley ate. I guess he didn't like it much as it would make him spit. And unfortunately, he often missed his most likely spitting-target: the ground, because poor, old Mary's lower legs (or hocks), would be stained brown.

Harley and Mary: Raking Scatterings

arley was a real character. One-of-a-kind, in human terms. Harley had his own, personal sense of style. His pants were either dark blue, or green, work pants. His shirts were always either tan or light blue. He never wore a belt. Probably a belt was uncomfortable around his rather ample middle. He held his pants up with a pair of olive- green straps that had vertical blue stripes and buttoned to his pants - Gallus's as he called them. Over all of this he always wore his charcoal grey beach vest. On his feet, in colder weather, were brown, heeled boots. In warm weather, he always wore black, high-top sneakers. On his head was his signature grey felt hat. It was not dirty, but it was quite stained from decades of wear.

Harley had many pockets but only carried two essential items. I'm sorry, it was three items. He carried no money or wallet because where he went he had no need of them. One pocket contained his red handkerchief with white designs. He would pull it out with his own special flip ready for use. Another pocket contained a razor-sharp jack knife. He did not use his knife for carving as he felt that carving would take too much concentration. Whittling, it appeared, was its only use. As he whittled, all the children would be drawn like a magnet, one on his lap and the others sitting close around. They would be laughing at his jokes or listening with rapt attention to his stories. Allen cautioned the children that all of

18

Harley's wild tales might not be true, but they had to be true because he was Grampa Harl.

Harley kept a little yellow round can with a metal lid, in his right-hand pocket. The can held that strange, brown, powdery substance that he ate. I, also, found out that the powder was the reason for the very prevalent lump which appeared in his lower lip. He would take the can out of his pocket, tap it four times with his finger on the metal lid, open it and take a "pinch" as he called it, and stuff it between his teeth and lower lip. Soon, the foul substance would start to make him spit. We, horses, always found this a very strange thing to do.

I know that the powder was foul tasting because Brud told me. His youth and curiosity compelled him to ask for a taste of the powder. So, Harley figured that the best thing to do was to satisfy the boy's curiosity and gave him a pinch of the stuff to try. Bravely, Brud chewed up and swallowed the powder. Immediately, the powder caused terrible distress in his stomach. He ran to the back porch where he could expel the liquid. Amused, and perhaps hopeful that he had turned the boy away from this odd habit, Harley gave Brud a little square, green, mint candy; the only kind of candy that Harley ever kept. He knew the mint would relieve the boy's stomach distress as well as remove the foul taste. Brud's experiment with the mysterious powder was over for good.

While Harley was keeping the children spellbound with his stories and jokes, Mary would share with Roany and me some of her and Harley's experiences and adventures. They would take the buggy and go on long trips either north or south on the Whipple Hollow Road or up the Fire Hill Road. She told us that she had to always be well aware of where they were going as she never quite knew what Harley might do. One day they went north on Whipple Hollow Road then up the Fire Hill Road for about three miles where they stopped at Chet Henderson's house. Chet would make a beverage from apples (and various other ingredients) that Harley truly loved. They called it Hard Cider. Mary would stand for hours, waiting, and she'd often fall asleep between the fills of the buggy. Many hours would pass while Chet and Harley talked and drank the Hard Cider. Finally, Harley would come out of the house, walking a little strangely, towards the buggy. He would climb in and they would head home. Mary thought that the cider must have made Harley very tired as she felt the reins gently go slack and she realized Harley had fallen asleep. She was glad that she had remembered the route she and Harley had taken to get here. She would find their way back home.

Later that day as Allen drove by Harley's house with his motor car, he saw Mary standing outside the barn, still with the buggy hitched to her. Her head was in the open window of the barn and she stood there, peacefully eating hay, with Harley still asleep in the buggy. Allen stopped and helped Harley into the house since he was still walking a little strangely. After settling Harley in his house, Allen unhitched Mary from the buggy and fed her. He put the buggy back into the barn. And while Mary, Roany and I really liked apples, we tried never to eat too many after that. We couldn't help but wonder if too many apples or too much hard cider would have similar effects.

* * * * * * * * * * * * * * * *

During haying season, after the hay had been picked off the meadow and stowed in the barn, Allen always did an extra job which he called "Raking Scatterings". Many times, after the children had greeted Harley and Mary, Harley would hitch Mary to Allen's Yankee Dump Rake. Back and forth over the entire meadow they would travel gathering any loose straws that had been lost in the process of haying. After the rakefuls of scatterings were picked up, Allen's fields were the neatest fields in all of the Whipple Hollow Valley.

When Ferne Marie was a little older she did the raking and would always choose me to work with. I think because she considered me as her own personal horse and thinks of me as her handsome white Charger. I can be that even though I'm pulling a Yankee Rake and not her own personal jewel-encrusted chariot. As we worked Ferne Marie sang to me as we travel back and forth over the meadow gathering scattered hay. Roany says Brud does not sing when they rake but I'm sure that's just as well for her as we have both heard him sing and it is not really a pleasure.

* * * * * * * * * * * * * * * *

I'd like to tell you some more about the children now. I loved them all and was very glad to be a part of their family.

Ferne Marie was a lovely girl with long, beautiful curls. Her expression was typically "Very Serious" and may have been caused by her desire to do everything right, and the responsibility she took upon herself for taking care of her siblings. With her constant desire to learn and then to teach what she had learned, the children often played school whether they liked it or not.

Kathy, another beautiful girl, had a heart of gold. Often, I saw her with a bouquet of flowers in one hand or she'd be out on her swing with a pair of skinned knees.

Brud was probably clumsier than most boys. Allen would say he was as handy as a cub bear wearing boxing gloves. I think he was more curious than most, always poking into things to see what he could find, often trouble, sometimes bees.

Jan, such a cute little gal, dancing, always running (she had to keep up with the others) and bouncing like Tigger in pigtails. You would always find her on Allen's lap or by his knee.

Every summer, a boy named Mike Horan came to the farm. He was from a place that he called the Bronx in New York City. He had fire-red hair and more freckles than he had room to put them. Freed from the city, Mike would revel in the country and simply enjoy being a part of our family and working and living on a farm.

Often a strange, blue motor car would pull into the yard. It had DESOTO written on the front. It kind of frightened me because it had two huge lights that blinked like eyes. From out of this odd machine would emerge a cute, laughing whirl of mirth girl. Her name was Lynne Smith and she would be with her brother Ron, who was pure mischief in the shape of a boy. Ron and Lynne were cousins to the Mills children and their arrival meant fun for the children.

Animals on The Farm;
Roman Riding;
and Collie's Story

*T*he farm seemed to be in a constant stream of animals coming and going with various lengths of stay. The chickens were kept mostly in a room in the barn, separate from us horses. What a noisy group with their constant cackling! And I've mentioned that annoying rooster. He was always awake early and insisted that everyone else be as well. It was evident, by not only the words Ferne Marie used, but also by the huge club she carried whenever she entered their coop, that she took no pleasure in taking care of them.

We often had Bantam chickens that roamed freely about the farm. Their nests were often raided by the boys: Brud, Mike and Ron Smith. They would divide up what they found and along with our horse droppings use them to throw at each other for a little fun and excitement.

There was an occasional duck but very few as there was no close water source for them to get into aside from our watering trough. Allen and Ferne knew I wouldn't tolerate that.

One thing I almost forgot about the chickens. There was another flock of them that Allen kept in the long barn across the driveway from the house. Ferne and Allen called them their meat birds. They were real tiny creatures when they came to the farm in the early spring. They were fed kernels of corn and something called growing mash. They grew rapidly during the summer and freely traveled the yard. The chickens mostly just roamed the yard, eating bugs and insects. Their numbers dwindled quickly as the year turned toward fall.

I remember one early evening when Brud and his mother were trying to put the meat birds back in their barn. They all went in quickly except for one reluctant bird. After chasing the bird around the yard for some time, Ferne picked up a stone and threw it at the bird. The stone hit the bird right in the head. The chicken fell over on his back and began kicking his feet in the air, then laid motionless. Brud began yelling, "You killed him, you killed him, and he's dead!" but the bird finally began to twitch and move, and after a few minutes he got up, staggering, and walked directly into the chicken coop.

At one time, there were also three geese who wandered slowly and proudly around the farm yard. They had a real purpose though; because as they wandered the yard, they were constantly watching for predators. If they saw an approaching predator, they would begin with their loud and incessant honking. They would keep honking until the danger passed, thus warning the other farm animals.

There were a few sheep who were very cute and playful as they romped around. I didn't like them as they seemed to see and eat the sweet clover that I liked. They would eat it so short that there was nothing left for us horses.

Then came a most humorous and odd-looking Billy goat. He was curious and strange and got into places where he shouldn't be. In this, he was kind of like Brud wasn't he? The Billy goat would eat anything; like small brush and weeds, that none of us other farm animals wanted. This seemed to be his purpose on the farm. One day he did the one thing that would cause him or any other animal to be immediately expelled permanently from the Valley. The most serious and unforgivable act was to hurt Allen's or anyone else's children. The Billy goat had butted Kathy in the stomach with his curled horns which came extremely close to her eyes. The goat had knocked Kathy down and made her cry, which was unusual. Even with her tender heart and caring nature, she rarely

24

cried; not even when she skinned her knees. So, that was it. The Billy goat would have to go! That very day while Allen was talking with Howard Steinberg a local cattle dealer, I saw Harry Wedin, Allen's hired man, secretly load the Billy goat into the back of Steinberg's truck. We wondered if he knew where he had acquired a goat.

So now I'll tell you about the pigs. There were always two of them. They might have been of some practical use on the farm, but all I could see was that they had voracious appetites. They ate, constantly, which caused them to get very fat and lazy. The pigs were filthy creatures who smelled bad. They laid around all spring and summer; lolling and rutting around in the mud. In the fall they disappeared. Maybe pigs don't like our cold winters.

I've mentioned our cats. I think there were too many of them. There seemed to always be a new litter of kittens being born somewhere in the barn. Mike Horan's greatest passion was finding the new litters of kittens. He would search and spend many hours looking for them. One day, he had spent a long time following the mother hoping she would lead him to the kittens. Later, Mike came into the cow barn quite discouraged. He told Allen that he had followed the mother cat but didn't have any luck. She wouldn't lead him to her kittens. Allen told Mike with his usual sense of dry humor, that he was following the wrong cat. He told him that he should follow the tom cat. Mike got up early the next morning determined to find the kittens. He watched closely as the Tom ate his breakfast in the barn and then climbed up on the window sill and went to sleep in the warm, morning sun.

Mike was afraid he would lose the cat, so he decided to skip his own breakfast. After the cat had finished a good long nap, he jumped out of the window and left the barn. Mike cautiously followed the tom cat around the back of the barn, through the garden, and the back yard and up through the corner of the meadow. Hours passed and so did lunch time. They went into the pasture and along the stone wall. Mike decided the cat was, actually, hunting probably for chipmunk or squirrel. He thought that when the cat caught a meal, he would then take it directly to the kittens. Now it was late afternoon and they were finally back at the barn. It was now feeding time again for the cats. The tom cat ate until he was full and then laid down for another nap. Mike, hungry and very tired, found Allen the in the barn and told him all that happened. Allen, with his sly grin, told Mike that maybe the old tom cat really didn't know where the kittens were hidden, after all.

I remember one time, when there was a large population of cats on the farm, a strange thing happened. A severe disease was attacking the entire population of cats. Some were very ill, and many died. Harry Wedin was living and working on the farm at that time. He had the same desire to drink the beverage that Harley liked even though it made them both walk funny after they drank it. Harry was holding his bottle and a very small tiger kitten. Harry thought that since the beverage made him feel so good that maybe it would help the kitten. He gave the kitten some of the beverage that he called whiskey. The cat showed some improvement. After several more doses for both Harry and the cat, (who we now called Whiskey...the cat, not Harry) got up and walked away. Staggered away.

* * * * * * * * * * * * * * * *

The story of Collie:

Ferne Marie was the first grandchild of Waven and Jessie Spaulding and the light of their lives. Waven and Jessie were Ferne's parents. Ferne Marie spent a lot of time with them at their home in Pittsford. She lived there for a time, so she could be closer to school. The bus did not go out as far as the farm.

One day as Ferne Marie and her grandparents were out in the yard, a beautiful red and white farm collie came off the hill near the house and went right up to Ferne Marie. As if by magic an instant bond was formed between the girl and the dog. Ferne Marie named her appropriately, "Collie". The two were inseparable and Collie settled right into farm

26

life. It was as if she was born to it. Everyone in the family loved Collie. She had a special skill: she could herd the cows. She could make the cows go wherever Allen wanted them to. Allen would say, "Collie girl, go get the cows" and off she would go, returning with the entire herd in front of her.

Collie was Ferne Marie's constant friend and protector. If the girl was wandering too far, Collie would get in front of her and gently push her back into the yard. Collie felt there were many dangers on a farm and she must protect Ferne Marie. She would even keep her from going down into the fields to meet Allen as he came back from working. She would only let Ferne Marie go, if Ferne Marie's mother said, "It's okay Collie Girl, let her go". They would then go romping off together, the little girl and her dog to meet Allen.

Ironically, it was Collie's desire to protect her little girl that got her in serious trouble. A neighbor girl, Beverly Trombley, came running up the road to the farm. She was going to play with Ferne Marie. As the girls ran towards each other, Collie thought that Beverly's intent was to harm Ferne Marie. Collie ran at the girl, knocking her down. Collie scratched Beverly and the girl's clothes got torn.

Collie had broken the same rule that the Billy goat had. So, she could no longer live at the farm. Allen was unable to do what he felt should be done so Uncle Bob Smith was asked to help. There are always times of sadness on a farm. This was an especially bad time but, no matter what, there was always work to be done. So poor little Ferne Marie, having had no time to grieve for her beloved friend, and with tears still glistening on her cheeks, went back to work.

27

* * * * * * * * * * * * * * * * *

The cows were the source of most of the work and were always bawling for attention and more food. The calves, though actually, were quite cute and fun. At the age of about two months, they were kept in a small pasture by themselves. They were always frolicking and liked to run.

And I, from my oak tree, would watch the kids, usually Jan and Mike, in a rather dangerous, but fun, game. They called it "Tail Riding". It was truly a funny sight to see. The game began with one of the kids grabbing one of the calves by the tail and hanging on as the calf, jumped and ran, trying desperately to rid themselves of the tail rider. Jan seemed to be the best at this game; her feet sometimes not even touching the ground and her pigtails flying out behind her. She would usually hold on the longest. Ron Smith would come in a close second though and he was always eager to join in the mischief when he visited the farm.

The cows, on the other hand, were work, work and more work. A great deal of effort went into just feeding them.

They were constantly fed huge quantities of hay and silage, which is chopped corn. They were also fed grain, which was a milled combination of seeds and corn. The grain was purchased from grain mills and brought to the farm in huge trucks. And of course, after all this feeding, came the inevitable manure. Cleaning up after the cows was a never-ending job. The cows created mountains of manure and likely would have buried themselves in it, if Allen hadn't worked so hard to get rid of it. Allen had to shovel the manure out of a long trough called the gutter. Then he would load it into a wheelbarrow, take the full wheelbarrow out of the barn on a raised walkway and dump it into either an iron wheeled wagon, with high sides or a heavy work sled also with high sides, depending on the season.

Sometimes when Harry Wedin was cleaning the gutter and had drunk some of his favorite beverage, he'd stagger out onto the walkway, pushing a huge load of manure, and as he was dumping the manure into the wagon, over the whole thing would go, manure, wheelbarrow and poor Harry. He would, eventually, climb out of the wagon while freeing the wheelbarrow, clean himself off and stagger on with his work.

After the wagon was loaded, my team mate and I were brought out and hitched to the loaded wagon. It was always a real heavy load. With Allen standing up in the wagon, he would drive us out to the field where he would spread the entire load on to the field with his manure fork and shovel. He did this chore, summer or winter, regardless of the weather. If it was raining, he would wear his long black canvas raincoat. On the coldest winter days, with the snow blowing and drifting around him, he'd work, in his heavy boots, bib overalls and as much wool layered over him as he could and still be able to work. On his head would be a red and black checkered, wool hat with the ear flaps pulled down over his ears. His hands would be covered with thick leather mittens with wool liners. Out onto the field we would go to spread the manure every day. His ability to just keep on, under any conditions, was amazing! I was very proud (and happy) to work with such a person as him.

I would observe all things going on in the cow barn through an open window. From here, I would see a most unusual practice. At daily intervals, Allen would extract this strange white liquid from the cows. It was milk. The extraction was done by hand and by a strange looking machine that attached to the cow and extracted the milk. The process seemed much like the way calves get milk from their mothers.

Hand milking was a slow and sometimes dangerous process. The Milker, usually Allen, sat on a stool with a pail held between his knees. The Milker would then squeeze and pull on the cow's teats until the milk started flowing. He would continue to squeeze and pull until he got all the cow's milk. With a lot of practice, a person could be pretty good and could milk the cows quite quickly. Now here is the dangerous part, some cows objected to this process. Often, they would kick at the Milker. If you were lucky, the cow would only hit the pail causing it to spill all over the Milker and everything else. Sometimes though, the cow's vicious kicks would hit the Milker squarely on the shin. Cows usually weigh between 900 to 1,200 pounds, so if one steps on your toe, as they sometimes did, the pain was very bad indeed. If the Milker received both of these objections almost simultaneously, he would forget the kick to his shin because his toe hurt so badly.

When Brud was a young boy, he was given his first heifer calf to raise. He raised her up until she had her first calf. The heifer needed to be milked for the first time. Brud bravely started to milk her. She stood quietly for the first few minutes, then she kicked, hitting Brud in the chest. She knocked the pail, the stool, and Brud, into the gutter, across the walkway and against the cement wall. Brud finally got up and went over crying to tell Allen what had happened. Allen said, "That's too bad but the cow still needs to be milked, so you need to go back and do it." To this Brud replied, "But what about this brown foot print on my shirt and the huge red mark underneath?" Allen said, "She is just being a little nervous and probably won't do it again." The cow, after a few more kicking attempts, seemed to get over her nervousness and Brud did finish milking her, although it took many more cows after her for Brud to get over his nervousness.

The milking machine was run by an electric motor which ran a small vacuum compressor. A vacuum pipe ran along the top of the stanchions and was connected between two cows and to the milking machine. The vacuum hose then went to the milking cap which covered and sealed the large pail. A pulsator caused a squeezing and pulling motion on the four teat cups that were attached to the udder of the cow and a milk hose then ran back to the pail. Allen would work three machines at a time. He said that four was too many and with two he was wasting too much time.

Allen did the milking twice a day, every day, with no days off and no time off. Except for the one year he took five days of vacation with the family at Burr Pond in Sudbury. From there, he traveled back and forth to do the milking while a neighbor did the rest of the chores. Allen had quit school at the age of sixteen because of his father's illness. He had begun farming at a very young age and continued until he sold his herd of milking cows at the age of sixty-two.

One day while tending the milking machine, the cow behind Allen turned her rear end directly toward Allen's back. Brud stood there watching, but unable to utter a warning. This sort of thing never happened to his father. The cow was depositing a pile of soft green manure directly onto Allen's shoulder. Allen stood up his face beet red with extreme anger. He uttered not a word. I think this action by the cow and lack of warning by Brud had exceeded all his limits of curse words. There was no time for repercussions to the cow, as there no doubt would have been. Allen's most immediate need was to clean himself off. He meticulously cleaned himself leaving only a light green stain on his shirt and went back to his work.

After Allen had finished milking, he would then have to dispose of the milk which he did in several different ways. I noticed that at times the children would come into the barn each with their own cup. Allen would then, milk by hand and fill their cups with the white foaming liquid. They would drink the milk and seemed too really like it, all except Ferne Marie. Apparently, she really doesn't like milk. The mystery to me was why Allen wanted so many cows as I'm sure one cow would have produced more than enough milk for the entire family. Some of Allen's big black and white cows would produce thirty to forty quarts every day and he usually milked about thirty cows. He fed a little bit to cats, which I think made them fat and lazy and not very ambitious mousers. Another small amount of milk was fed to the calves.

Feeding calves seemed to be chore that everyone wanted to do. First off, the little creatures had to be taught how to drink from a pail. I can't imagine any animal not knowing how to drink. The children would have to put their fingers into the calf's mouth. The children said that the calf's tongue was scratchy and tickled their fingers. With their fingers in the calf's mouth they would then gently force the little creature's head down into the pail. After several sessions in and out of the pail, the calves would eventually figure out that the source of the milk was actually in the pail and would drink by themselves. They would often drink too fast causing them to choke. They would cough and blow milk all over everything even the children. The calves would also butt the pail and spill milk everywhere.

All the rest of the milk, gallons and gallons of it, was put into large metal cans. The cans were then put into a huge tank of almost freezing cold water and kept there until it could be trucked away from the farm.

The milk, I learned, had some magical power. I would see Allen pick up these new born calves, put them at their mother's side and support them while they suckled milk from their mothers. Almost immediately the milk would give them strength, they would be able to stand without Allen's help and soon even walk around on their wobbly little legs. Maybe this magical power was the reason why Allen worked so hard to keep it so clean, white and pure and then had it trucked away from the farm to be sold.

The cows were always needing some sort of attention, sometimes special attention. Attention that Allen could not

32

give. At these times, an extremely tall, thin man was called to the farm. He was so tall that he had to walk all bent over so he wouldn't hit his head when he was in the barn. His name was Bill Philipsen. He was the Veterinarian. He would come quickly whenever he was called to the farm. He would wear a long denim coat with many pockets which bulged with pills, syringes and other things he might need to use. He always carried a black bag with even more stuff crammed inside. He wore high black boots that he would clean and disinfect before and after leaving the barn. He would do everything from a single injection to the often long and tiring job of helping a cow give birth and always charged the same fee of five dollars.

Another animal was kept on the farm with the cows. He was not kept in the pastures only in the barn or the barn yard. He was called the Bull. He was a huge arrogant creature especially when you consider his only worthwhile function was to mate with the cows. He would walk around bellowing, snorting and pawing the earth as if the world revolved around him. Allen did not own the bull but kept him on a not-for-pay lease agreement. Allen kept the bull, grew it and fed it for the use of its mating services. He was kept on the farm for only about two years at a time, then he would go back to the cattle dealer from whom he had been leased. This constant changing of the bulls was mostly to prevent inbreeding in the herd.

The last bull on the farm was named Old Doby. He was a huge, mostly-white, bull, although I remember Allen didn't like mostly-white cattle. Doby seemed to be gentle and more docile than the other bulls we had over the years.

One day when the cows had come back into the barn, Old Doby remained outside. Allen said, "Brud go out and chase in Old Doby". Brud went casually out into the yard to get the bull. As Brud approached the bull, Old Doby began to snort and paw the ground, then aggressively started towards Brud. Brud did the bravest thing he could think of and that was to turn and run like hell. Oh, please excuse the word as the children and I are not supposed to use curse words. Brud knew that even though he was running as fast as he could, he would not be able to make the corner and escape into the barn. There was a hole under the gate to the barnyard and Brud dove right onto his stomach sliding head first through the mud and slipped out of the yard, now safe from the bull. Allen, seeing what had just happened, jumped off the outside walkway and ran over to Brud shouting, "Are you alright? Are you okay?" Brud said that he was okay. Just a little scared. Again, Allen's face flushed with that bright red color.

Allen went inside the barn and grabbed his heavy cattle cane and went out after Old Doby. He applied the cane to the bull while screaming a whole line of curse words, many of which Brud had never heard before. As I stood in amazement watching, I think Allen would have killed the bull right there had the bull not gone directly into the barn and into his stanchion. Brud by then recovered from his fright, came back into the barn. Allen said, "Go down and tell your mother to call Steinberg and tell him to come and get that bull right now." That was the last day a bull was ever kept on the farm. Allen used artificial insemination exclusively after that incident.

When the children were quite young, a neighbor, Jim Harrison, gave a pony to the kids as his children were grown and he no longer wanted the pony. The pony proved to be a mean little character and he would kick and bite. I was happy when Ferne and Allen decided that he was unsafe to have around the children and had to be taken back to the Harrison's.

Waven and Jessie Spaulding were visiting the farm on the day that Harry Wedin was to take the pony back to Harrison's. Waven also seemed to like the same beverage that made people walk funny. I observed Harry and Waven sharing a container of the beverage.

Waven decided he would help Harry with the pony. They both came out to our pasture. The pony tried to bite and kick as Waven held the pony while Harry attempted to get on the pony's back. Harry would get on one side of the pony and immediately go right over his back on the other side. This was repeated many times with the same result. Sometimes as the pony objected to the mounting procedure, Harry would go tumbling right over the front or slide off the back. Eventually though, they got the pony back to the Harrison farm.

There came to the farm, for a period of time, a tall lanky riding horse. Brud had bought the horse and named him Pal. He was full of tricks and mischief and just loved to run. He was kept in the barn with Roany and me and would share the pasture with us. Sometimes, if the cows were in the same pasture with us, Pal would flatten his ears back and nip at them. I think he did this just to make them run so that he could chase them. This seemed to be great fun for him even though Allen did not approve of it.

Pal would escape from the barn by picking his rope with his teeth until he could get it untied. Brud would tie the rope with a knot on the bottom, thinking this would prevent Pal's escapes. This worked to a certain extent in that it took Pal a little longer to untie the rope. He had another trick to use though. If he had a rider on his back he'd slowly lower his head to the ground, hoping to send his rider tumbling over the front of him and onto the ground.

The trick that seemed to work better for Pal, was to just lay down if he had a rider on his back, forcing the rider off and allowing Pal to escape. Pal would try this trick with Brud but as he laid down and forced Brud off, Pal would then stand up and as he was getting up, Brud would swing his leg over Pal's back. When Pal got up he would find Brud sitting on his back.

Pal tried this several more times and finally gave up this trick altogether and he and Brud became good friends. Pal continued this bad habit with the girls and Ferne stopped them from riding him as she felt it was too dangerous. The last time that any of the girls rode Pal was when Jan was on his back and he laid down again. Allen saw this happen and he came running from the barn and he as very angry. He jumped on the horse and made him run. He kept him running at full gallop until the horse was completely tired out.

Allen rarely rode us horses for pleasure, but I do remember one time that he did after Allen and I had finished cultivating the potatoes. (I worked singly for this job). The mail and his newspaper were delivered to a small metal box beside the Whipple Hollow Road at the bottom of the hill. Allen decided it would be better to get on my back and ride down to get the paper than it would be to drive down with his motor car. As we came around the big corner on the way back from picking up the paper, Allen decided that he might as well read the newspaper as he rode along. It was a warm day and I was walking along slowly, enjoying the valley and soon I felt the reins go loose as he laid them on my neck to free his hands up to read the newspaper.

All of a sudden, I heard a loud, rattling sound and it was just above me and on my back. In my fright I forgot that Allen was even there. Terrified of this rattling, crackling creature that had somehow gotten on top of me, I began to run. This caused some of the paper, mail and Allen's hat, to go flying out into the meadow. The rest of the paper was spread out covering Allen's face. While trying to gather up the paper, which caused even more rattling, which made me run even faster, Allen discovered that the reins had slipped down my neck and over my head so that he could not reach them. The only means left for him to stop me was several repetitions of "Whoa" each followed by his familiar curse words. We, finally, stopped in the safety of the farm yard. Allen had to walk back and collect the things we had lost along the way.

There was another thing Allen did sometimes when we had finished our work in the meadow and the equipment was to be left there for later use. He would unhitch us, get up onto our backs, and, standing with one foot on my team mate and one foot on me. With us at full gallop he would ride us back to the barn. Must have been an impressive sight to see! He called it, Roman Riding.

****

There were many wild animals who came around the farm. There were early sightings of coyotes and foxes who tried to sneak in and steal the chickens. Many deer were seen, and all of the family hunted in the fall. And, of course, the cute but dreaded by us horses, woodchucks. They were dreaded because they made huge holes and tunnels in the fields where we worked. There was great danger of one of us stepping in a hole and breaking our leg.

One day when Brud was driving us and we were hitched to the hay wagon. Roany stepped in a woodchuck hole and went down clear over her knee. I think she would have broken her leg if she wasn't hitched to the pole and supported by me. She limped for quite a while after that and Dr. Philipsen had to come and look at her leg. I believe this to be the only time he was called in for a horse injury or illness. Roany had sprained her leg. Dr. Philipsen gave Allen some Bute tablets (Phenyl butanone an anti-inflammatory analgesic), charged his usual five dollars and left. The injury didn't stop Roany, (and around here, if there was work to do, you just keep going; hurt or injured or not), so she went right back to work.

Daily Farm Life

*I*ts early morning as I watch from underneath my oak tree, Allen is in the barn milking the cows. The lights are just coming on in the house, which means Ferne is up and starting her day. What a busy woman; she never rests! The first thing is to get the fire in the kitchen cook stove going, it is fueled by wood and is used to cook all the daily meals that the family eats. This morning, she comes out to the woodshed to get an armload of the small sized wood that is best for cooking. She is already going at her special pace that she will keep up all day long. It is a pace somewhere between a walk and a run. No other human person seems to use this pace. I call it the Ferne Mills Scoot.

When she needs wood for her stove, she usually has only to go to a large wood-box that is kept on the back porch but this morning, it seems Brud has forgotten his only household duty, which was to keep the wood box full. The girls help Ferne with all the other household duties along with some of the barn chores and much of the field work. This inequality (Brud not having to do as much housework as they did) was voiced by the girls. And I must agree with them. Roany and I shared all of our work equally. I've noticed that this notion of inequality is solely a human one. An unwritten code where humans' separate females as unsuitable for a particular job, or for a male to complain that he is doing "women's work". However, I sense a growing new independence in this generation of girls and I feel this code will change.

The children are now awake and getting ready for school. Ferne has breakfast ready for the family. Allen has finished milking the cows and is just coming into the house. As he enters the back porch, he notices the empty wood box. The usual morning greetings pass between the family members. Allen gets a dipper of hot water from the reservoir on the side of the cook stove. He puts the water in his wash basin and washes up for breakfast. Everyone gathers at the table and starts eating. When they are almost finished, Allen says casually, "I noticed the wood box is empty". Brud stopped eating immediately, he knew a most severe punishment was coming. Allen did not punish the children physically, but his expression of disapproval always hurt much worse. He merely said, with his typically calm logic, "Well Brud, you know better". Brud quickly finished eating and filled the wood box before the school bus came.

The school bus was an extreme concern to me, at first that is, but I got use to its comings and goings. It was a huge, completely metal encased motor truck. There were two wooden benches that were attached to the interior walls of the bus where the children sat, facing each other. It was dark inside as there were no windows and the children said it was cold in the winter. When the bus came to the farm in the morning, the children would come running out of the house and disappear into its dark interior. I could only think of the cattle truck which would, at certain times, take a cow from the farm, never to return. I would worry all day until late afternoon when the bus would return. The door would open, and my happy, beloved children would come tumbling out and I was relieved and happy again.

Now with the kids off to school, Allen is back to the barn and the breakfast dishes are washed. Ferne might have time for another cup of coffee while she makes telephone calls for Allen. One of the cows is in heat and Allen needs the Artificial Breeder to come. He, also, wants her to order more grain for the cows. So, she will only have time for half a cup as she must get to the barn and help with the chores. So off she goes at her "scoot" to the barn. First, it's feeding the cows, then she drags huge bunches of loose hay the full length of the barn and gives each cow a generous amount. She is feeding the cows while Allen is cleaning the gutter.

Next, she starts carrying basket after basket of sawdust. She gets the sawdust from the "Dark Hole" as Allen calls it. It is the empty space underneath the barn floor where the loads of hay are unloaded and stored in the summer time. She spreads the sawdust under each cow, so they will have clean bedding and then leaves piles along the walkway wall to be used later. Next, she goes into the Milk House to wash the milking machines and the strainer which is like a huge funnel with a removable strainer and disposable strainer pads to keep impurities out of the milk. Also, Ferne has to wash the Bulk Tank where the milk is kept, awaiting pick up.

Then Ferne goes back to the house. She must pack a lunch for Allen and herself. Allen wants to fix fence today. They will be far from the house and won't want to waste time coming way back for lunch.

In the late afternoon Allen and Ferne will also have to do the afternoon feeding and cleaning and get ready to milk again.

The kids are now home from school and Brud seems worried about something. Ferne finds out that he has had a school assignment for some time. The assignment was to bring a kite to school and fly it during recess; everyone was to bring one and participate. The kite was to be brought to school tomorrow. Brud didn't think he could make one on his own and his parents wouldn't go out and buy one. Ferne said that the girls could start making supper and she and Brud would build one in Allen's shop.

To begin Ferne got two, one-inch square, sticks; about three feet long. Then, folding her tongue between her teeth (as she always did when a task required extra concentration), she drove two large nails through the sticks forming a cross. The huge nails went so far through both boards that she cinched them over on the back side. The kite was rapidly gaining weight. She cut a piece of the heavy green material from a broken window shade and nailed the shade to the frame with roofing nails. They added a tail and a long string. Brud could see that unless there was a hurricane tomorrow, this kite would never fly. So Brud, trying to avoid embarrassment to himself and his mother, broke the kite and left it on the bus when he went to school the next day. He told his mother that the kite had gotten broken. He is probably still carrying his guilt today.

After completing this project with Brud, she went back into the house to finish up the supper and get it on the table. As she was scooting to the table carrying a big platter of pot roast, potatoes, carrots, onions and gravy, the family's big gray house cat called Smokey got in her way. As she was coming to the table, she tripped, falling flat on her stomach. She didn't spill anything, but the platter made a loud crash as it hit the floor right in front of the cat. The cat spun in the air and headed for the porch. The cat was too frightened to stop and dove right through the window; breaking the glass as he went.

Ferne picked herself up, along with the platter of food and the family ate their supper. After the meal was finished, Ferne had to quickly get ready for a meeting at the Florence School. She was President of the PTA (Parent Teacher Association). Vee Poremski, a neighbor, would come and drive them to the meeting.

She returns well after most everyone's bedtime including hers. Only Tip, her little white dog, is still awake and she takes time to pat him before she goes to bed. She notices that the girls have cleaned up and done the dishes. Thanks to those girls! She scoots off to bed as tomorrow might be a busy day.

We, horses, were kept in our own section of the barn. Both of us had our own stall and there was one extra stall for visitors and later for Pal when he arrived. In the front of the stall where a large amount of hay was put for us to eat there was a huge metal bowl for our grain. These bowls, I was told came from the stables of the Whipple Hollow Church, located about a mile up the road from ours on the left. The church stables, I understand, were burned down by an angry parishioner.

The grain we were fed was a mixture of oats and corn parvtially ground and then mixed together with sweet brown molasses and yes, we horses do get to eat dessert. Allen makes sure we get good quality hay. He feeds us coarse hay, mostly Timothy with very little clover. The dry clover leaves, he feels would make us cough. Our hay is selected and kept separate from the cow's hay. In a place above our stable there is a loft area that is called the scaffold. This is a very difficult and hot place in the summer to put hay. When the wagon is empty, Ferne and the children will climb down from the scaffold covered with hay chaff and soaked in sweat. When I think of it, maybe the work, sweat and hay chaff is the glue that keeps this family so closely stuck together.

Our feeding time seemed to be of considerable interest to all the kids, especially Brud and Mike. They would sit on the edge of the manger and watch and listen to us eat. They seemed to enjoy watching us chew on the long stalks of hay and grind the grain with our teeth. Just out of boyish curiosity Brud has gotten Mike to eat both cow grain and our sweet feed. He says that the cow grain is easier to chew but our grain tastes better. A boy's curiosity is a strange thing and it usually got them hurt or something got broken sometimes simultaneously.

We get our water from the big trough down by the cow barn. The source of the water is a spring located high above the farm in another small valley. The spring supplies enough water for the house, milk house, a water bowl for every cow and the watering trough which is always full and is constantly running away. This is all done by gravity feed with no mechanical pumps.

The children would watch in amazement at the large quantities of water Roany and I could drink after a hot day working in the fields. Allen and the kids would often go out to the gully during a time of prolonged dry weather. The gully would be running slowly at some places with just a trickle of water. Allen and the kids would try to catch brook trout as they were swimming back and forth in the shallow pools. They would eventually catch one or two in their hands and quickly put them into a pail of water. They would bring the fish home and put them in the watering trough. Allen felt the fish would eat insects and keep it clean. Sometimes a lucky cat would sit on the edge of the trough and grab a fish as it swam too close to the surface. This would necessitate another trip to the gully to catch a replacement.

What We Wore

No style necessary here, anything we wore had a purpose; nothing just for show. The most important factor was fit. Everything had to fit perfectly. This was to prevent injury, sores from irritation or lameness. First came the shoes. Each horse had two sets: one set for summer and one for winter. For the summer shoes, Allen would have Ferne call Dawson, the black smith, as Allen called him. He seemed to have no other name, just Dawson, maybe because he only worked with horses and we only had one name too.

Dawson would arrive driving an old black panel truck, much like the truck that the children rode to school in only a little smaller in size. Dawson was a serious, stern looking man who never smiled. He was firm but never mean with us horses. He did get rather gruff though and would often push Dolly, though probably that was because of her natural laziness; while she was being shod she would lean on him too heavily. We were shod down by the garage where Allen kept his motor car.

Dawson was a man of average height and build. He seemed to always stand and walk with a slight stoop, probably from working on horses so much. He had white, wild-looking hair and several gold teeth. His gold teeth and his strange-looking eyes glistened out of the darkness of the garage. Dawson always dressed all in black from the strange leather cap to the black leather apron that he tied around his waist. Everything he used and even the white of his skin was covered with a black sooty ash. Dawson never seemed to be

44

happy. Possibly because he had no horses of his own. I had the sense that Allen didn't like him as there was very little talk between the two men.

Dawson would begin his job by opening the back of his truck. Inside was a metal bowl with small holes in the bottom. A soft coal was put into the bowl and set on fire. A thick, black, smelly smoke would be in the air. He would then turn the crank on a bellows that the bowl sat on. When the coals turned a cherry red glow, he put a thick, new, steel, summer shoe onto the coals. He would then ask Allen to lead us so that he could observe how we walked. He would clean the bottom of our foot and trim our hoof of excess. Another new shoe was used to check for fit and make sure he had filed our hoof flat enough. Dawson would use tongs to remove the red-hot shoe from the coals and by hammering over his anvil, he would bend hooks in the ends at the heel of the shoe, then hammer the soft hot metal so that he formed a toe clip at the front. He would then dip the hot shoe into a pail of cold water causing a loud sizzle. Here comes the frightening part especially for a young horse; the still somewhat hot shoe is placed on our foot. As Dawson holds the shoe in place with his tongs, I again hear a faint sizzle, I can see smoke and the smell of burning hoof. I only feel a slight warmth and thankfully, no pain. After the shoe has been cooled again in the water; it is then attached to the hoof by nails which are driven through the holes in the shoe and into the thick hoof wall. The nails are clipped and clinched and will stay on for a long time. The process will continue until all four feet are shod.

I can tell Allen very much respects Dawson's skill as a Blacksmith. Allen asks the price of shoeing; the shoeing process includes: trimming, shoeing, and the shoes themselves. Dawson is paid the fee of ten dollars per horse and he goes on his way.

Before winter and icy conditions, Allen will put on the winter shoes himself. The shoes are heavier but don't need the heating process, so he can do it himself. The winter shoes have the same small holes for the nails; but also have several larger holes and sharp chisels are driven into these holes. Allen calls these chisels Ice Calks. There are two ice calks at the front and sometimes one at each side. These calks will give us a good grip when we pull the heavy sled even over solid ice. I like the feeling of lightness and freedom sometimes when I am barefoot, but nothing beats the sound and feel of a new pair of shoes. I like the heavy clunking sound when we pull the hay wagon into the barn and the grinding of the gravel under our feet. I feel a sense of pride and strength when wearing a new pair of shoes. For you motor heads: that is what REAL HORSE POWER is all about.

In the barn, we wore a halter which was just a few straps: one over our head in back of our ears, one over our nose, one up each side of our face and a throat latch. The halter kept us in our horse stall and was used for leading us.

Our work outfit consisted of the collar, harness and a bridle. The fit and function of this outfit was of great importance because it was through this outfit that the strength and power of the work horse was guided and released. We provided the strength to move all the equipment necessary to plant and gather all the crops that were needed to keep the farm animals growing and producing and to move anything else that the farmer could not move by himself. It is no wonder that when we are shod and in harness that we walk so proudly.

The bridle consisted of a head stall, check rein and bit. The check rein was attached to the bit and hung over the hames; this kept the horse's attention and prevented the horse from grazing while working. This was quite necessary, particularly with Dolly, as she was always taking every opportunity to stop and eat, even while working.

The bit is a round metal bar which goes in our mouths and is attached to the head stall. The driving reins are attached to the bit to control our movements. The fit of the collar is of extreme importance. It had to fit perfectly around the neck and at the base of the neck resting lightly on the shoulders. It is from the neck and shoulders that the horse gets most of his pulling power. Wooden or metal bars called Hames were buckled over the collar. A series of specially placed straps and padded metal rings make up the harness. The harness required constant attention for wear and broken straps. Allen was always sewing, riveting, or replacing, broken parts. The harness had to be placed and adjusted properly on the horse for comfort and control of the horse.

I remember the first time that Brud was able to complete the job of harnessing us by himself. Allen was greasing the mowing machine as he had just finished using it. Allen told Brud to get us horses into the barn and get us cleaned up for harnessing. He got Roany and me in and cleaned us up. Then, he decided he would harness the team. He was nine years old, at the time, and big for his age, but not really big enough to do this job. But he had watched Allen harness us many times and was sure he could do it.

Brud started with the collar and found he was too short to put the collar on and buckle it at the top of our necks. So, he put it on bottom side up and then slid it up our necks near our heads. He was then able to spin it over and then slide it back down against our shoulders.

I signaled to Roany that it was going to take a lot our patience and understanding to endure this process.

Brud had to drag the harness over to us because he couldn't carry it. He was able to climb up on the boards at the side of the stall, and by pushing and pulling each section; front, middle and back, get the harness over our backs. And then with many trips around and under our bodies he was able to do the buckle and get the harness on properly. The process was then repeated on Roany and then both of us seemed to oblige him by lowering our heads just enough, so he could get our bridles on.

At last, Brud brought us out of the barn and properly hooked the driving lines to our bits. Roany and I were very proud in our new shoes and with the young boy driving us out to the wagon. I know Allen was proud too when he saw us coming and I know Brud was feeling like a King.

The Gully

Most people would define a Gully as a brook or mountain stream but to our family, it was, and always will be, referred to as the Gully.

The Gully begins high in the mountain, west of the farm, beyond the western boundary of our land. It runs down the mountain through a steep notch between two hills and emerges almost in the center of the valley. At this point, it turns south, traveling along the valley floor, and then disappears at the extreme southeastern end of the farm.

All along the gully from where it enters the valley to where it disappears at the other end, nature has created a very special playground. It is always changing but somehow still remains the same. People and animals, both domestic and wild, are drawn like a magnet to this life-giving vein of liquid. For as long as we have been here, everyone wants to visit this magical place.

Allen and Brud try to catch the Brook Trout that live in the pools all along the Gully. The most successful fishermen seem to be the raccoons who catch the fish easily when, in dry weather, the water flow gets low and the pools become shallow.

Everyone seems to have their own special places along the Gully where they like to just sit and listen to the flow of the water and be soothed by its sounds. My special place is the extreme south western corner of my pasture. Roany and I go there many times when we are not needed for work. There is a steep path that leads through the Hemlocks and down to the Gully and it is always cool there. Huge boulders surround the small clearing where we enter the Gully to get a drink of the crystal clear pure water. I enjoy hearing the clink of our metal shoes in the loose small water-worn stones at the edge of the Gully.

When Carroll Mills, Allen's uncle, was home from the Army he often came to the Gully to bathe. He goes to the deep pool near the Sugar House. He calls it his bath tub. Even when there is snow on the ground, he goes there to bathe.

People explore the entire length of the Gully, finding unusually shaped stones and imagining what it was like in ancient times also enjoying this beautiful natural place.

One day as Roany and I are bringing the last load of hay to the barn, I see Ferne and the children heading out across the flat meadow, so I know they are going to the Gully to play. Lynne, Ron and Mike are with them so Ferne has seven children with her. When they get to the Gully's flat pool below the big elm tree, they are all soon in the water. They start building a dam to increase the depth of the pool. Although it takes almost constant work to keep the water from breaking loose the dam, there is still time for exploring upstream and splashing and playing in the increasing depth of the pool.

Harry Wedin helps Allen unload the hay and when they are finished, Allen gets the picnic basket that Ferne has prepared. Allen, Harry, Roany and I bring it out to the Gully where Ferne and the children are playing. Roany and I stand and watch as the family enjoys their picnic at the Gully.

There is another area south of the sweet apple tree where the family will sometimes go for picnics. It is always

cool at this place near the Gully where the water cascades over a low ledge into the pool below.

The Gully is a very special place to rest and rejuvenate mind, body and soul now and for generations to come.

Working the Land
and
Fixing Fence

Winter is just beginning to leave the valley. The snow is starting to melt and disappear from the valley and surrounding hills. The gully is running swiftly again. The hay mows are getting low but there is still enough hay to last us all until the lush, green grass comes again. Spring is coming, and we will all be busy, especially us horses.

When the frost is out of the ground, the plowing begins. I think about the early years when Allen plowed the fields with a walk-behind land plow. Allen is an expert with the walk behind land plow as I am told he has been doing it since he was a young boy even before I was on the farm. He takes us to the field and begins plowing one furrow at a time, straight and true. He drives us with the reins tied together hung around his neck. Both of his hands are on the wooden handles working to keep the plow running straight. He has to keep speaking to Dolly, telling her to stop "just walking" between the traces and pull. It makes it more difficult for him if the team is not pulling together.

I remember one other spring when we had finished plowing, the crops were in and most everything was up and starting to grow. There was one small field that Allen was going to plow to plant millet; a type of fast-growing grass that Allen would cut in late July and feed to the cows to supplement the feed they were getting in their pastures.

This spring, there was a great feeling of excitement and joy as Ferne has just announced that she was going to have a baby. She told the children that they would have to be patient as the baby wouldn't be born until fall. This was the spring of 1947.

That same spring a strange new machine arrived at the farm. It was a funny looking little grey colored machine that was delivered on a large truck. Allen climbed up on the machines back as if he was about to ride a horse. Then a loud roar started coming from the machine and smoke came spewing from the backend. He drove the machine off ramps which had been attached to the truck. Allen called this machine a tractor and it came with several attachments which included a land plow, a set of harrows, cultivators, mowing machine and something that Allen called a saw rig. This saw rig was attached to the back of the tractor along with all the other implements and was used for sawing fire wood into stove lengths. Allen was hoping that the tractor and all of its equipment would prove to be worth the huge price of two thousand two hundred dollars that he had paid for it.

I stood watching from the oak tree feeling doubtful and amused as Allen drove the tractor with the plow attached

out to plow the millet field. Then, I watched in amazement at this strange, new development. A louder roar issued from the tractor and Allen lowered the plow, which made two furrows at once. He plowed the entire millet field in much less time than we could do it. Well, I guess that's enough reminiscing for now. As I said, spring is here and there is much work to do for all of us.

As soon as the frost is out of the ground, the huge job of fence fixing begins. Allen fixes the fence around the perimeter of the farm's two hundred eighty-five acres plus the fences that separate different pastures and the outside of the meadow. The fence around the meadows keeps the cows out of the growing hay fields. Allen also fixed the fences around Harley's land. Harley had seventy-seven acres with both outside and inside fences. During the week, Allen and Ferne, with Jan tagging along because she doesn't go to school yet, fix the inside fences that they can get to with the tractor and trailer attached carrying all the posts, wire, and tools needed to fix the fences.

When the weekend comes, the older kids are out of school and the fencing adventure begins. As soon as the cows are milked, and morning chores are done, Allen says, "Let's go up and fix the mountain fence". The trailer is loaded with all the things necessary for the job. The older children, Ferne Marie, Kathy, and Brud climb into the trailer. Harry Wedin usually goes along to help, too.

Ferne and Jan will stay behind because it is much too difficult for little Jan to climb up over the Peak, which is what they call the mountain they will work on. Allen drives the tractor as far up the mountain as he can get. Then Allen, Harry and the kids load up with all the tools and posts that they can carry and head off on the long climb along the fence line to the top of the peak. They stop briefly to fix the fence as they go along. It takes a long time to patch the broken wires and replace the broken posts.

After they reach the top and are heading down the other side, Allen tells Harry and the kids to keep going and he will take a short cut and go back and get the tractor. As Allen is taking the short cut back to the tractor, he purposely crosses a ledgy, moss-covered area. He knows that growing among the moss, he will find a quite rare, and very fragrant, spring flower. It is called trailing Arbutus. This flower grows in only a very few places on the farm and Allen knows them all. So even though he is in a hurry to get back to the tractor, he stops long enough to pick a big bouquet to take back to Ferne because it is one of her favorite flowers.

Reaching the tractor, Allen drives it down to the farm house where he would pick up Ferne and Jan and the lunch of fried chicken that she had packed for everyone. Allen then drives back up the mountain taking the lower road with plans to meet up with his fencing crew.

Harry and the kids are just coming into the lower road when they hear the tractor coming. They are hot, tired and hungry and have fought the black flies which are bad this time of year. Everyone is more than ready to rest and enjoy a picnic in the woods.

After lunch and a short rest, they all gather up more fencing equipment and follow the fence line down onto Blueberry Hill. Ferne, carrying a few posts and more wire, joins the fencing crew. Jan is tagging along close on Allen's heels. It looks more like a safari than a fencing crew.

The last downhill stretch will take them into the North Meadow. Allen leaves them again as they start down the hill. He will go all the way back and get the tractor and then eventually meet them in the North Meadow. When Allen arrives in the meadow, the fencing crew all climb in the trailer. Jan on the tractor with Allen. They all are tired but happy to have finished the mountain fence.

* * * * * * * * * * * * * * *

I recall one particular job of fencing when Allen, Harry and Brud were fixing fence out in a rocky area below the steep side of Blueberry Hill. Brud had come along to carry some

53

of the tools. As Allen and Harry were repairing a stretch of fence, Brud was exploring in the shale rock ledge nearby. In one rock, Brud found many square chunks of iron pyrite, "fool's gold" I've heard it called, embedded in the rock. One of the tools Brud was carrying was the staple hook. The hook was a small metal bar with a short "L" on one end. The tool's actual purpose is to be driven under a fence staple and then used to pry out the staple. Brud found that it was also the perfect tool for digging out the chunks of iron pyrite from out of the rocks.

Brud suddenly noticed that Harry and his father had finished the repairs and had moved along the fence line. Stuffing the pieces of pyrite into his pockets, Brud ran to pick up the staple bucket and catch up to his father. After they had moved a considerable distance down the line, Allen discovered that he needed the staple hook. Allen asked Brud for the hook. Brud, finding that the hook was not in his hand, looked in the staple bucket where it should have been. Finding that it was not in the bucket, he came up with his usual intelligent answer at times like this: "I don't know". Allen said, "You had it back in those rocks, go back and find it and don't come back until you do". As he went back down the fence line all sorts of thoughts were going through the young boy's mind. What would he do and where would he go if he couldn't find the hook? He would never be able to go back to the family and farm.

As the boy hurried back to the ledge he imagined what he might do if he didn't find the tool. Maybe he could live with Grandpa Waven and Gramma Jessie. Grandpa was always busy and made things out of wood in his garage, maybe Brud could help with that. And Gramma Jessie was a wonderful little woman. She always said that anything you had, like a new pair of shoes, were "Pips". She could also make the best baked beans and wonderful baked spaghetti and meat balls. They lived in the city of Pittsford and were "City Slickers". That would never work, he would turn into a city slicker too. Maybe he could go and live with Grampa Harl. He told wonderful stories and he had Mary and the Buggy. But

Grampa Harl could only make fried potatoes and green Kool Aid. Always delicious, but he thought, could he really live on just fried potatoes and Kool Aid?

Then, he thought of the one thing that might help. He was told in Sunday school that if you needed help, you only had to pray. He thought and remembered all the words to the "Lord's Prayer". He repeated it over and over several times, but no hook was found. He thought of another prayer although he didn't think the words would apply to finding a staple hook, but this was a desperate situation, so he started in, "Now I lay me down to sleep-" and suddenly, there was the staple hook laying right on the rock where he had left it. He clutched the precious hook in his small fist and went running back to his father. Even now, I bet he still remembers that in all situations, he always has prayer.

Spring Time

*I*t wasn't all work on the farm for the children in the spring and I enjoyed just seeing them playing outside in the yard. Sometimes they would be just out for a walk to enjoy the spring sunshine. Jan would be with Ferne Marie, either being pushed in a stroller, toddling at her side or being carried by the strong little girl. Kathy and Brud would be hand in hand as they were pals. The little boy was Kathy's little Brudder, her pronunciation of the word, "brother". She shortened it to" Brud", creating the nickname that he carries today.

The children would head down the road; Collie trotting beside them always watching for danger. When they get down to the steep ledge bank near the turn, Kathy spots Mayflowers growing by the thousands on the bank. She drops Brud's hand and starts picking flowers. Kathy loves all flowers and Mayflowers are her favorite. Brud is busy poking in the mud beside the road, looking for insects or worms. Ferne Marie and Jan keep going toward the turn. Collie gets nervous and starts to gently push them back because she feels they shouldn't be going that far. Kathy has gone high into the ledge, after the prettiest blue and pink Mayflowers. Suddenly she comes running down the bank and starts running up the road and yelling for Ferne. Kathy has gotten into red biting ants and her legs are covered with them. She knows she needs help, but she won't drop her flowers.

* * * * * * * * * * * * * * *

One fine, spring day, I hear a strange sound coming from the corner of my pasture above the apple trees near the old dam. It sounds like a motor is running. Out of curiosity, I go up to take a look. There is a huge boulder up here with a split in it. It has a shelf in the split that forms a seat and that is where I find Brud. It is him making the motor noise. He is driving what he calls "Cadillac Rock" and I must admit with more than a little imagination, it does look like a car. Soon, he gets bored with his driving and goes up a little farther into the secluded little valley below Blueberry Hill. He calls it Wild Horse Canyon, where, in his imagination, lives the Black Stallion.

* * * * * * * * * * * * * * * *

In the spring of 1950 a cousin, Dick Granger, came to visit during his school vacation. Although Dick was only a young teenage boy, he had acquired great skill at carpentry, which he had learned by working with his father, Adrian (Peanut) Granger. During his vacation, Dick built a cute little playhouse for the girls. It was four feet by six feet with a front porch and a window. He built the playhouse just south of the house near the woodshed. He built it out of scrap lumber he had found around the farm. It was a cute little house but unfortunately lasted only a short time. In the late summer of that year, a huge storm with very strong wind came roaring through the valley. They called this storm a Hurricane.

We horses stood huddled in an open corner of the pasture, having decided that we weren't safe under the oak tree. Suddenly, we saw the little playhouse lift into the air. It hit the electric wires as it flew and went crashing into the meadow behind the barn that is just north of the house. That storm also took the entire back half of the roof, rafters and all, of that barn as it roared and raged through the valley.

* * * * * * * * * * * * * * * *

I'm sure the children were sad to see the playhouse go but there were always many games and adventures for them on our farm. There were numerous, excellent hiding places, so Hide and Seek was a game I saw them play a lot. I could always tell from the running and laughter that when Lynne and Ron Smith were over, the kids had even more fun.

The children also enjoyed a game they called Baseball. The ball games would often include friends, cousins and neighbors. The location of the baseball field often had to be changed, from one game to another, depending on the shortness of the grass and which fields had been mowed.

Brud loved baseball but as the older girls grew to be less interested in the game, he had to find ways to improve his baseball skills by himself. Throwing the ball up on the barn roof and then catching it when it came down was a pretty good way to practice but Allen put a stop to it for fear of breaking the slates of the rooftop.

Jan could throw a baseball pretty well but was not quite good enough yet for Brud to practice high fly balls with. So Brud came up with an idea. He sent Jan up the hill in back of the house. From up there she could throw the perfect simulation of a fly ball and she would throw balls from that hill until her arm got sore.

Brud felt that the worst game to play was a game that Kathy liked called Hop Scotch. This game was truly NOT fun for Brud, but it was for Kathy, so he would do it for a short while.

However, the boy hated a game of Ferne Marie's that was called School. For Brud, playing School was the absolute worst. It was clearly mandatory and always seemed to coincide with a rainy Saturday; as if that weren't bad enough. Ferne Marie would announce that everyone was going to play School. What?! The boy thought. There can be no such thing as "playing" school! There was only real school and Brud had just been through five, yes, FIVE days of it. Protests were futile from any "Nin-com-poops" as Ferne Marie sometimes called her sibling students. She tolerated no whining nor any excuses. And, at least in Brud's mind, the rain and School seemed to go on and on, forever it seemed, and without recess.

* * * * * * * * * * * * * * * *

One spring day, a strange looking little red machine was delivered to the farm. It looked like a trailer but had strange looking disks and spikes sticking out from the back of it. Allen hooked onto it with the little grey tractor and pulled it down to the manure chute. The next morning after the stables are cleaned and all the manure was dumped into the little red machine, I watch as Allen pulls it with the tractor out into the field. He adjusts some huge levers at the front of it and then starts pulling it along. The disks and spikes start spinning and the manure comes flying out the back. The machine is a manure spreader and he can spread the whole load in a matter of minutes. There were times when I resented the little grey tractor and the ever- increasing jobs it could do but it seemed to be faster and easier for Allen and allowed him to do more work in less time. Even I must admit, I needed more help as the years passed.

Allen practiced the method of crop rotation. Each spring Allen would plow up a section of the field. The first and second year, Allen would plant corn in this section. The third year, after this section had been plowed and harrowed and picked clean of stones, it would be seeded with a mixture of Clover, Timothy and Oats. The oats would grow quickly, holding the weeds back and protecting the grass seed coming underneath. The oats would be cut as a hay crop.

The process of preparing a field for a hay crop included plowing and harrowing and after this Allen would pick up all the stones that he felt would damage the harvesting equipment. Picking stones was a very tedious and difficult job for my people. The only equipment that my people could use was a manure fork. If the stone would fall through the tines on the manure fork it had to be picked up by hand and put into the box of the wooden wagon that Roany and I pulled. When the wagon was full, we would bring the stones off the field where they were unloaded and left in piles.

One day, Allen was harrowing with the tractor and disk harrows in a section where he was going to plant corn. Harry and Brud were picking stones off a field that was to be seeded with the hay mixture. They had filled the wagon and were unloading the stones in a pile. Harry Wedin was standing nearby, using a fork to empty the wagon. Brud was standing in the wagon box throwing stones off, one at a time. In an effort to make the job more interesting, Brud was trying to hit a stone in the pile with the one he was throwing. He threw a stone and it hit a strand of barbed wire that was hooked from one fence post to another. The wire stretched and then hurled the stone back towards the wagon. The stone struck Harry right in the back of his head. Harry fell to the ground and laid there unconscious and perfectly still.

Roany and I had become very nervous at the sight of Harry falling after being struck by the rock. Brud was crying and yelling. Not knowing about unconsciousness, his only thought was that he had killed poor Harry. With no one to help, Brud had to deal with his mounting fear by himself. He thought that by his having killed Harry, he would surely be put in jail for the rest of his life or worse yet be put into the Electric Chair! He dropped to his knees beside Harry, sobbing, pleading and praying for a miracle.

Harry began to move. Soon, Harry sat up and asked what had happened. Still sobbing, Brud told him what had happened and how sorry he was. Harry said that it was okay and that it was only an accident. When Harry finally recovered enough, he and Brud went back to picking stones.

After the field was cleared of stones, Allen would get out the corn planter. It had a seat for the driver to sit while he guided us horses. There were two canisters, one on each side of the driver, mounted over the specially designed wheels. Mounted in front of each wheel is a small "V" plow and behind the plow is a tube that drops corn seed from the canisters into the small furrow. Then the wheels, by design, cover the seed creating long straight rows of corn as we horses, working with the long pole between us, pulled the planter back and forth over the entire field. The long pole of this and many other machines would eventually be shortened to be pulled by the tractor. Actually, I didn't mind the tractor doing these jobs without me as they were noisy. Rattling and clanking sounds came from everywhere and it was quite boring, pulling machines back and forth over the fields.

****

Among the most important jobs during the spring was preparing and planting the vegetable garden and potato piece. The potatoes and vegetables were essential to help feed the family. The family needed the gardens. They needed to grow enough vegetables to last throughout the year. Some of the vegetables were canned or frozen to eat during the times of year when they couldn't be grown outside. The potatoes were stored in the cellar to last all through the year. Just like our hay was stored so that we had food even in the winter. We horses were still used to do some of the work in the garden and potato fields. Usually the job required that one horse

61

work singly. The first job, after the land had been plowed and harrowed, was to mark the rows. This was done by using a wooden 4 x 4 crosspiece with four wooden stakes, all spaced equal distances apart and attached to the 4 x 4 crosspiece. There was a set of shafts that the single horse was hooked between. Allen had made the wooden row marker himself. The marker was pulled over the ground making four equally spaced rows at a time.

When the garden and the potato piece were planted, the whole family would be involved in this project. The seeds would soon sprout and start to grow. Ferne could hardly wait until she could have a cucumber and radish sandwich.

After the garden started growing and the rows could be seen, we would start the cultivating job. The cultivator would dig the weeds out of one row at a time and was pulled by a single horse with single whipple tree hooked at the front and center of the machine. I was chosen for most all of the single horse work. I guess because I walked so steady and straight. We would cultivate the garden, potato piece and sometimes the corn if the kale weeds were crowding it out.

Allen would work the handles, keeping the cultivator digging and holding it in the center of the row. I walked and pulled the cultivator down the center of each row. I needed some guidance in order for me to be able to keep walking in the center of the row. The children were all too small at that time to see well enough to drive me from the ground. One of the children would ride on my back and guide me using the check rein for control. This was great fun for the children and I enjoyed having the children so close. They would talk to me from up on my back and pet me at the end of each row when we would take a short break and look back at our progress.

I felt really sorry for little Ferne Marie when she reluctantly gave up her job in the cultivating process to her younger brother. I know there was no feeling of chauvinism or disrespect for women when Allen let Brud take over the job as I know these feelings were not in Allen. He only knew that a man should provide for and protect his family and he wanted his son to know and learn this as soon as he could.

Brud got quite skilled at controlling a work team and driving horses with the reins but I would often hear Allen say, "Hey! Hey! Hey! Pay attention. Keep Dick in the center of the row", when Brud was on my back.

Twice during the growing season, the potatoes had to be hilled. This was done with a horse-drawn shovel plow. The shovel plow was pulled by a team of horses. The plow had two plow shares that attached to a wooden bar. The two shares straddled the row of growing potatoes. They were angled from wide at the front of the share to narrow in the back. The horses walked one in the middle of each row. As the plow was pulled over the ground the dirt funneled to the back of the share and did a neat job of hilling the potatoes. When we were working with the shovel plow in the early years, Allen worked the handles of the plow while Harry drove the team from the ground. Later on, when Brud was big enough to drive the team from the ground, he took over the job.

During the late spring and early summer, there was a near-constant job of weeding to be done either in the garden or the potato piece. Sometimes I would see the whole family out in the corn piece pulling kale weeds.

Trout-fishing also began in the spring. Brud would get very excited with the anticipation of bringing in a huge catch. When he was a small boy, he wasn't allowed to go to the gully by himself. He was allowed to go by himself down to a small brook, more like a drainage ditch, that ran from north of the farm house through the pasture and the north meadow. Trout would run up the small brook from the Whipple Hollow Brook where it eventually connected.

On the first day of trout season, I saw Brud out looking for fish worms. After he had found enough worms (probably two or three), he grabbed his fish pole and went running for the brook. When he got to the metal culvert where the meadow road crossed the brook, he baited his hook and dropped his line in the water. Suddenly, he felt a sharp tug on his line and pulled an eight-inch trout out of the brook which immediately came free from the hook. In shear panic, Brud threw his pole and went scrambling after the fish that was flipping and flopping along the bank of the brook. After several catches and losses of the slippery fish and getting himself covered with mud, and his boots full of water, at six years old, he had caught his first trout all by himself! Then, clutching the fish so tightly in his little fists that he made the poor creature's eyes bulge, he went running and screaming to the house. I thought Brud had been hurt as he was yelling so loudly, and I guess Ferne did too as I saw her come running out of the back door. After admiring and praising Brud for his huge catch, she asked, "But where is your fish pole?" Brud said, "Oh, no, I must have left it back at the brook". He left the fish with his mother and went running back in his sloshy boots after his pole.

Oh great! Here comes Allen, I have to save my wool-gathering for later. It must be time to cultivate the potatoes. I've been noticing a few weeds starting to grow there. Let's go to work!

Where are the Calves?

*A*llen always paid close attention to his cows and always knew when they were due to have their calves. If he could, he would have the cow in the barn at her time of calving. In the spring and summer, they would occasionally have their calves in the small, night-pasture where they could easily be found. It is a cow's nature at calving time to leave the herd and go off by herself to give birth to her calf. She would then leave the calf hidden and go off to feed; returning to the calf occasionally so the calf could nurse. If the cow came up missing when the herd was in the day pasture, that meant the cow could be anywhere within a territory of one-hundred acres. It was important to find the calf soon after it was born as the calf developed strength quickly, and without human contact they would resist human control. Finding the newborn calf right away was also a serious matter because the mother cow needed to settle back into the milking routine and to being back with the herd. There was also a rather grim possibility that a predator would find the calf first.

So even though it was serious work to find the cow and calf, I know for the children, it was an exciting game of hide and seek. The only difference was that you were seeking a valuable little animal who had been alone with his mother somewhere in a huge playground of nature, full of adventure and excitement.

Sometimes, I would see the entire family heading out together to search a section of the pasture. I always wished that I could go along but I knew that a big horse would probably frighten the cow and her calf. I liked to watch the family, working as a team, spread out to cover more ground, more quickly. Jan always tagged along beside Allen as this was where she most wanted to be, and she knew that her father would be the most likely to find the calf. Ferne and the other children would be searching nearby. Mike Horan always eagerly joined the search when he was at the farm during the summer. This was a great adventure for him. In New York City where he lived, his environment was tall buildings and concrete sidewalks.

One day, I saw Kathy and Brud heading out into my pasture in search of a cow and her calf. The cow had not come back with the herd, and Allen knew that she must have calved early. So, he sent the two children out to search for them. They found the calf in the far corner of the pasture laying under a small pine tree. The cow was a short distance away feeding peacefully. While Kathy kept the calf's attention, Brud worked his way around behind the calf and made a leaping grab. Successful, the young boy held tightly as the calf struggled to get away. Brud told Kathy to run and get Dad. He didn't know how much longer he could hold on to the wriggling, and maybe a little frightened critter. Kathy ran as fast as her little legs would carry her down through the pasture and into the barn.

Kathy soon returned with Allen. They hurried up through the pasture to get the calf. When Allen and Kathy got to where Brud was, he was still holding the calf tightly. Allen told Brud to release the calf and the calf hopped up and scampered over to its mother where it laid down, refusing to move. Allen picked it up and carried it back to the barn with the cow and kids trailing along behind.

After a calf was found, sometimes it would cooperatively follow its mother, as the children led her back to the barn. But there were times when the calf would have to be coaxed and pushed all the way. With its sense of adventure, a calf hunt was fun for the children.

Brud often got distracted by things in nature. During one particular calf hunt, when Brud had searched all morning for the cow and calf, he came into the little valley at the base of Blueberry Hill. He discovered a mother fox playing with her pup. Moving very quietly, Brud got very close to them. The little fox would jump on his mother and nip at her ears. Suddenly, the mother fox sensed danger and jumped to her feet, alerting the pup. The young fox ran straight at Brud, passing him only by a couple feet and then hid at the base of an over-hanging rock. The mother fox, with her hair standing on end, came growling and snarling towards Brud. He reached down and grabbed a big stick expecting to have to defend himself against the oncoming fox. He suddenly realized that if he would just move away from the pup, the mother probably wouldn't attack. Not taking his eyes off the mother fox, he moved up the opposite bank away from the little fox. When the pup and its mother reunited, Brud knew the stand-off was over. A short run would take him to Cadillac Rock where he could rest and calm himself down. Perhaps take a short ride.

Haying Season
(and Wild Strawberries)

*J*une meant school was out and that wild strawberries were ripening. I would see all four of the children heading out to scour the edges of the meadow or, if I was lucky, in my own pasture, for the red juicy berries. Ferne Marie and Kathy would return with their pails full or nearly so. Brud's pail would be empty or nearly so as he seemed to be easily distracted from picking strawberries by most anything else that he could find to do or explore. His interest in strawberries would return, when his mother baked a huge, wild strawberry, shortcake or her famous white cake, spread thickly with a creamy, delicious, pink wild strawberry frosting. Jan would also return with an empty pail but it was evident she had found plenty of berries to pick because of the red stains covering her cute little freckled face from ear to ear.

The end of the school year meant more visits from Ferne Marie's friend and school mate, Kathryn Parrow. Kathryn's and Ferne Marie's interests and imaginations involved playing cowboys and wild horses which was great fun for all the children, even the younger ones if they cooperated as directed by Kathryn and Ferne Marie.

Lynne and Ron Smith visited more frequently in the summer; Ron often bringing his BB gun with him. I would see the two boys, Ron and Brud, head out both heavily armed, each with a BB gun and hundreds of rounds of ammunition. They would practice their shooting and stalking skills as they hunted the elusive red squirrels, chipmunks and frogs out near the gully. There would be much shooting with rarely, if ever, any success. I can remember once, when "Dead-Eye" Ron fired his trusty Red Rider BB gun from his hip and took a swooping Swallow right out of the air. Both boys marveled at Ron's sharp shooting skills but were very sorry that he had, actually, hit the Swallow.

Summer in the valley was simply, beautiful. The longer days gave everyone more time for adventure and fun, and I loved naps in the shade under my oak tree. On a farm, though, good weather was good weather to work in, and in the summer, haying was the focus. Haying was an extremely stressful time for Allen though he never seemed to show it. The gathering and storing of a good quality early cut hay crop was critical for good milk production from the cows and meant a successful or a failing year of farming and the whole process despite good planning was totally weather dependent.

After the hay was mowed, it took between two to four days to properly dry the hay to the point where it was safe to be put into the hay mow in the barn. If it was too green, it would mold in the hay mow, making it unpalatable and unhealthy for the cows. In the worst case, it could over-heat in the mow causing spontaneous combustion. When this happened the entire mow of hay would burst into flames, burning the entire crop, the barn, and any animals in the barn. Needless to say, Allen was very careful with the hay drying process.

This very tragedy happened one day on a nearby farm just as we finished unloading a load of hay in the barn. Harley and Mary were visiting, and the children were gathered around him and the horse and buggy. After Allen had backed us and the wagon out of the barn, we noticed a huge, black cloud rising up over the hill at the south east end of the valley. Allen yelled, "Sherman's barn is on fire!". Harley and Brud quickly unhitched us from the wagon and put us in the pasture.

Allen and Harry hurried off towards the Sherman farm in Allen's motor car to see if they could help. They were able to get all the cows out of the barn safely. A few minutes later, Allen could not believe what he was seeing as two large pigs came tumbling out of an open window. Wilma Sherman, George's wife, had caught the pigs in their pen. Wilma, a short, slightly stocky, woman, had to lift each of the frantic, squealing pigs, each weighing much more than she did, up and over her head and then hurl them out of the window to safety from the fire. Wilma climbed out the window herself, just ahead of the ever-increasing flames. Allen had thought this would be an impossible task for such a small woman.

Ferne, Harley, and the children had come over the hill in the buggy and stood in Harley's meadow, watching as the flames leaped high into the sky. The fire had started with an explosion of heat from within the hay mow. By the time the local fire department could arrive to put out the flames, all that could be done was to make sure that the house did not catch fire also.

Friends and neighbors gathered at the farm in a show of support and to help however they could. The most that could be done, however, was just to watch as the flames ate away the center of this farmer's livelihood. His barn was gone. But the most important thing was that the family and animals were all safe. As darkness settled into the Whipple Hollow Valley, the only light was the still glowing embers of the fire.

In less than twelve hours, George's cows would have to be milked, but without his barn, how would he ever manage to do it? A neighbor, Earl Rider, had sold his dairy herd the previous fall, so his barn was empty, and it was less than two miles away. George's cows could be milked there, but they would have to be herded the two miles up the road to the Rider barn.

The next morning, Allen hurried to finish the milking. The whole family had eaten a quick breakfast and were all in the barn to help get the chores done as fast as they could. The cows were put out into the pasture and after we had finished our grain, we were put into ours. Brud excitedly explained to us that, just like real cowboys, they were going on a real cattle drive. There would be no one on horseback, however, as these were dairy cows and needed to be moved slowly and calmly.

A little later that morning, George's family and Allen's family began moving the cows up the Whipple Hollow Road, which at that time was gravel-surfaced and had very little traffic. Some of the people stayed in the rear of the herd, slowly moving the cattle forward, while other people would travel ahead to keep the cows out of yards, side roads, or openings in fences. Neighbors who were at home came out to help by keeping the cattle out of their yards as the herd passed. Finally, the herd arrived at the Rider barn. The cows would stay there until early fall when the Sherman's barn was rebuilt.

Allen made time to help his neighbor. He didn't really have much spare time at all but that was the way things were done. Neighbors helped each other.

Allen was constantly studying the weather, trying to determine if he could get a field of hay dried and into the barn without getting it wet. Unlike us animals, people don't seem to have much of a sense of approaching weather changes. Allen seemed to be able to though; perhaps those who must work with, and through changes in the weather develop this ability. Rarely did Allen let the hay get wet. If he thought there would be a three-day period without rain, he would mow a field that he would be able to get into the barn on the third day. He would mow more on the second day if the weather was still promising.

If the hay is a heavy crop or the weather is threatening rain, Allen will tell the family, "It's time to spread the hay". The entire family will head out to the field, each one carrying a three-tined pitch fork. Even Jan had her own special fork; Allen had shortened the handle, so she could use it. The mowing machine had cut the hay and as the seven-foot cutter bar passed through the hay it would be left behind, laying in neat seven-foot-wide swaths or rows. The hay laid among the stubble. To hasten the drying process, the hay needed to be picked up with the pitch fork, flipped over and laid back down on the other side. It took some amount of practice and some frustration to become skilled at spreading hay. Allen

72

made sure that everyone had plenty of practice.

I was always amazed when they started spreading hay, knowing that they would spread the entire field of hay. Allen would take the first swath with Jan in between him and Ferne; then Ferne Marie, then Brud and then Kathy. Mike Horan would help when he was at the farm and he also required a short-handled fork. As the family was spreading hay across the field, I would see Allen step over and help Jan with her swath to keep up her enthusiasm and to make sure the little girl was not getting too tired. Ferne often would be wearing her apron as she was always ready to drop her housework and go and help Allen whenever he needed her.

Ferne Marie would be flipping and spreading each fork-full of hay so perfectly and efficiently. Her swaths would be the best-looking swaths on the field. She would always stay a short distance ahead of her brother. Brud would be frantically thrashing and slashing with his pitch fork trying to catch up and pass Ferne Marie.

I'm not sure that Ferne Marie was even conscious of his efforts to pass her, but by keeping ahead of him, she knew that this would keep him focused as she knew that he was easily distracted. In this instance Brud was displaying the foolish characteristic of human behavior of male dominance. I knew it was Brud's frustration that not only that she could beat him at spreading hay but most everything else too. Like being able to carry the big sawdust basket when he couldn't even lift it, and the worst thing of all was that she could hit a baseball more than twice as far as he could. I hope that this generation of young women can help him through this non-sense idea that some jobs are strictly for men and some strictly for women and that boys are better at "men's work." If he doesn't learn the mistakes in his philosophy, he'll run the risk of becoming, as Ferne Marie says, a "Nin-Com-Poop".

Kathy works just a bit behind everyone else. She works steadily and without complaint, except for maybe a slight grumble, now and then, when she has to untangle her swath from the tangles being created by her brother with his wild thrashing.

The family worked their way all the way to the other end of the field; pausing to look back at their progress: a forty-one-foot strip of the field all spread. After a short break, they start down the other side and soon there are eighty-two feet; all spread. Another couple of repetitions and I think, wow! They are really going to do this; the field is almost finished. Allen has a horse-drawn machine that is called a Hay Tedder, but he hardly ever used it. His opinion was that the machine didn't do a very good job.

A few more hours of work pass and they have spread that entire section. Just another example of working as a team. In humans and in horses, working as a team not only gets the job done faster but it also strengthens the team. As a Work Horse, I know how important this is.

Allen removes his blousy, train engineer's cap that he always wears if the weather doesn't require a hat with ear flaps to protect from cold and wind. He wipes the sweat from his brow and says, as he often does when someone has completed a difficult task, "You have got courage."

* * * * * * * * * * * * * * * *

After lunch Allen puts my harness on and brings me out to the Yankee dump rake. I will be used singly for this job. The Yankee rake has two wooden- spoked wheels with steel rims. The wheels are mounted on a long axle which has a series of long, closely spaced, rake teeth. Each tooth is about four feet long and bent in a half circle. When the rake teeth become full of hay as the rake is pulled along, a foot pedal is tripped causing a cog to engage with a gear in the wheels, allowing the rake teeth to dump and release the raked-up hay into a neat row.

When Allen first got the Yankee rake he took great pride in it. It was brand new and did a very clean and efficient job of raking hay. Allen had only had the new Yankee rake a short time though when John, Allen's brother, who, being twenty years younger than Allen, was quite a young boy. He was using the new Yankee rake in the big meadow south of the farm buildings. Being a job where a single horse could be used, Harley had assigned Nellie (as in "Nervous Nellie" you might say) to work with John. Nellie was a blood-bay mare who looked just like Mary.

Like Danny, Nellie was a little nervous and skittish, but she had a fast walk and worked quite well on the dump rake. John had been raking and had stopped to remove a large stick from out of the hay. He threw the stick into the bushes which spooked Nellie. She hadn't noticed John throw the stick, you see, she only knew that she had heard a sudden crash in the bushes nearby. Badly spooked, Nellie ran, the rake attached behind her and John running behind the rake; running as fast as he could, and probably faster.

Nellie and the rake ran into a stone-wall and caught a wheel on the gate post which broke the wheel from the axle. The axle dropped to the ground on one side causing the rake to hit against Nellie's heels, frightening her even more. In through the barnyard she went, hitting a post there with the other wheel causing even more damage. Nellie finally stopped at the other end of the barnyard. She could go no further. Luckily Nellie was not seriously injured in the run-away, just a few bumps and a small cut on her heel. Allen and John worked together to repair the rake using wheels and parts from an older Yankee rake.

John spent most of his short young life working with Allen. It seemed as if they were always together. Allen lost his precious little brother in 1948 when John's automobile was hit by a train in North Clarendon. John was only sixteen years old.

* * * * * * * * * * * * * * * *

There was a stony meadow just north of the barn and house. It used to be an old farm orchard and there are still a few apple trees growing there. It is from that orchard, as well as his own, that Harley teaches the children the fun of "Apple Shooting". Harley and the children would go up to the apple trees, usually carrying a pail. The pail would be filled with the small apples from the trees. Harley would then select a long slender branch from the apple tree and would make a point on the most slender end of the stick with his ever-present jack knife. An apple was stuck on to the point and the stick was then whipped over head in a throwing motion. The apple would fly off the point and travel great distances. The apples were not supposed to be shot at anyone as the sting of apple would cause quite a lot of pain. I know this because I would, sometimes when Harley wasn't with them, I'd see Brud, Mike and Ron, who was particularly fond of the game (most any game really), head up to the apple trees. Soon the apples would start flying and I would hear the occasional yelp of pain. It bothered me most when Jan would join in but, somehow, she never seemed to get hit.

Allen and I raked this steep meadow, and Ferne Marie, Kathy and Brud would come out with their pitch forks and start tumbling the hay, Jan would most certainly have been with them, but she was too young for that job, so she stayed with Ferne. Tumbling required that the rake-full of hay be wrapped in a certain way so that the size of the tumble was consistent and that the tumble held together while it was being pitched or loaded onto the wagon. Kathy did a good job of tumbling while Ferne Marie's looked more like a piece of artistic sculpture, with the exact number of straws in each tumble, it looked to me. In contrast, Brud's tumbles looked like thrashed together bunches of hay that had been played in by a pair of chimpanzees.

Brud thought Ferne's work was neater simply because Ferne Marie's pitch fork, just made better tumbles. He would sometimes grab her fork first thinking she wouldn't notice and with that particular fork he would be able to make the same artistic tumbles. It didn't work, of course, no matter which fork he used, it made no difference. If Allen didn't rewrap Brud's tumbles and just pitched them onto the wagon, some of the hay would fall to the ground, while the better share of the leftover hay in the fork, cascaded over his head, causing him to expel a string of choice curse words. Most often these words and phrases were simply a way of getting someone's attention. At other times, though, Allen used these words to express anger and frustration. At these times, I don't think the use of the curse words were to get someone's attention but really was to express some degree of anger or frustration.

As Ferne Marie and Kathy were finishing up the tumbling, Allen took Brud with him and Danny would be brought out and hooked up to the wagon with me. Allen's hay wagon was somewhat different than the high wooden wheeled hay wagons that most farmers used. Allen had made the wagon himself. He used the front wheels and steering mechanism from an old pickup truck. He had a long reach pole from the rear wheels and the rear end of the truck that connected to a pivoting bunk and reach pin at the front. A shallow wagon

box was attached to the bunks and a flat rack was bolted to that. The wagon rack was about twelve feet long by nine feet wide. The wagon had rubber tires which traveled over the ground much more smoothly than the large wooden wheels with steel rims. The wagon rack ended up being much lower to the ground which made it easier to pitch the hay onto it and there was a decreased chance of tipping over and you could put on a larger load of loose hay.

Harry Wedin arrived just as Allen and Brud had finished hitching Danny and me to the wagon. Allen and Harry would pitch the hay on and Brud would drive us and load the wagon. The tumbles had to be placed in precise locations on the rack and in layers so that the load would travel well and not fall off.

The shallow box in the center was filled first, then a tumble was put on each of the four corners. Two tumbles were put on the middle of the rack with one overlapping the other. Another tumble, called the binder, was put between the corner and the middle tumbles which would lock the whole side together. This pattern was repeated until the load was finished. A typical load was usually between six to ten feet high. With its contents packed in so carefully, the load traveled well and without loss even on steep grades.

They had picked all the tumbles on the steep side of the meadow and gotten all of them on the top by the apple trees. The load was getting heavy as we started straight down the steep, north end of the meadow. Because of the steepness of the grade, Brud stopped to drive us so hold us back with the reins, so that Allen and Harry could place the tumbles on the wagon.

Unfortunately, Danny just couldn't hold the heavy load against the pull of the steep grade and even I couldn't hold that much weight combined with the steepness of the grade, by myself. The weight of the wagon kept pushing us down the hill as Allen and Harry struggled to keep up while still loading the tumbles.

Allen yelled a couple times at Brud to hold the horses, but he saw that the horses and the wagon were still moving ahead. Allen yelled a couple of curse words before he repeated, louder, and with no small amount of anger, "Hold those horses!" Trying to control us, and fighting both the weight of the wagon load, as well as inevitable gravity, was challenge enough and then Brud's father began cursing over what was, at this point, mostly out of his control. Brud was frustrated as well. It was more than the young boy could take, I guess. I never saw him so angry.

When we reached the bottom of the hill and could now stand comfortably, Brud wrapped the reins around the buck stick and jumped from the wagon. He erupted with his own string of curse words ending with, "Drive your own horses!" and ran crying to the house. As he ran, he suddenly realized the words he had just used and to whom he had used them. With his vivid imagination, he could see himself forever burning in Hell's fire. Maybe that would be preferable to what his father might do. He thought that surely his punishment would be severe

By the time Brud reached the house, he had stopped crying. Ferne knew that something very serious had happened, farm work can be dangerous, and accidents are not uncommon, but she could not get a word out of him as he sat quietly on the couch waiting for whatever fate had in store for him. Soon Allen came into the house. He didn't speak either. He came over to where Brud sat miserably on the couch. He sat down next to him. After several moments of only silence from both of them, Allen said, "Brud, it's really hot out there and I really need your help loading that hay". I knew everything was okay again when I saw them both coming back to the field and I noticed that the boy was walking in Allen's shadow.

* * * * * * * * * * * * * * * *

With the passage of time, machines began to take over a lot of the work that we horses had been doing. Allen got more equipment that he could use with the little grey tractor. He bought a mowing machine for it. The mowing machine was mounted on the back of the tractor and he could mow the fields much faster with this machine.

Allen also got a machine that he called a Side-Delivery Rake. The pole that we used to hitch to was shortened so that he could pull the rake with the tractor. The rake was a ground-driven machine. Ground-driven means that as the wheels turn over the ground they also turn a sprocket with a chain to another sprocket causing another desired action of the machine. As the rake traveled over the ground, the wheels spun with a combination of gears, chain, sprocket, and two wheels with four long bars with many teeth attached. The rake would pick up a swath of hay and with a rolling action, leave the hay in a neat, long windrow. I noticed that after the rake picked the hay up out of the stubble that the hay would finish drying more quickly.

At the same time, Allen bought from our neighbor, Red Poremski, another machine that Allen called a hay loader. The combination of the side delivery rake and the hay loader made a huge difference in the ease and efficiency of our haying process.

Before Allen purchased the hay loader, he and Norm Cham pine, Allen's teen-aged nephew, had gone over to the Red's farm to see the machine. While they were there, Red's cute little blond-haired daughter had been pestering Norm. Norm picked up the little girl and swung her around. Red, not thinking what would happen, said to his farm collie, Topper, "Sic 'im". The dog jumped quickly and sunk his teeth deep into the calf of Norm's leg.

Allen brought Norm back to the farm and it was decided that Norm needed to see a doctor. Ferne and Allen took him to the doctor's but left the children with Harley as they were too young to be left a home alone.

It was early evening when the children were left with Harley. He knew he could keep them amused by telling stories of his past. So, as he sat on his porch under the webs of the guardians of his house, the huge grey spiders and there were hundreds of them, he began telling the children stories. He sat, peacefully rocking in his chair with his walking stick leaning against the porch railing. The stick was a piece of hickory, hard and strong with his initials carved into it. This he referred to as his "cudgel". He never used a fire arm for either hunting or defense; he didn't need one as long as he had his cudgel. He had dispatched any beast from a rattle snake to a silver-tip grizzly bear with that cudgel, at least that's what he told the children.

Harley told the children about Rabies, a disease, he said, that was caused by animal bites; bites like the one Norm had gotten from Topper. People who get bitten by a rabid animal, froth at the mouth and go around biting other people, giving them the rabies too! He also told them about the albino lady with white hair and pink eyes that lives in Center Rutland, and about the lady in Fair Haven who had been scalped by Indians and now always wore a scarf to cover her bony white

skull. Ferne was somewhat upset with Harley because when they returned, the children wouldn't go near Norm and she had trouble getting them to go to sleep that night.

* * * * * * * * * * * * * *

As time passed, machines began to do more of our work, as well as that of people. For instance, the hay loader was a big step forward in our haying process. The hay loader hooked directly behind the wagon. By this time Brud was getting quite skilled at driving the work team as it took close attention to ground speed and staying centered over the windrow. As the hay loader passed over the windrow, a rake lifted the hay and directed it to a chute which had bars and teeth which pushed the hay up the chute and onto the wagon. As Brud drove the work team, Allen would move the hay away from the loader and place it on the wagon in the same layers that he used when he pitched the hay from the ground. As Brud drove, while standing on the buck stick at the front of the wagon, Allen would load the hay right around him. I can imagine the site of Allen standing on top of his huge load of hay and Brud driving from his little hole down at the front. The side delivery rake and hay loader took the place of the dump rake which would now only be used for raking scatterings. The tumbling process was no longer needed, and Allen no longer had to pitch the hay on to the wagon from the ground. The whole haying process could be done more quickly now.

I always get a certain amount of excitement as Roany and I pull a huge load of hay up the hill between the house and the long barn and garage. Our shoes seem to echo as we pass between the two buildings. I like the clink of stones and the grind of the gravel beneath our metal shoes. As we pass by the house, the girls are already out and running up over the back lawn to the barn. Ferne will come trailing along with Jan by the hand.

As the girls run to the hay barn, they will shout "Which bay?" Allen will shout back where he wants to put the load. He will yell something like, first on the left or second on the right. Ferne Marie and Kathy will climb up into the mow that Allen has indicated. Ferne will then toss Jan up into the hay mow. She will still be climbing up herself just as we come into the barn, our hooves making a hollow, thumping sound and our trace chains jingling.

The hay barn was divided into six sections, they were called mows or bays. There were three mows on each side of the barn floor. Each mow is about forty by forty feet square. As the hay crop was put into the barn, Allen had to plan where in the barn he wanted the hay from each field to be stored. In this way, he could insure that the cows were getting a variety of good quality hay, at all times. When we stop at the appropriate bay, Brud will climb up into the mow. Jan will be passed down to Allen in the wagon and she will stand by the buck stick where she will "supervise" the unloading process.

I once again stand in amazement watching the family work all together as a team. The hay must be arranged carefully for storage. Each person works with a pitch fork; moving each tumble of hay to its appropriate place in the mow. Allen pitched the hay off the wagon and up to Ferne who will then pitch the hay down to the children who are spread out in the bay, (bay means basically a very large room for stowing hay). A row of tumbles is put around the edges of the bay first, then a row of tumbles is placed front of these. This pattern continues toward the center until the last tumble is put in the middle and the pattern begins again. Storing the hay this way was important for two reasons: one, it kept each mow separate and straight; two, it was easier to take the hay out to be feed to the cows rather than if it had been just a huge, tangled mess.

When the level of hay got low enough, Jan climbed down from her "supervisory" position and onto the barn floor. She would snatch a couple hand fulls of hay and somehow, she would always get the best. She would bring it to Roany and me. I think she liked the tickle of our whiskers and the feel of our big floppy lips as we carefully took the hay from her tiny, little hands. Roany and I thought the best we could get was to be fed by the cute, little, pig-tailed girl.

When the wagon is empty, the family climbs down from the mow. Jan is hoisted up to Allen who then expertly backs the big hay wagon out of the barn. He drives us down to the front of the house, where we rest under the shade of the huge maple tree. That maple tree is a wonderful place to rest after pulling in a load of hay. Ferne would bring out ice water or Kool-Aid, a sweet, fruit-flavored drink, I know about Kool-Aid. Once, Brud had a big smear of it around his mouth and on his cheeks, so out of curiosity, I took a lick as he hooked up my check rein. It tasted like the wild strawberries that I find in my pasture. I'd like to try a whole bucket full sometime. Must be it's not good for horses or I think one of the children would have brought some to me.

Roany told me that when she and Brud were raking scatterings, he would often just let her wander with very little guidance. That was probably because he would be day-dreaming about becoming a baseball star. Or maybe he would be day-dreaming about all the pretty, little, blond-haired girls, that like the pretty, little yellow wildflowers grew all along the Whipple Hollow Road. There were quite a few girls that lived on the road, all the way from the Carlson girls to the Poremski girls, all the way to the Florence Church. When Brud told me about these thoughts, I would tell him that just like the flowers that are pretty and smell nice, it's better to just enjoy their looks and fragrance but not get more involved than that. I'd remind him about the time he insisted on riding in the back of the empty sawdust truck with pretty, little Esther Carlson and ended up with his eyes full of sawdust.

Roany would tell me also as she and Brud were raking, back and forth across the field, she would feel the reins go slack and drop to the ground, trailing along behind her. She would stop, realizing that Brud had fallen asleep and she was afraid he might topple from the rake seat.

* * * * * * * * * * * * * * * * *

When the first crop of hay had been harvested and stored, it was time for Allen to trim the entire perimeter of his meadows. He would first hitch Roany and me to the horse-drawn mowing machine as we could get into areas that the tractor could not go. The mower pulled quite easily, and I liked the metallic clicking noise of the knife as it moved back and forth in the cutter bar. Allen will then use his scythe to mow more closely to the stone wall or the fence line.

I   enjoy watching Allen use the scythe; swinging it back and then bringing it forward, cutting the hay so evenly you would think it was done by a machine. He carries a sharpening stone in his back pocket that he calls a whet stone. He stops frequently and whets his scythe. He says that keeping the blade sharp is the secret to cutting hay with a scythe.

There is probably a reason Allen has two scythes and he won't let Brud use the one he uses. Watching Brud use the scythe would be funny if it wasn't for how frustrated he gets. He swings and slashes with the scythe causing very little damage to the surrounding vegetation but doing a great deal of damage to what once was a sharp blade. When Brud mows, I do not hear the rhythmic swishing sound of the blade slicing through the hay but instead the clank and clunk of the blade striking the hard rocks and sound it makes as the blade is imbedded into the gravel. I am sure Brud will someday be really good at hand mowing; but I feel that will have to wait until they come up with something besides a scythe as I feel he will never be able to keep one sharp enough to actually cut anything with it.

As Allen mowed the edges, we would often be pulling the wagon along behind him. One of the children would be hand-raking along behind him. Hand-raking seems to be another tedious job. Jan quite often seems to do the hand-raking, I think because it keeps her closer to Allen and keeps her from doing much house work which seems to be a chore she would rather avoid if at all possible. Brud and Mike load the hay on to the wagon then take it out into the pasture where they spread it out leaving it in small piles for the cows to pick through and eat.

One day as Allen was mowing the edge of the meadow north of the farm house, he pulls his hat off and hurls his scythe, sending it twirling high into the air as he slaps himself with his hat. He yells to Brud, who is sitting on the hay wagon with Jan and Mike only a few feet from where he was mowing, to get the horses away from there. It didn't take Roany and me long to get ourselves and the children away. We knew that Allen had gotten into a nest of bees. Yellow-Jackets! From a safe distance away, we watched as Allen ran around wildly, still slapping himself with his hat.

But the children couldn't see the bees from that distance and thought that their father was going mad. He dropped his pants and continued to slap himself with his hat, shouting loud curses into the wind. Finally, due to the lethal swatting of his hat, the Yellow Jackets gave up the attack. After treating his numerous bee stings, Allen picked up his scythe and went back to mowing, only conceding a small amount of hay near the Yellow Jacket nest.

Something in the Berries; An Illness; and The Doodle Bug

A break from field work did not mean a time of rest for Ferne. Now she could devote a good part of her day to gathering and putting away the vegetables from her garden. I see her go out to the garden with her bushel basket. She usually brings at least Kathy or Ferne Marie to help her. Today, both girls are helping her pick string beans and when she returned, her basket was heaping full of beans.

Brud had just finished morning chores and he and Jan head outside to play baseball. Ferne tells them that baseball will have to wait today as everyone is going to help prepare the beans for canning. Brud attempts to inform his mother that there are certain jobs that men do and certain jobs that women do and that preparing beans is a woman's job. Ferne dumps the contents of the basket in the middle of the dining room table and informs Brud that boys need to know the work that goes into putting food on the table as well as putting food by for the times when none can be freshly harvested. She tells him that both girls and boys like to eat, so he needs to sit down and get to work.

Ferne Marie washes and prepares the jars to be filled while Ferne gets her huge oblong canner filled with water and gets her wood-fired cook stove stoked up. The water must be kept at a constant boil for the canning process. Kathy, Jan and Brud are cutting the ends off of the beans and cutting them into the proper length to be put into the jars. Brud wonders as he is working, if there really are other people in the world working on a literal mountain of string beans and actually thinking they can finish them all.

Altogether, Ferne would can one hundred quarts of string beans, peas and tomatoes so that she would have enough vegetables put away for the coming year.

One year, there seemed to be an abundant crop of wild blackberries. Harry Wedin knew where many of them grew, on the north end of Blueberry Hill. He took the children, each one with their own picking pail and Harry with a picking pail of his own and a large milk pail. Harry and the children went up on the hill to see how many they could get. As they picked the black berries, Ferne Marie, who is a great little berry picker, matched Harry pail for pail. All the pickers' pails were dumped into the huge milk pail. It wasn't long at all before they were finished. The milk pail and all the picking pails were heaping full. Even Brud's pail was full, though his interest in berries didn't go beyond the pies and short cakes that would be made with them.

That year, Grandpa Waven said that there were a lot of berries in his back woods which bordered Sugar Hollow in Pittsford. Grandpa Waven led the entire Mills family and the Smith family to the location of the blackberry bushes. They were heavily laden with an abundant crop of berries. The picking pails were soon filled and were dumped into the milk pails.

Ferne was so intent on getting all the berries that she had found in a huge patch of bushes, that she hadn't noticed that everyone had moved farther down the wood road, picking as they went. She heard thrashing on the other side of a patch of berry bushes that had grown so tall that they were way over her head. She remarked to Allen that this was the best berry picking she had ever seen. Somewhat upset that his only response was heavy grunt and more thrashing of the bushes, she moved around the patch where she could see him. Allen wasn't there but the noise in the bushes continued. She turned to see a big, black bear busily (and hungrily) munching on the blackberries. She quickly decided to concede these berries to the bear and headed down the wood road as fast as her legs could carry her. That summer, Ferne canned eighty quarts of black berries.

****

From the sale of gravel out of their pit, Allen and Ferne decided they would buy a huge chest freezer. This purchase provided a whole new dimension to putting food by and meant a lot less time stoking the wood cook stove in the heat of the summer.

One day as I watched from the oak tree, I saw Ferne Marie and the children come out of the house. Each child was carrying a berry pail. If there is a berry anywhere, Ferne Marie will find it. I think she can smell them from a mile away. I think she can probably stand outside and just like one of Allen's hunting hounds, who can catch the scent of an animal blowing in on the wind, she can catch the fragrance of berries and pinpoint their exact location. On this day, she wants blueberries, and she knows that on the steep point of Blueberry Hill, they will find them.

I follow the children for a little way and they take the path by Brud's Cadillac Rock, then turn and go up the hill above Wild Horse Valley. Before heading up the hill, they stop to check and make sure the initials of their grandfather Harley, and his brother Arthur, are still visible in the huge rock that had slid down the ledge. Years ago, when they were young boys, the two brothers had carved their initials in the rock.

The children scramble up the steep path to the top of Blueberry Hill. This path is so steep that only white-tailed deer, and children after berries, ever used it. In no time at all, Ferne Marie found the blueberries. Brud grumbled about how small they were. Ferne Marie informed him that actually, the tiny, wild blueberries have the best flavor. Then, Brud began grumbling about how many of these tiny little berries it was going to take to make a pie, and that they could never pick that many. She tells him if he picked as much as he grumbled they would have enough by now.

But Brud is still muttering to himself about how long it is taking to pick all the berries she needs. So Ferne Marie announces that no one is leaving until they have enough berries for a pie, and if Brud doesn't start picking, she will make sure he gets NO pie. Those were exactly the right words to inspire Brud and he begins to pick the berries. When she is satisfied that they have enough, she says that they will have to take the long way back because she doesn't want to take the chance of spilling the precious blueberries, going down the more direct, but steeper, path.

* * * * * * * * * * * * * * * *

During one hot summer, a very strange thing happened to the family. For myself, I can only equate it to the times when I had lost one of my team mates. During those times work had to be done but everything was more difficult, and nothing seemed to go right. I had not seen Ferne going to the barn to help with the chores, nor had I seen her hustling back to the house, from the barn, to do her work there in quite a few days. I also noticed that Allen was spending more time in the house. He'd emerge with a mop and pail, dump its contents and go back into the house. We had never seen him do that. And where was Ferne?

I learned that Ferne had a severe gum disease and that it had made her very sick. All of her teeth needed to be extracted. If that wasn't bad enough, Ferne had a problem in her blood that made it, so her blood would not clot properly, making certain medical treatments and procedures dangerous. There was an additional complication. Ferne was extremely allergic to the penicillin she'd been given to fight

90

infection. She became very ill and her entire body was completely covered with hives. Her feet swelled to the point that she couldn't walk on them and so she had to stay in bed.

The two little girls, Ferne Marie and Kathy, along with Allen, (who still had a farm to run), did the best they could to care for Ferne and do the cooking and house work. As for poor little Jan, she was, actually afraid of her mother, who now had no teeth and was covered in red blotches.

Brud was even too young to know why his mother was now spending so much time in bed instead of taking care of all his usual needs, from a scraped knee to a big slice of apple pie, and everything in between. For breakfast, he was even having to eat cereal that Ferne Marie and Kathy made for him. He considered cereal to be like the grain that the cows ate. Cereal was nowhere near the breakfasts of home fries, eggs and toast that his mother usually made for him.

Then one day, a wonderful thing happened. A huge motor car, called a Buick, drove into the yard with a curly, little head just peeking through the steering wheel. The car stopped and out hopped cute, little Grandma Jessie Spaulding, with her rosy cheeks, reddish nose and ever-present grin. To use her own words, she was a "Pip"! As soon as her feet hit the ground, she was in a hustle to get into the house. In fact, I think that's where Ferne gets her own speedy, little hustling gait.

I know it makes Ferne feel better just to know her mother, Jessie, is there to take charge. Soon after she arrives, the wood stove is popping and out of the oven came her delicious, molasses cookies that Ferne Marie helped her make. The supper to follow will be the special baked spaghetti and meat balls that only Jessie can make. She might also make her famous baked beans, known from the hunting camp in Chittenden, to the church suppers at the Methodist Church in Pittsford. Ferne Marie will not eat them though; she insists that never will a bean pass through her lips.

There were no treatments, at that time, to relieve Ferne's allergic condition. All she could do was wait until the antibiotic had cleared her system. I think maybe the one thing that

91

helped Ferne through her illness was the day I saw Allen cutting, with his jack knife, a beautiful pink thistle. He carefully cut all the sharp thorns from the thistle and then brought the beautiful, pink, flower into the house and gave it to Ferne. I am sure that she felt that if Allen could uncover this beautiful pink flower from all those thorns and cared enough to bring its unique beauty back to her, she could get better for him, and she was soon back to her busy, wonderful self again.

There was a strange machine that arrived at the farm one summer. It was a 1930 Model A Truck. Its frame and drive shaft had been cut into, shortened and welded back together. Harry had bought the machine and after his first attempt at driving it, he decided that for his own safety and concern for other people's property, he should give it to Brud.

Brud repainted it black and silver and called it his Doodle Bug. Because the battery was weak, he parked it on the hill just the other side of the fence from my oak tree. I could look it over closely from my pasture and could see it could be a source of real danger, but I hoped that this machine would present no real harm to anyone from using it. It had no emergency brake, in fact, it had no front brakes at all and the rear brakes were probably only good enough to stop a bicycle on really dry almost level ground and would do little to nothing to stop a vehicle of this size and weight. This seemed a bit of a bad sign to me. Brud would put a big rock in front of the rear wheel to keep it from rolling down the hill where, out of necessity to get the thing moving, the Doodle Bug had to be parked.

In order to start the Doodle Bug, Brud would first kick the stone away from the wheel, then climb into the driver's seat, turn on the switch, shift into neutral and let the contraption roll down the hill. By the time it came to the gravel road, it would have picked up a good amount of speed. At this point, he would shift it into second gear and pop the clutch. Loud bangs, pops and black smoke would erupt from the exhaust pipe of the un-muffled engine. When the engine started, Brud would be off on a trip around the meadows.

Allen and Ferne were not very happy with Harry's gift of the Doodle Bug to Brud. They could see that the vehicle really could be a source of trouble; some restrictions would be needed concerning its use. Allen knew that the best restriction would be for Brud to buy his own gas, which was quite expensive at that time. Nearly twenty cents a gallon.

The Doodle Bug did have some worthwhile use as it could pull smoothing harrows and stone-boats. Roany and I used to like to watch Brud drive the Doodle Bug around, to patrol the meadows and shoot woodchucks from the driver's seat. This was not done out of cruelty. A horse stepping into an unseen woodchuck hole would badly injure our legs, and horses, as you might know, spend a great deal of our time standing. We sleep, eat, work, and relax while standing. A leg injury is very serious to a horse.

For Brud's patrols with the Doodle Bug, speed was not required, which was good because the vehicle had no springs. Passengers had to sit on a wooden tool box with a metal seat attached. This was quite uncomfortable if the vehicle wasn't moving slowly. Also, the steering on the car was very loose and became quite uncontrollable at any great speed.

From the other side of the fence, I saw trouble coming one day, but was powerless to stop it. Brud came up to start the Doodle Bug. First, he kicked the stone away from the wheel, jumped into the seat and shifted it into neutral. However, this time the machine did not start to roll down the hill as usual. Brud was thinking that maybe a little push would be enough to start the Doodle Bug rolling, but the machine would move not at all. So, he went around to the rear and gave it a mighty push. Just as the Doodle Bug began to roll, Brud's feet slipped and he fell to his knees.

I watched in terror as the machine went careening towards the back of the house with Brud running behind trying desperately to catch it. Gaining speed, the car crossed the gravel road, and headed across the back lawn. In the very nick of time, Brud managed to jump on the back of the moving vehicle. He had no time to gain the seat before going over the stone wall and crashing into the porch. With the vehicle moving, at some speed, now, Brud reached over the seat and gave a vicious pull on the steering wheel to the left. The Doodle Bug went along the wall and down over the bank, heading straight for the garage. From his position behind the seat, Brud gave the wheel a quick pull to the right, sending the machine down the road at which time, Brud was able to climb over and get into the seat. He quickly turned on the switch, shifted into gear, and let out the clutch. The engine back-fired and started. Brud sat with the engine idling and both he and I were able to catch our breath. He from running, and no doubt imagining all the terrible outcomes of this excursion, and me from a terrible fear that something Very Bad was about to occur.

Undaunted, Brud then proceeded on for a pleasant drive around the meadow. Pleasant, that is, until he got back to the farm yard where he was met by Allen. Allen asked if the Doodle Bug had started easily after rolling down the hill. Allen said that, by the tire tracks, which Brud had forgotten all about, the vehicle had rolled quite a distance before it started. Allen told Brud to park the Doodle Bug and leave it there until he could afford to buy a new battery for it. This kept us all safe for a while as it took some time for Brud to scrape up the ten or fifteen dollars needed to buy the new battery.

After a new battery was purchased, the contraption was roaring through the valley once again. It was not used to pull any haying equipment, as Allen feared that the sparks that spewed from the cars' exhaust would surely set the hay on fire. Night-driving was not permitted. The Doodle Bug had no lights and it was dangerous enough even when you could see where you were going.

Ferne Marie was very busy studying and working at Castleton College, and had very little interest in the Doodle Bug. Like Kathy, she seemed more interested in boys and real cars than the ridiculous old machine.

Jan was curious about the Doodle Bug and really enjoyed riding with Brud, but she was afraid to drive the noisy vehicle herself. Along with its other troubles, steering the car was difficult even at a slow rate of speed, and for her, the car was uncontrollable if she tried to go fast. The passenger seat was actually only a wooden tool box with a metal seat bolted to it. There were no springs on the vehicle other than on the front end. Not very comfortable at all. Jan would most often stand behind Brud and use the back seat to hold on to. Being a smart girl, she no doubt noticed that from that position she could jump from the vehicle if she needed to.

Mike and Ron also drove the Doodle Bug. Taking some really wild rides. Ron really needed to have someone with him, as it is well known that with anything he does, Ron likes to be right on the razors edge of danger and how will he know if he has gotten there unless he goes over the other side? This philosophy combined with the Doodle Bug made it necessary for Ron to travel with a partner.

Lynne, who was always up for anything that was a little bit wild and exciting, convinced Brud that she could drive the Doodle Bug, having watched Grampa Waven drive his Doodle Bug when they rode with him into the woods of his pasture. However, the seat of Brud's Doodle Bug was bolted down and could not be adjusted to fit her smaller size. Lynne's feet could just reach the clutch, which she would need to shift the vehicle. It was fortunate, for lack of a better word, that the brakes were largely useless because she could only reach them with a great deal of effort. The gas pedal she could reach not at all.

Just then she noticed that, just like Grampa Waven's Doodle Bug, Brud's had a hand throttle, just to the right of the steering wheel. Problem solved! She shifted the vehicle into gear, pulled down the throttle, and let out the clutch. Away they went! Careening across the meadow. From under the oak tree and above the roar of the engine, I could hear laughing and squealing as Lynne struggled to keep control of the steering wheel. After a while, Brud was able to work up enough courage to let go of the seat he was clinging to and with one hand he pushed the throttle up, slowing the vehicle down and allowing Lynne to gain more control of the steering.

The Doodle Bug lasted only one summer at the farm which, in my opinion, was more than plenty. Two serious incidents spelled doom for the troublesome contraption. The first involved the old fellow who traveled around the countryside, stopping at all the farms. He would buy old rags, metal and dead batteries that were of no more use but could be recycled. On this particular day, he was driving his old, rusty, red pickup truck up the road when Brud came speeding around the corner of the corn piece, up near the road. It was a near thing, but luckily the old fellow was able to stop in time to avoid being crashed into as Brud sped along, rounding the corner of the tall corn piece and sliding onto the road; tires spitting gravel. Brud was worried about what the old fellow would say to his father when they both drove into the yard. Allen simply raised an eyebrow as the old man handed Brud a pitch fork saying, "I think you lost this when you drove out in front of me."

The second, and deciding incident happened one day as I was grazing in one of the small pastures. I heard the Doodle Bug start up. From where I was standing, I could just see Brud and Ron Smith or Mike, I couldn't tell which one was riding with him. I could see Brud and his passenger as they passed through the gate. I could tell by the sound of the still-running engine that they had passed the spring, which was as far as the Doodle Bug was supposed to go but it continued to climb up the steep Company road. This road is so steep that even Roany and I have all we can do to hold back even a small load of wood with Allen pulling on the steel brakes of the wagon as we descend the hill. As the boys reached the upper log-header and turned around for the return trip, it occurred to Brud that the brakes would be of no help at all on the steep grade back that they now would have to go back down.

He shifted into the lowest gear that he could, hoping not to damage the engine. He thought that if he could keep to the inside of the curve at the "Y" in the road, (where a man named Dimick had lost his log truck over the bank and would have gone down over the steep ledge and into the gully below if not for the truck getting hung up in the trees) they would probably be okay. The boys skidded in the gravel and loose shale as they just made the curve. The road straightened after that, but it was still very steep. Now, if the engine didn't blow, they would make it back and might be able to start breathing again.

Soon after these incidents, Allen convinced Brud that he should sell the Doodle Bug to a man in Brandon who wanted to use it in his wood lot.

Harley's Corn Dodgers; and Hilling Potatoes

*T*he potatoes are now bulging the sides of their hills. First, the ground needs to be loosened with the cultivator. Brud guides me, riding on my back as Allen works the cultivator. We go over the entire piece again with the single-bladed shovel plow. With Brud working with me and Allen working with the plow, we go between each row and push the loose dirt up next to the potato plants.

As we work the potato piece, I can see Jan and Ron heading over the wood road to Harley's house. They like to talk with Harley and he likes to share his mint candies with them. He invites them to stay and have some biscuits that are just coming out of the oven. Harley calls them Corn Dodgers. Ron says they are like muffins, except they are much harder than muffins.

Harley, who had no teeth by then, tells the kids that the Corn Dodgers are better if they marinate in maple syrup for a little bit. While the Corn Dodgers are marinating, Harley makes some of his famous green Kool Aid to drink. Harley adds a little more sugar to the Kool Aid; so that it will go better with the Corn Dodgers, he says. After the Corn Dodgers have taken on enough of the marinade, he scoops them out. Kool Aid and Corn Dodgers in hand, Harley and the kids go out to the porch.

They eat, watching the huge, grey, spiders working in the webs above. Some spiders are poisonous and can be rather unsettling to some, but I've watched spiders in my stall and their webs are quite beautiful. They also catch and dispatch the flies that buzz around my head.

Harley tells stories about the Indians that used to inhabit his land. He shows them Table Rock, where the squaws took their disobedient children to spank them. He shows them Council Rock, where the Chief stood and told his braves of his plans to frighten the settlers and pillage the entire Whipple Hollow Valley.

After they finished the delicious Corn Dodgers, Jan and Ron head back to the farm. They ran all the way across the pasture and around the wooded road, just in case there might be a few Indians around, still hiding among the trees.

* * * * * * * * * * * * * * * *

When the shovel plowing was completed, everyone would go out to uncover any plants that had gotten buried and to make sure none of the new potatoes were poking out of the hill where they could get sunburned. While they are out in the potato piece, Allen digs into a few hills of Early Reds. Early Reds are fast maturing red potatoes. In each hill, he finds many small red potatoes, he can see the white flesh of the potatoes through their tender, pink, peel. He picks up every one, even the very tiny ones. He thinks these are the best potatoes to eat. Ferne carefully washes the tiny potatoes. She cooks them with fresh-picked peas and serves them in warm milk, butter, salt and pepper. Even Allen enjoys this summer delicacy though he really doesn't care much for any kind of vegetables other than Ferne's fried parsnips.

The Sweet corn is harvested around this time and take it from me, there is a difference between Sweet corn and Field corn. The taste of sweet corn is much sweeter. I'd snatch an ear of sweet corn any chance I got. I'll bet most people have never tried Field corn, but I agree with Mike Horan, who has:

it doesn't matter as long as it's corn. It must have been quite a thing for him to be able to pick a fresh ear of corn, right off the stalk, and eat it. I understand this is not something you can do in the city where he was from. I have seen him eat an entire ear of Field corn raw right out of the stalk with the juice spraying his freckled face and running down his chin, he will profess how good it tastes.

Ferne picks a bushel of ears of corn at a time. She has the children husk the corn. Brud doesn't mind this job but he is somewhat lax about removing all of the corn silk. Ferne will can some of the corn, and put some in the large chest freezer, which takes up most of the room on the back porch. The freezer was a good purchase. They would no longer need to rent a freeze locker in Pittsford. All the frozen foods, stored right on the back porch, just outside the kitchen. It also was a place to store venison. Allen shot a deer every year in November during hunting season. He was hunting for the dinner table. Sometimes the gunshots in the woods would unnerve me, and I never really got used to it, but I could see that not only would the deer feed the family, it was one less deer to get into the garden and fields.

Hunting for Ginseng

Late July and August is the best time to hunt Ginseng. Grampa Harl called it "Ging Shang". He may have not known the correct pronunciation but Brud said Grampa Harl could spot a ginseng plant growing in a patch of wild buckwheat from a hundred yards away. By late July, Ginseng has a small cluster of green berries that become a brilliant red color in August. Ginseng is not easy to find among all the plants of the undergrowth of the forest. There are many plants that look similar and they grow in the same areas. Grampa Harl said to pay attention in the patches where wild buckwheat grows. Not every plant that is found still has it's bright, red berry to draw your eye. One day Harley and Brud were searching the steep side of Blueberry Hill, and Brud shouted, "There's one!" and immediately spotted another of the elusive plants. Harley said, "That's right, now that you have found your first Ging Shang plant, you will always know it when you find it."

From a soft denim bag that Grampa Harl always carried when he hunted ginseng, he took out a long, metal spike. He showed Brud how to carefully free the root from the earth before pulling on it; he said not to break the root, because the shape resembled that of a man and that ginseng was the Chinese word for man, (person) root. He told Brud that the Chinese believed that the root would bring them health and wellbeing. Harley believed this to be true because no matter if you found the plant or not, just knowing that you could if you needed to, made you healthier.

101

The roots were carefully washed and dried, and then sold; bringing in as much as sixty dollars a pound at that time. Wow! Easy money, right in the woods! If you have ever seen a dried ginseng root, you know that it does indeed resemble a human figure. A small figure, and when they were dried it took a lot of roots to make a pound. One summer Brud found a pound and a half!

Harley and Brud searched Pittsford Ridge, from the Markowski Farm to Grampa's Knob, for Ging Shang. Harley showed Brud where the Robbins' logging camp was located and told him about the winch and rail system they used to lower logs down the mountain. He also showed Brud Sheep Mountain, where Austin Allen Mills once grazed large herds of sheep and, of course, the gold mines of Harley's brother Arthur.

I hope children will always be able travel the woods with their grandparents. They will be better for having been there even if they don't find any "Ging Shang".

The Hurricane;
A Strange Old Man;
and
The Whirly Gig

*I*n the late summer of 1950, the strong winds of a passing hurricane blew the entire back half of the roof of the long barn next to the house off. Allen got Joe Shuteck, a little old carpenter, from West Rutland to help him fix the roof.

Allen took Dolly and me up on the mountain to get rafters for the roof. Allen cut the rafters and we skidded them out to the wood road where Harry Wedin helped load them on the wood wagon. I didn't like skidding very well as a rolling log could easily injure a horse's back legs. These rafters would be small, so I wasn't worried nearly as much as I would have been with big logs. Allen got Lee Lewis to help put the roof on the barn. He was a strong young fellow and could lift the heavy rafters into place with ease.

The same year that the hurricane came ripping through the valley, a strange old man arrived one day. He was driving a surrey with fringe dangling from the edge of its roof. The surrey was pulled by an old white horse. The horse was very sad and looked very tired. He seemed resigned to whatever fate had put him in his situation and I never got his name. I gave him space to rest and just be, here, in this (mostly) peaceful place.

The old man's name was Cameron. I got the feeling right away that Allen did not like or trust the old fellow as he said, "I think, he bears watching". The old man told Allen that he was going to be visiting Harley for a while and wanted to leave his horse and surrey at the farm until he left. Allen reluctantly allowed him to leave the horse and surrey. I think it was because Allen felt sorry for the poor old horse who obviously needed food and care.

Danny and I shared our barn with the old horse. He used the spare stall in the barn with us and the old man stayed with Harley. The old horse had a ravenous appetite and would eat huge amounts of hay, bolting down his grain as if he never had any before. I had to caution the old fellow, for fear, he might choke from eating his grain so fast.

The old man, Cameron, was quiet and didn't join in hardly any conversation. Nothing wrong with being quiet but he never did any work to help Allen, not even just for giving his horse a place to stay. This old fellow seemed to just be looking, and lurking, around the farm. I, definitely, sensed that Allen felt the man was likely up to no good.

One day the old man showed up at the farm just as Dewey Balch arrived. The three of us horses were in the barnyard when Dewey and the old man came out of the cow barn and into the yard. Dewey, with his large pot belly, hat cocked over to one side of his head, and a cigar stuck in the corner of his mouth, was a local livestock dealer. I have found that all livestock dealers have these cigars stuck in their mouths. They seem to chew on one end of the cigar until the juice starts to drip from the other and at this time they take a stick which makes fire, out of their pocket and light the dripping end of the cigar on fire. Dewey puffed on his, sending plumes of bluish black smoke (which, to me, anyway) smells worse than our horse crap piles, warm and wafting into the air.

Dewey and the old man began to circle the old horse. Dewey made a remark about the condition of the horse and he even looked in the poor old horse's mouth. The old man grew angry over the low price that Dewey offered for the horse, and then got even angrier when Dewey stood his ground on the amount. The old man reluctantly accepted the money and the horse was quickly loaded into Dewey's livestock truck and disappeared from the valley. Danny and I worried about the old horse and wondered why he had not let us know anything of his former life. I will forever remember his sad, haunted eyes.

The selling of the old horse bothered Allen even more, as he felt this probably meant that Cameron had decided to settle in for a long stay with Harley. Shortly after the sale of his horse, the old man mysteriously disappeared from Harley's place and the Whipple Hollow Valley altogether. We never knew where the man had come from or where he went. The only thing he left behind was his surrey, which led to some trouble which I will tell you about presently.

The surrey was blown over the bank and probably rolled over a couple times during the hurricane. The top and the seats were thoroughly smashed. Allen was wondering what he was going to do with the wreck when Grampa Waven and Gramma Jessie Spaulding came to visit. Grampa Waven said that if the surrey was brought over to his house, he could make a Whirly gig out of it. Waven said that would take care of the wreck and then the children might have some fun with it.

Waven took the seats completely off and left only enough width of floor boards in the center so that if a person's legs were long enough to reach the front axle, you could steer the Whirly Gig with your feet. A rope was also attached to each axle which would aid in steering and could be used to pull the Whirly Gig back up the hill in the meadow across the road from Waven and Jessie's house.

The Whirly Gig gave a wild ride down the hill and across the meadow. At this point the driver would have to turn and stop, just before the stone wall. It was a lot of work to get the Whirly Gig back up the hill. It took at least two kids, and of course, the more kids, the better, to get vehicle all the way up the hill again. Many of the grandchildren took the wild ride to the bottom of the meadow.

One day after Brud and Ron Smith had taken a couple rides down through the meadow, Ron got to wondering how the Whirly Gig would go on the road from Waven and Jessie's house, then by his house and down over Keough Hill. Brud thought about the pond at the bottom of Keough Hill. He also wondered how they would get the Whirly Gig back up that hill. They finally decided that although they were not supposed to ride the Whirly gig on the paved road, probably one quick trip down by Racine's and then around Whittemore's corner would be all right and besides, they knew that Gramma Jessie was taking her afternoon nap, so she wouldn't see them.

The two boys calculated all the engineering details. Because Brud's legs were longer, it would be better if he was driving when they made the sharp corner by Whittemore's. They also thought that because Ron was more nimble and quick, he would more easily be able to give the Whirly Gig a mighty push and then jump on the rear before they picked up much speed. Everything had worked perfectly, and they were both comfortably seated and rapidly picking up speed. With every revolution of the huge wooden wheels, their speed increased. Ron thought maybe he shouldn't have pushed quite so hard at the beginning of the ride.

As the two boys, and their now, very fast vehicle approached Racine's, they began wishing that Grampa Waven had been able to build some kind of braking system for the Whirly Gig. As they rounded the curve, a little wider than they expected, the back wheels were sliding slightly on the smooth pavement, Ron began to yell in a high voice, "Hold it inside! Hold it inside!" Then, one factor which they had not thought about, but was now forefront in their minds, appeared. Coming from the opposite direction was a car. The car pulled over to the edge of the road and stopped. The head of what appeared to the boys to be a real, live witch popped out of the drivers' side window and began shrieking at them as they zoomed by, narrowly missing her car.

Brud and Ron thought that the best thing they could do was to somehow stop this thing and get it back to Grampa Waven's meadow. They steered over to the edge of the road, slowing a bit. Ron jumped over the back, hung on tight and applied his PF Flyers to the pavement. Finally, they skidded to a stop at the entrance to the old Sanatorium. They turned the Whirly Gig around and headed back to Waven and Jessie's.

As they pulled the Whirly Gig back into the meadow, they could see the angry, white-haired lady, who turned out to be a neighbor of Waven and Jessie's, standing with Grandma Jessie. She was waiting for the boys to return. Her hands on her hips. Neither of the women were smiling. The woman muttered angrily about what should be done with careless, irresponsible boys like that, finally got into her car, stuck her head out of the window and shrieked something that sounded like curses.

Gramma Jessie, in an unusually cross and angry voice, told the boys to park the Whirly Gig in the yard and not to touch it again. Park it and come into the house. She would speak with Waven later. When they came into the house, nothing more was said about the Whirly Gig. In her sweet Gramma Jessie voice, she asked them if they would like some milk and molasses cookies. After that day, the Whirly Gig, disappeared. Just like it's last owner.

Picking Berries
with
Grampa Harley

*H*arley and the children head out as Grampa Harley knew many things about nature and the kids loved to go berry picking with him. Ginseng or berries, Harley was good at hunting. Most often, he would be successful. The children were fascinated by Harley's stories and all the things he knew about. I have heard humans say that life is really about the journey, not the destination. I think Harley would have agreed.

This day, the hunt was for berries. Harley and the children head out to the south pasture, each with a berry pail and Harley with his ever-present cudgel. I could tell this was going to be one of Harley's longer trips; on his back, he carried his trapping basket and the lunch that Ferne had packed for them. The group crossed the gully and disappeared into the woods.

From the bottom of the gully to the logging road above is a steep climb. Harley led them up by using several switch backs; zig-zagging upward, which is easier than just going straight up, a steep path. He called this "coonin' it" because that was the way raccoons climbed steep hills and ledges. Harley said the racoons had to climb this way or they would roll like cobble stones all the way back down to the bottom. It seemed strange that a creature that could climb trees would need to do this but if Grampa Harl said a thing was true, it was. They had reached a road and were in a grove of thickly growing hemlocks.

The heavy canopy of branches and the layer of needles underfoot is a cool, quiet place to walk. Harley showed the kids a large hemlock tree that had taken a direct hit of lightening. The top of the tree was gone, and the large trunk was blackened and mostly shattered.

They stopped and carefully looked down into Austin's gorge. From up there on top of the ledge, they could see the silvery ribbon of the gully far below. They traveled along the road that runs parallel to the gully and then went south towards the West Rutland State Forest.

They came out at a CCC Camp. CCC, Harley told the children, stands for Civil Conservation Corps. It was a program started by the federal government to provide jobs during The Depression when jobs were scarce. The door to the camp was unlocked. Grampa Harl said it was always left that way so that anyone passing through could find shelter. He took off his trapping basket and laid his cudgel on top of it.

Harley and the kids went back outside. He pointed out the tall, slim red pine trees that were planted in perfectly spaced rows. They looked like huge pencils that were stabbed into the ground.

When it was time for lunch, they all went back inside the camp. As the children ate lunch, Harley told the kids more about the CCC (Civil Conservation Corps). They were paid to do work such as building bridges, roads, buildings, and planting literally millions of trees all over the country. They also worked in forests, to keep them accessible. Along with providing jobs, the program brought attention to the conservation and preservation of natural places and resources.

As they ate lunch, Brud picked up Grampa Harl's cudgel. It had two rings running around the circumference of the cudgel that had been carved into the wood. In the wood between the rings Harley had also carved his initials HNM, Harley Nelson Mills. The bark had been rubbed surprisingly smooth from its constant use, and with the rubbing of his powerful hands. Brud thought: what a marvelous, magical tool, and one that could also be used as a weapon. But no one else carried a cudgel quite like the one Grampa Harl did.

The real surprise of the berry picking trip came just before they left the camp area. Grampa Harl showed them a cold spring just a short ways from the cabin. From a pipe in the ground ran a steady stream of cold, clear water. This, Harley said, was the Fountain of Youth and that if anyone drank from this spring they would stay young forever. So, the children all drank from the spring, especially Brud, who drank all the water he could hold. He wondered why Grampa Harl didn't drink any. He thought it was probably because Grampa Harl had just taken a big pinch of snuff.

Harley and the children trooped down through the Sherman's pasture where they finally found some blackberries and quickly filled their pails; their heads filled with all that they had learned from their Grampa.

Chatting with Jan;
the Rhythm of the Rake;
and
Ferne's Calf Deal

*R*oany and I are pulling the hay wagon with the hay loader attached to it. Brud is up on the buck stick, driving as Allen loads the wagon with Rowen. Rowen is the second cutting of hay. The aroma of the Rowen is to die for! It was hard to concentrate on our work as we traveled up and down the windrows picking up the hay.

I snatch a mouthful when I get a chance, but I know that more than that wouldn't be good for me. The goofy cows will eat great amounts of the Rowen which caused them to make a lot of milk. My digestive system is much more sensitive than theirs and if I was to eat a great amount of Rowen, it would get impacted in my stomach and cause me great distress. I guess I understand how it must be for Ferne some days as she gathers, puts away and cooks, food with all it's wonderful aromas. She stops to have a small supper by herself. During the meal, Ferne will be too busy to sit and eat with the others. She likes to concentrate on serving her family.

After many loads of Rowen, Roany and I are done working for the day. Allen, with Jan close behind him, drives us into the barn yard. He stops us at the big concrete watering trough where there is always an ample supply of constantly flowing, fresh cold water, that comes in through a supply pipe and goes out through the drain pipe. Jan watches intently as we suck in huge amounts of water. She watches as we raise our heads and let the water dribble from our big lips.

Allen takes our check-reins off our hames, so we could drink. and as we drink, he unhooks the driving reins from our bridles, coils them up and hangs one rein on Roany's hame and the other rein on mine. When we were finished drinking, we went into the horse barn where our harness and bridles were removed, and Allen fed us hay and allowed Jan to fill the grey enamel dish with grain and empty it into our grain bowls. She sat on the wooden plank that supported my grain bowl and marveled at the feel of the plank made smooth by the rubbing of my lips. Allen had to start milking but Jan asked if she could stay and talk with me for a while. Allen said it was okay and that he would come up after we finished eating and let us out of the barn later.

Jan told me about the fun she had as she rode on the dump rake with Grampa Harl. Harley and Mary had worked all afternoon raking scatterings on the same field where we had picked up the Rowen. The little girl often talked to me. This day, Jan told me about listening to all the different noises that she heard as they traveled back and forth over the meadow. Jan hadn't even noticed that I had stopped eating. I was just enjoying the gentle stroking of her small hand on my neck and the sound of her voice as she talked. She told me she loved the smell of horses. She talked about the lulling, comfortable, back and forth motion caused by Mary's slow, plodding gait. Jan said that the clopping of Mary's hooves combined with the other sounds she heard while they worked, made music if you really listened. There was the constant squeak of the fills rubbing the plank where they were attached; the jingle of the trace chains, and the tapping sound they made when they bumped against the fills; the rubbing noise of the hames against the padded leather collar and the creaks of the leather from the harness. There were other noises too: the steel rims rolling over the ground, and the slight scrape of the hubs turning on the axles as well as the tinkle of the rake's many teeth, and crackle of the straws as the rake's teeth traveled over the field.

Perhaps Grampa Harl did not talk much as he drove Mary back and forth across the meadow because he was listening to the music too. Occasionally, he'd reach down and gently touch Jan's head or caress her pigtail with his huge, work-worn hand. When he stopped to empty the rake where the hay loader could pick it up, he would take the opportunity to calculate the direction of the wind. He had a special passenger, so he wanted to be sure to spit his snuff juice so as not to hit her with it.

Jan stopped talking long enough to notice that both Roany and I had finished eating. Jan thought that if she stood on the feed dish she would be able to slip our halters off and let us out of the barn herself. We stood patiently while she accomplished the task, then she let us outside. I watched, as the little girl used all her strength, to slide the heavy wooden bolt to lock the door, otherwise the goofy cows might wander in and mess up our barn.

As Jan went into the cow barn to tell Allen that she had let the horses out and locked the door all by herself, I had the thought that all children should be able to touch a horse and ride with their grandfathers and listen to the rhythm of the rake.

In order to insure a healthy herd of cows, Allen sold all the bull calves that were born on the farm because if he used a bull from his own herd for breeding, the herd would end up inbred and that can cause many problems.
Howard Steinberg, a local cattle dealer, would travelled around to the farms, buying and selling cattle. He would buy calves as well.

One day when Allen was going to be away doing an errand, he told Ferne that if Steinberg came around, she should try to sell the newborn bull calf. Allen told her to ask for twenty dollars. He warned her that Steinberg would want to pay less; he never paid the asking price. Ferne was excited, she liked a little sport, and dickering with the cattle dealer would be fun.

When Steinberg arrived, he asked, "What does Allen want for the calf?". Very firmly, Ferne said that Allen wanted twenty for him. Steinberg coughed and nearly swallowed the stub of cigar that he had been holding in his teeth. "Calves are way down," he said, "I can't give you more than fifteen for him." Determined to succeed, Ferne replied, "Oh no, that's not enough.

Steinberg coughed again and said, "I just can't afford more than eighteen." "Well, Allen is going to be really angry if I don't get twenty for it," Ferne said. Howard Steinberg walked around the calf, kicking the sawdust with the toe of his boot while mumbling something that Ferne could not hear. He produced a roll of bills from his pocket and peeled off a twenty-dollar bill and four one-dollar bills. Still sputtering, he loaded the calf in and left. Ferne counted the money again, then tucked it in the pocket of her apron and with a sly grin on her face, she went into the house.

White Washing
the Barn;
and
an Electrocution

Allen sold his milk to a large milk processing company, H. P. Hood. The milk was brought to a transfer plant in Florence where it was loaded along with many other local farmer's milk and shipped to Massachusetts. This practice did not work well for Allen, and he often expressed his concern that his milk, which he had so carefully worked to keep clean and pure, was dumped in with all the other farmer's milk. He had seen some of the other barns and several of them were not clean at all. People, particularly children, drank this milk. A farm whose animals and surroundings are clean and taken care of properly, produce good milk; along with many other types of food. Inattention and carelessness, most definitely do not lead to cleanliness.

The milk company had many regulations that farmers were supposed to follow. One of these regulations was that the inside of a cow stable had to be white washed at least once a year. White-wash is a mixture of lime and water. This mixture would clean surfaces to rid them of dirt, and any germs that would might make the cows sick.

Every summer, H.P. Hood sent a spray truck around to all the farms with whom they worked. A white spray truck would arrive at the farm, and everything about the truck and its equipment, including the two men who emerged from the truck were dressed all in white. The two spooky looking men, if that is what they were and not some alien creatures, would take their huge gun and long hose into the barn.

The two creatures, peeking out of small slits in their hoods, would spray anything that hadn't been removed from the entire barn before they arrived to do their job. The cats, having caught on to the invaders by now, would come streaming out the doors and windows, where ever they could get out of the barn, or risk being sprayed by the very aggressive cleansing of the white-wash agents.

Some farmers did not clean their barn out at all before the white washers arrived, and it wasn't the job of the white-washers to do. Cobwebs, splatters of muck on the walls, literally everything present, would just get sprayed right over. On Allen's farm this rather lazy approach was not permitted. He wanted all cobwebs swept down and all manure scraped from the walls, all dirt and sawdust had to be swept up and disposed of before the white-washers arrived to do their part.

Allen did not pay the children for most of their chores. He and Ferne felt that farm families should all work together and share both successes and failures. He did pay them to clean the barn before it was whitewashed, if, they'd done the cleaning to his satisfaction.

The children were eager to clean the barn and earn a little extra spending money to use at the Rutland Fair, which usually came soon after white-washing time. If they planned it right, their Uncle Rich, because he delivered milk for Seward's Dairy to the Fair, could get them into the Fair for free. Not having to pay the admission, made it possible for the kids to go to the fair. They could use their no doubt, hard-earned money for ride tickets and fair food: special treats available only at the fair.

The chore of sweeping down cobwebs in the barn was difficult and time-consuming, working with a broom. So Brud discovered that by cutting a large bunch of baling string into shorter lengths and attaching them to a short pole, he could clean the cobwebs very quickly. Allen came into the barn as Brud was flailing away at the cobwebs. He told Brud what a great job he was doing, and that his baling string tool was a really good idea, but what was he going to do with all the dirt and cobwebs that had rained down on him? It almost looked like Brud had used himself to dust down the ceilings and walls.

* * * * * * * * * * * * * * * *

On the following day, Brud was back in the barn. He was scraping manure splatter of the walls. He was using a wrecking bar which has a flat blade on one end and a crook on the other end. The crook made a great handle and the angle of the blade worked really well to scrape the walls. Allen had a radio in the barn and Brud had turned it on, so he could listen to music while he worked. He had stopped to take a break and was standing with the metal bar resting on his shoulder, his back to the radio.

As I've told you, Brud was easily distracted by the natural world. This day, as he was taking a break, Brud was watching a cow chewing her cud (a big mixture of grass, or as in this case, hay mixed with the cow's saliva). Fascinated and distracted, the boy watched the cow chew her cud for a while. After chewing for a while the cow then swallows the cud and he would watch the wad slide down the cow's throat. Then in a few seconds he could see another cud come sliding back up her long throat and she would begin chewing again.

As Brud was watching the cow, he stepped back, this movement caused the metal bar, still resting on his shoulder, to touch the end of the radio's aerial wire. He immediately felt a huge electrical shock to his shoulder and severe pain to every joint in his body. Brud immediately thought " Electrocution!? No one survives Electrocution!" He had heard things about the Electric Chair. He wondered if smoke was coming out of his ears, but he couldn't see them.

Brud sat down on a bench in the milk house. He'd been electrocuted; seriously and actually electrocuted. His joints ached, especially his knees. He was surely dying. He wanted to try for the house, but what if he didn't make it? So, he sat there in the coolness of the milk house, thinking that this was as good a place to die as any...besides, he couldn't take one more step, but surely, he would be found here.

He sat for a while. The aching in his joints was nearly gone and he was feeling much better. Brud began to wonder if he was some sort of miracle now. He was, as far as he knew, the only person to have been electrocuted and had lived to tell about it!

Harvesting Corn; and the Mystery of the Electric Fence

*L*ate summer to early fall, there is much to do on a farm with harvesting and preparing for the long, New England winter ahead. Allen peeled back the husks on several ears of corn and noticed that the kernels were starting to dent and harden so Allen, along with Jan and Brud, went down to see Axel Carlson. Axel was a tall man with a red face and a rather large stomach. He seemed to love children and had a loud thundering laugh that seemed to come all the way up from his ample stomach. Allen wanted to discuss with Axel about helping each other fill their silos again this year, at that time, Axel had an ensilage blower and Allen didn't.

Allen and Axel shared labor and equipment for the job of getting both of their silos filled. They made an agreement that worked well for both of them and made the job a little easier, and more efficient. The two farmers shared labor, and, for the use of Axel's equipment, Allen would pay for Axel's milk to be delivered to the Florence Milk Plant. Axel's son, Eric, picked up Allen's cans of milk from a platform at the bottom of the hill, at the edge of the Whipple Hollow Road, where he'd load it into Axel's big farm truck.

The children liked to go down to see Axel and his wife, Clara. The children knew her as "Gramma Carlson." They also knew that she made wonderful donuts. Said donuts may have been one of the reasons for Axel's ample stomach. While they were in the kitchen, eating donuts, Axel would go over to a high shelf and take down a jar. This jar contained his spare coins. He let Jan reach in and she took out a few shiny pennies. He let Brud reach in and he took out a large coin, a silver dollar.

With the agreement to share work, equipment and milk delivery, they all went out to take a look at Axel's cattle. Brud ran ahead. He wanted to check out the huge ramp that rose high above the Whipple Hollow Road from one side and up into the hay loft of the barn on the other side of the road.

Axel kept only Jersey cattle which were small, tan-colored cattle that gave very rich milk but not in the quantity that Allen's black and white Holstein's did. Axel had a new born heifer calf and he gave the calf to Brud. Brud raised the calf and she was the first Jersey on Allen's Farm.

Allen was not using artificial insemination to breed his cows, at that time. So, when one of Axel's Jersey's was old enough, she was bred to Allen's Holstein bull. The first time, the Jersey gave birth to two pure black calves. They were both Heifers and Allen reluctantly allowed Brud to raise the larger one of the two. Allen felt there was a weakness inherent in twin animal births that he did not want to continue in his herd.

The black cow had twins twice after that and Brud raised one of these heifer calves and her first birth was also to twins; a pair of large bull calves. Allen had large Holstein bulls, and the cows had had so many multiple births, Allen felt that breeding those cows stressed the cows' bodies out too much. None of them lasted very long in the herd, except the original little Jersey cow that Brud had raised.

* * * * * * * * * * * * * * * *

Okay, back to the corn, you know by now how I love it! Our upland fields could be worked earlier in the spring than Axel's. That meant that our corn was usually ready to harvest sooner than his. The ensilage blower was brought up from Axel's farm, it had several sections of eight-inch pipe, enough to make up forty feet; the necessary length to reach from the top of the ensilage blower to the spout section that went into the silo window. The pipes were bolted together and there was a pulley hitched into the top of the silo. The long pipe was raised to the top of the silo. When the spout could be positioned into the window, the pipe could be then bolted to the blower. Sections of distribution pipe were then hung from the spout to direct the flow of the silage around the inside of the silo. There was a large pulley on the back of the blower; this pulley spun six large knives with a paddle behind each knife, in a compartment that the pipe was attached to. The spinning pulley also powered sprockets that ran a bed chain in the trough that brought the corn into the blower.

The spinning blades would chop the corn stalks, cobs and all, into half inch lengths. The paddles threw the chopped corn the entire forty feet up the pipe and into the silo. All the power to run the blower was created by our tough little grey Ford tractor. A belt, eight inches wide and twenty feet long, went from the pulley on the blower to a pulley that was run by the power take-off shaft of the little grey tractor. Axel also had a Ford tractor. With the two rigs and all of us working together, we could maintain an almost constant feed to the blower.

The tractor was put in neutral with the brakes set to hold it in place while the engine ran at nearly full throttle for long periods of time. To some of you, this might seem like an awful lot of mechanical description. I just want to point out the very serious business of working around farm machinery, or any machinery.

One day during the corn harvest, Eric Carlson hooked up the grey tractor to the blower and started unloading a load of corn. Dolly and I stood hitched to another load waiting to pull it up to the blower. Dolly and I were on a small incline below the grey tractor. Eric either forgot or neglected, to set the wheel brakes and did not chock the wheel on the tractor to keep it from rolling. As Eric was unloading the other load of corn, the belt slipped off the pulley on the blower.

Driverless, the tractor started rolling down the hill directly towards our wagon. As I saw the tractor rolling towards us, I knew there was nothing I could do but stand firm and try to prepare for the collision. When we were hit, I turned to my companion to see if she was alright and saw that the incident had not disturbed her. She was still napping. There was no real damage, only a dent in the grill of the tractor.

Allen, however, was quite upset. He took meticulous care of his land, animals and equipment. He hadn't put even a scratch on his Ford tractor. There was another incident with Eric involving Allen's tractor. Eric was cutting corn. He was using Allen's tractor, which was attached to Carlson's Corn Harvester. Eric turned too short at the corner of the corn piece and drove the point of the Harvester right through the back tire of Allen's tractor. It was at this point that Allen decided that he would get his own blower and fill his silo by himself. After Allen got his own ensilage blower, he had to set up the blower by himself.

Brud had expressed to me how frightened he was during the set-up and tear-down process of the blower. He would have to climb up the silage chute, forty feet, to the top of the silo. Brud was still quite a young boy, and his legs were too short to climb the chute from step to step. He had to pull himself up with his arms until he could get a knee on the steel step to help get him to the top. The edges of the steel steps made his knees black and blue. He'd have a rope tied around his waist as he climbed, but it was really more a tool than a safety measure. When he reached the top, he would enter the roof area through a small window. He would then crawl across a twelve-inch plank that spanned the sixteen-foot diameter of the silo. As he crawled across the plank, he couldn't resist taking a heart-thumping look at the forty-foot drop to the concrete below. After untying the rope from himself, he ran it through the pulley and dropped both ends down to Allen. When the spout was finally through the window and hitched to the blower and top of the silo, Brud would make the crawl back across the plank, down the chute, to the ground.

Before the corn could be brought to the blower, it had to be cut and tied into bundles by the Corn Harvester, which we, horses, pulled. It pulled quite hard because of the weight of the machine. It was all ground-driven by one big wheel on one side of the machine and an idler wheel. Two points straddled one row at a time. The corn was pushed, by a series of sprockets and chains, to a short cutter bar that cut the corn stalk, and while it was still standing, it was pressed against a metal bar. When the bar filled up to about a dozen stalks of corn, a needle came around the stalks and tied them into a neat bundle and then kicked the bundle out onto the ground.

The team driver sat on a metal seat that was mounted to the machine over the big driving wheel. Even after the pole was shortened on Allen's Harvester, so that he could pull it with his tractor, he left the seat attached, and usually one of the kids rode on the seat, watching the machine operate.

On Allen's farm, the hay wagon was used to bring the corn to the blower. We, horses, were used to pull the wagon. I just love the smell of corn (have I said I like corn?) and it was quite distracting working in the middle of all that wonderful stuff. Sometimes, one of the children gave me an ear of corn while the wagon was being loaded. Dolly though, would sometimes just snatch herself an ear if Allen passed close enough while carrying a bundle of corn. Along with the stolen ear of corn, Dolly would also receive a generous helping of Allen's ever-ready curses.

The blower made an extremely loud noise as it chopped the corn. I remember even I was frightened the first time I heard it start up. First, the tractor would start up and there was a hissing sound as the long belt traveled over the pulleys. Then, the spinning knives and paddles made a loud whirring noise as their speed increased along with the RPMs of the tractor. The whirring noise changed to a loud roar and a clattering noise would then start as the sprockets and bed chain were put into gear. The sound increased to an astounding level when the bundles of corn were put on the bed chain and fed into the blower and then there was the sound of the chopped corn streaming up the pipe.

I knew I would have to stand solid and still, like a tree does, it's roots grounding it firmly, when Dolly left, and spooky little Danny was added to the team. He would jump every time the blower was started and continue to fidget until the wagon was empty and we were moved away from the noise.

With all that was happening, from the first start of the pulley on the tractor to the last kernels of corn falling in the silo, there was great danger for anyone near the area. I was always worried about Brud when he was unloading the wagon and feeding the blower. Brud was a rapidly- growing, clumsy boy, probably ranking pretty high on the scale of normal clumsiness. He seemed to always be slipping or tripping over his "paddle" feet. I knew Ferne always worried too. But Allen had to be doing the work needed inside the silo. Allen cautioned Brud and showed him where the safety bar was on the blower and how to operate it, so he knew Brud would be okay.

One day, Allen had all the children helping him load corn on the wagon. Little Tippy, the house dog, had gone along to help Brud and Allen. They were loading the corn bundles onto the wagon while Kathy and Ferne Marie brought the corn bundles over closer to the wagon. Jan was up on the buck stick standing on the third slat to get her up high enough to drive us horses. His Lordship, Little Tip, must have gotten bored with supervising the loading process and decided to explore the interior of the corn piece that Allen had not finished cutting. Soon, we heard the fierce yapping of Tip coming from inside the stand of corn. We all thought that by the fierceness of what we were hearing that we would at any moment see the "Little Lord" come dragging a Mountain Lion out of the corn by its tail. The fierce yapping changed to yelps of distress and Brud said, "Maybe I better go in and help Tip". Allen, who had already caught the smell of a skunk coming from the corn, said, in his usual calm way when he was advising Brud, "Well, Brud, I don't think you're gonna want to do that".

Little Tip came out of the corn with his beautiful white chest and cute little face covered with a nasty, foul smelling stain. He rolled and whimpered and whined and couldn't understand why no one in his family wanted to help him. I couldn't help but give a big horse laugh (more corn in the corn) as little Lord Tip headed humbly back to the house with his tail between his legs. Surely, Ferne would fix this disgusting situation. Ferne bathed him in mouth wash, but he still was banished from the interior of the house for a while. What a disgrace! He surely did not feel like a King now, only a skunky, minty-smelling mutt. This condition did finally disappear, and he was back to his old Lordly self once again.

In the late summer after the Rowen had been cropped and the corn had been harvested, the new growth of the meadows would already be green and lush again. A few ears of corn had been lost and were scattered about the corn piece. Allen did not want to waste this lush green grass or the corn that was left on the corn piece, so he would turn the cows out to graze in the meadows and clean up the corn piece. There was a fence around the entire perimeter which kept the cows contained to the meadow. He had to put up an electric fence to keep the cows from entering the yard and punching holes in the lawn with their sharp hooves, eating Ferne's flowers and leaving their huge green messes all over the yard. Cows seem to be creatures of very little self-pride and will just gorge themselves grazing on the lush green grass which causes them to give more milk, but they will also expel these huge, green, gooey messes wherever they wander.

Brud, who seems as yet, to have very little concern for where he puts his rapidly growing feet, was running and slipped on one of these huge cow messes once, sliding on his back through the foulness. He got up covered from head to foot in the green mess and went to the house, seeking help from his mother. Luckily, Ferne stopped him before he reached the interior of the house and took him to the watering trough where she cleaned him up with an old broom.

* * * * * * * * * * * * * * * *

There was an electric fence which effectively kept the cows out of the yard. If touched, an electrical charge would travel through a single strand of wire. The result was that anything that touched the fence would get a zap of electricity to discourage further progress.
One day, Allen watched Ferne Marie touch the charged wire and lift it up for Kathy, Brud and Jan to slide under the wire of the fence. Why hadn't the girl gotten a shock when she took

hold of the wire? He thought maybe there was something wrong with the fence. Before anything else, Allen would have to test the fence. Allen was carrying a pail of water so he asked Norm Champine, who was working for Allen at the time, to help carry the pail of water. Allen reached over and firmly grasped the wire and felt a slight tingle, so he was sure the wire was working, and when the electrical charge increased as it passed through the metal bucket of water and into Norm who yelped in pain, he was very sure it worked. It remained a mystery how Ferne Marie could have touched the wire and not have gotten the expected electrical shock.

Sometimes the cows would be brought out to graze in the meadow not far from where the road curves to leave the valley. The road meets up with the Whipple Hollow Road. When the cows were grazing down there, they had to be watched so they wouldn't wander into the road. When we had Ferne Marie's collie dog all Allen would have to say was, "Go get them, Collie Girl", and she would go and bring them back. In fact, whenever Allen wanted the cows to come to the barn that's all he would have to say. She would go and head the whole herd back to the barn. They would slowly amble along toward the barn ahead of Collie as she trotted back and forth behind them, giving a small bark if they forgot what they were doing and began to stray.

After Collie left the farm, the children would often be sent after the cows who often were reluctant to leave the lush grass when it was milking time. They would often be in the farthest corners of the meadow. Brud, who had made quite a pet of one of the big docile creatures, thought he would get on her back and ride her back to the barn. This worked quite well several times and was a rather pleasant ride while the cows ambled along toward the barn.

One time, however, Brud sat on the cow's back as she passed too closely by the house. As the cow poked along, Brud was dreaming of being a famous rodeo bull rider. Ferne came out of the house on her way to the barn, and with her, trotted little Tip. Tippy decided that this just wasn't right to see Brud sitting on a cow's back and he needed to do something about it. He started towards the cow barking in his fierce yapping voice. The cow jumped and then Brud realized that unlike rodeo riders, he had nothing to hang on to. He was thrown from the cow's back and came down flat on his own back, losing his breath on impact. Ferne came over to where Brud was laying on the ground, but he was unable to speak to her with the wind knocked out of him. Ferne decided right then and there, that there would be no more cow riding from now on.

Picking Potatoes

Brud and Harley are out looking for Ginseng. Ferne Marie and Kathy are helping Ferne can tomatoes. Allen and Jan are out at the potato piece. The potato plants have died, and the leaves have turned brown. Allen bends over with Jan squatting beside him intently watching as he digs with his fingers into the side of a hill of potatoes. Jan squeals with excitement as three nice potatoes come rolling out of the hill.

There has been several dry days and the weather forecasts say several more before another rainy period moves in. Allen said that if it wasn't for everyone being so busy, he would go through the potatoes with the cultivator to loosen the dirt and then he would start digging the potatoes tomorrow. He said he needed someone to ride me and guide me as he worked the cultivator. Jan said, "Daddy, I can ride Dick?". So, they came back to the barn, put on my harness and we headed out to the potato piece.

I am hitched to the cultivator and Allen puts Jan up on my back. Jan had sat on my back before, but she hadn't realized how high up she was or how wide my strong back was as she sat with a hand on each hame. Jan took up the check rein and we began to work. I felt her tenseness as she squeezed tightly with her short little legs on my wide back. She found that by looking between my ears, she could keep me going straight between the rows. Although, it was fun, and she had done an important job, she was glad that they were finished because her legs were really tired.

Allen dug all his potatoes by himself, using a potato hook. Earl Rider, a neighbor, offered the use of his potato digging machine but Allen told him that he would dig them by hand. With the potato hook, he would have the potatoes rolling out of the hills with very rarely bruising or picking one with the sharp point of his hook.

Farm work is not easy, and Allen had been hurt as a boy. One day he became a target for a mean, and older, boy that he went to school with. The boy pushed Allen off a high stone wall. He fell on his arm and it was broken. He finished school that day and received no medical attention other than what his mother, Kate, could give him when he got home. For this reason, his right arm was forever after slightly bent at the elbow and he could not straighten it out in the normal way. Allen had to re-learn how to do things with this physical challenge. He learned and adapted so well that most people were not even aware of it.

Any tool which Allen used, from the needle that he would use to pick any slivers that the children would get in their tender flesh, to the sixteen-pound post maul that he used to drive fence posts into the ground during fence fixing time, was used and maintained correctly. Watching Allen drive a fence post was amazing to watch. He would start with the head of the sixteen-pound hammer sitting on the post. He would swing the heavy maul with his arms fully extended, with a small adjustment to take into account his stiff arm, in a circular motion from the top of the post down to his feet and then coming in an arc high above his head and down again hitting the post squarely on the top driving the post into the ground. I believe if anyone had the strength to use a maul in this manner, they wouldn't have the skill or confidence to hit the post as he did. I used to worry every time he used the maul; what if he misses the post? He will surely break his leg.

Oh! great! Here comes Allen. It must be time to cultivate the potatoes. I've been noticing that a few weeds have begun growing there.

Digging potatoes, just as planting them had been, was a family project. I enjoyed watching my family work together on all such family projects; but this one was particularly exciting because no one knew what treasures would be released from the earth.

Allen would get a one row head start before Ferne and the children would start picking up the potatoes. You need to let a freshly dug potato sit where it is, in the warm sunshine, for a short bit in order to dry the moisture of the earth from them. When they were dry, Ferne and the children would begin picking them up and putting them into bushel picking baskets. When the basket was filled, Ferne would empty the sixty pounds of potatoes into burlap bags to be transported up to the house and put into the cellar. The yield from the potato piece was usually more than enough to last the family for the entire year, with enough to give away to Waven and Jessie, Harley, and some of the other relatives. Occasionally one of the children would find an oddly shaped potato and would show it to everyone else.

One year there were many unusually large potatoes and Grampa Waven took several of the really large potatoes to a restaurant where he knew the owner and chef. He had the chef make them into French Fries and gave them to the family who he had brought with him to enjoy the treat. Brud had never eaten French Fries before and thought these were the best potatoes he had ever eaten.

Kathy was particularly good and fast at picking up potatoes, maybe because there were no flowers growing in the bare earth of the potato piece. Ferne Marie sometimes would squat down and pick up two handfuls of the rich brown loam, warmed by the sun; holding its warmth for a while and then letting it sift through her fingers. I know from watching her that this little girl would always have a great interest and enjoyment in planting seeds and seeing what she could produce from the goodness of the earth.

We had finished the potatoes, Roany and I pulled the wagon loaded with bags of potatoes back to the farm house to be stored in the cellar.

Allen said to the family after supper, "Let's go for a ride!" The whole family except for me, of course, piled into the blue Plymouth and headed out of the valley. They rode out to a nearby town called, Ira, and then back to West Rutland. When they got back to West Rutland, Allen said, "Let's celebrate", so he stopped at the only local snack bar. The snack bar was owned by Clarence and Stella Smith, who were Ron and Lynne Smith's grandparents. This was the only place locally were you could get soft ice cream. Clarence and Stella gave each one of them a free ice cream cone. Brud wondered why they didn't do this more often since it was free. Couldn't they celebrate this way when each type of vegetable was harvested? Radishes alone could be reason enough, he thought.

Lynne Rides Pal; and Someone's in my Watering Trough!

Lynne and Kathy were cousins and they were great pals too! Lynne came to visit one day and asked if she could ride Brud's saddle horse, Pal. She had no experience with a saddle horse, but Lynne was always up for a challenge. She figured that if she kept Pal at a walk, she would be fine. Pal was a tall, long legged horse. He was full of mischief and loved to run.

Lynne mounted the horse and sat quite comfortably, only much higher above the ground than she expected. She took one rein in each hand and started across the meadow. Pal was not trying any of his usual foolishness or tricks to unseat his rider. Lynne was enjoying the warm summer breeze that rippled the horse's mane when suddenly, she saw a snake in the grass, right in their path. Pal, who was blind in one eye did not see it, however, until it was much too close to him. The snake startled Pal and he decided to run. Lynne immediately dropped the reins, grabbed the saddle horn with both hands and yelled "WHOA!" several times. This is generally a good word to yell if you want your horse to stop. Maybe Pal mis-heard her in his panic, because "Whoa" was just making him run faster!

Brud had run out to the meadow, and stood there, waving his arms in an attempt to stop Pal who was now running full-tilt. Pal ran right past him, heading for the safety of the barnyard. Even with the seriousness of the situation, Brud couldn't help thinking how Lynne looked like one of the little monkeys clinging to the backs of ponies he had seen at the Rutland Fair. Once Pal was back in the barnyard, he stopped abruptly. Lynne, however, did not. She flew over the horse's head and finally came to a stop herself, on her back in the soft mud of the barnyard. She was able to clean herself off somewhat in my watering trough and then went to the house to finish the job.

My watering trough actually became a part of a wedding celebration once. There had been some kind of celebration in the Smith branch of the family. A wedding celebration of Bob's brother, Ralph. Humans like to celebrate things and I liked to observe their customs and traditions, which often seemed strange to me. But interesting! On this particular afternoon, the blue Desoto with the blinking eyes, came rolling into the driveway. Gussie was driving and Bob sat in an unusually casual fashion in the front passenger's seat. Ron and Lynne came tumbling out of the back seat as usual. They were dressed in their good dress-up clothes which were already quite rumpled from the day's activities.

Bob also came tumbling out of the car. His dress clothes were even more rumpled than Ron and Lynne's were. They were quite nasty-looking as well. It was said that he had gotten sick from eating too much food at the wedding. To me he smelled like Harry and Harley do when they drink beverages that contain alcohol. Bob was even walking in the same, strange, stumbling gait that afflicted Harry and Harley after having those kinds of drinks.

Ferne and Gussie helped Bob through the barn and out to my watering trough. They sat him right down in the cold water of my ever-flowing concrete trough and Ferne scrubbed him clean with a scrub brush. The cold water of my trough seemed to work a miracle on Bob and he could soon walk normally again. Hopefully, I won't get thirsty until the water in the trough clears out.

The wedding celebration reminded me of another celebration. It was called the Spaulding Family Reunion. And though they'd had to travel some distance, even Waven's younger brother, Ken Spaulding and his family were here. Everyone gathered in the door yard before heading out to the gully for a picnic. Everyone was dressed in fine dress clothes and were clearly enjoying visiting and laughing with each other.

All the men had the same foolish habit that Allen did. They would all put something in their mouths, light it on fire and blow smoke at each other. What a foolish habit to foul the same air you are trying to breathe!

Many of the men were also drinking alcoholic beverages but Allen never did. I guess it was because he had been so affected by the problems drinking caused, not only for the drinker but for all the difficulties a habit like this caused their families. I thought that it must be some sort of illness that only humans got. Why else would you drink something that made you sick and caused problems? Allen cautioned his children by saying, "It's in the blood, so you better be careful of it". Allen himself had to help with the farm chores when he was much too young, (about nine years old), and took over most of the farm operation when he was in the ninth grade to take care of the family when his father had two separate surgeries.

All the children were running and playing various games while the adults were visiting. Jan and Susan Spaulding were up in a section of the barn over the cow barn which had been given over to the children to use as a play house, after the one built by Dick Granger blew away in a hurricane. The two little six-year old girls were thoroughly involved in their play and didn't realize that everyone else had left for the gully already.

All were enjoying being together at the gully, but after a little while, Ferne noticed that Jan and Susan were missing. In a panic, Ferne and several others headed back to the farm which was the last place anyone had seen the two little girls. As Ferne and the others hurried back across the meadow, they

135

met the two little girls coming towards them holding hands. Ferne scooped up the two girls and said she was sorry they had been forgotten and asked them where they had been. Jan said that she and Susan were fine and not worried at all themselves. They had been playing in the Playhouse and they knew everyone was at the Gully for a picnic.

Time to
Fill the Woodsheds;
and
Gathering Butternuts

At the end of summer and the beginning of the new school year, the potatoes had been dug and stored in the cellar and all the corn was in the silo. It was time to fill the woodshed for the coming winter. Before Allen, and Lawrence Champine installed the big wood furnace in the cellar of the house, there was a wood kitchen stove and a pot-bellied stove in the living room that also burned wood. Wood burns better when it has had time to dry. But winter in Vermont can be quite severe, with freezing temperatures and deep snow, so it was very important to get all the wood stored that you could.

The wood had to be cut to stove lengths, and, as with most chores, it was a family project. The children attended school, so the wood project began on a Saturday.

First, Allen would get the wood wagon out of the barn. This wagon was very much the same as the manure wagon. It also had wooden wheels with steel rims. The wood wagon had a flat rack and was about four feet wide and twelve feet long. There were no side racks only a row of stakes on each side of the wagon bed. The stakes held the wood in place on the wagon. The wood was cut into four-foot lengths and the twelve-foot wagon bed allowed Allen to load three tiers of wood on the bed of the wagon. This made about a cord and a half per load. If we were pulling a load of all hard wood, (like oak), it was very heavy. The soft wood such as that from a pine tree and as Harley always burned pine which made a light load and was an easy load to pull.

To make the wagon pull easier and make the wheels last longer, Allen repacked the wheels each year before using the wagon. This involved jacking each of the four wheels off the ground and removing the large nut that held the wheel onto the axle. A big washer that went against the nut was taken off and the Babbitt and oakum rope like packing was removed. The wheel could then be removed, and the axle and hub were cleaned of old grease and dirt. New grease was packed back into the wheel hub, more grease was put in, and new Babbitt and oakum rope was pounded back in place. The washer and nut were then replaced, and after all four wheels were done, the wagon was ready for use.

I enjoyed pulling the wood wagon even the heavier, more demanding loads. Going up a very steep hill with an empty wagon was not much of a worry at all. Since my chat with Jan about the way noises made music, I liked to listen to the sound of the steel rims of the wheels turning in the gravel, the light bumping sound of the steel hubs moving against the axle. Listening to the music...then would come the trip back down that steep hill. But I liked even that. Hearing that music.

We were driven out to the various locations where Allen had cut, split, and piled the wood the previous winter. Sometimes, the wood was piled in the open pastures, but more often we were traveling on the old logging roads in the deep woods in back of the meadows. These roads were rough, and had many water bars. We would draw loads of wood all week long, making huge piles of four-foot lengths of wood stacked near the woodshed, ready to be sawed into stove lengths. That part of the job was done on the weekends. So that the kids could help.

Allen would have sharpened each tooth on the three-foot diameter circular saw blade. The saw was hooked to the back the little Ford tractor. The saw was powered by a belt and pulleys on the saw rig and the tractor. The blade was spun at an extremely high speed to cut the wood that was pushed into the blade from the saw table.

By eye, Allen measured the wood to stove length and then put them on the saw table and pushed the wood into the spinning saw blade. Ferne, or sometimes Harry (then Brud when he was old enough), stood on the other side of the spinning saw blade to hold the end of the wood that was being cut off. The cut end (approximately twelve inches long) was then thrown into the woodshed. I always worried when Brud was the one taking the wood away. He had a fear of losing a finger or hand in the spinning blade. I hoped this fear would help him to be careful and stay focused.

The other children brought the wood from the pile over to Allen. If the sticks were small, he would cut four or five at a time. If the sticks were very heavy, the children would each take an end of the heavy stick and help each other get the wood over to Allen. This would go on all day until the entire pile of wood was sawed. Farm kids are kids like any others, but I think working together helps children learn that helping one another, working together, and, by and large, managing to cooperate is important.

After we finished filling the woodshed at the farm, we moved the whole operation over to Harley's place. Harry Wedin cut most of Harley's wood and piled it to dry in the pasture before the sawing could begin. The pine that Harley used was light, and made a hot fire, which may have been what made Harley's Corn Dodgers such treats for Jan and Ron.

Harley had a wood burning cook stove in the kitchen. Harley's wife, Kate, had a summer kitchen (where it was cooler there for her to do her cooking and baking, in hot weather) and that had a wood-burning stove. It took a large amount of pine wood for their supply. We would draw many loads of wood up to the house from Harley's lower pasture which was across the brook from his house. Sometimes, Allen would saw right from the wagon as soon as we got back to the house with a load. The pine wood sawed easily, and I loved the smell of the pine sawdust. After Harley's wood was sawed, Allen went to Waven and Jessie's in Pittsford to help them.

Waven had an old Doodle Bug which had a flat rack on the back. He would take Lynne and Ron with him to help him load his wood on the rack and bring it down to the house from Waven's back pasture. Waven wanted only small, hardwood for Jessie's cook stove. The rest of the house was heated by two stoves that burned kerosene.

Before Allen got his big truck, he would drive his Ford tractor with the saw rig attached all the way over to Pittsford where he would leave the tractor and saw rig and Jessie would give him a ride back to the farm in her Buick. Allen would go back on Saturday and with Waven, Herb and Glenn Spaulding and Bob Smith and they would saw Waven's wood.

After Allen got his big truck, he could back the truck up to the stone wall in back of the farm house and drive the tractor and saw rig onto the truck. When he got over to Waven's, he would unload the tractor at the steep bank in front of the house.

Waven would have a huge pile of small wood. Which he called popcorn wood. He called it popcorn wood because after he'd gotten the cook stove very hot, by burning many small sticks, they could have popcorn. Waven put hard corn kernels in a wire basket and would shake the basket over the surface of the very-hot stove. In no time at all there would be a basketful of popcorn. I never tried it myself, but where there's corn, I'm interested.

I'm sure it was quite a project this sawing of the wood at Waven's with Allen at the saw table, Brud taking wood away from the saw and Waven bringing the wood to the saw. Waven cut his wood into lengths that were anywhere from three to eight-foot lengths. Waven would bring over a huge bundle of random length sticks to the saw blade. Allen would have to straighten the ends of the bundle of sticks on the saw table before he could saw them. It would be impossible for Brud to hold all the sticks as they were being cut off. By not holding all the sticks tightly, some of the sticks would kick violently from the saw blade, throwing them to the ground. The flying sticks would seem to always hit Brud on the shin. Despite the black and blue marks all over his shins, Brud thought that the lunch of Jessie's baked spaghetti, her famous baked beans, and chocolate cake, were worth the black and blue marks.

* * * * * * * * * * * * * * *

There were many things to store for the winter, and in September the nuts would start falling from the Butternut trees that grew in my pasture. There was one large tree that produced butternuts twice as big as any of the others. This tree grew in the upper corner of my pasture. If you wandered under the tree when the nuts were falling, the nuts would hurt quite a bit if they hit you.

Allen would keep track of the butternuts and when they had pretty much all fallen from the tree, he would get the family to help him gather them up. They would all come into my pasture, some carrying baskets and others carrying bran sacks. Though there were many other butternut trees, everyone went directly to the tree where the BIGGEST butternuts were, laying on the ground. They usually got four or five bushels from that one tree. One year, they picked up seven and a half bushels. That one tree would usually yield enough butternuts for all the cooking that Ferne needed them for, which included her Famous Christmas Chocolate Fudge, Allen's favorite Maple Cake with Butternuts in the cake and Maple Frosting with Butternuts decorating the top, and a few for snacking besides. Any nuts that were left on the tree, Allen felt should be left for the squirrels.

Butternuts have a green, fuzzy outer layer that is very sticky when they first fall from the tree. Allen would usually wear his leather work gloves and Ferne wore a pair of white cloth gloves, but the children would just pick up the butternuts bare-handed. Their hands would soon become black and sticky. Brud seemed to be able to get plastered all over with

141

the black sticky goo. When they were finished picking up the butternuts, Allen hitched us up to the wagon and we would draw the butternuts down to the barn next to the house. In the upper loft area was where the butternuts were spread out on the floor to dry; the sticky fuzz will change, and the skin will become brown, dry and wrinkled.

After Allen and the family had gathered enough butternuts for the family's use, he would let other people who wanted butternuts gather whatever nuts they could find. Donald Champine worked with a woman in Proctor, who expressed to him that she loved butternuts but couldn't find any. Her name was Carmine Genola and Donald told her that his Uncle Allen would let her have some if she would gather them.

One Sunday after they had been to church, Carmine and her mother arrived at the farm to gather butternuts. Carmine was a pretty and a finely shaped young lady. It seemed unusual to me that Brud (who was about eleven or twelve years old at the time) volunteered to help the women gather butternuts. The boy never really seemed to care that much about gathering butternuts before. Maybe he just wanted to learn about Italian culture from the two ladies, or maybe it was just to help them gather the nuts, after all he was a very kind, curious, young boy.

Harley and Kate Mills, Allen's father and mother.

Waren and Jessie Spaulding, Ferne's mother and father

Ferne and Allen Mills

he family house and barn as it was then

The farm in winter

Early winter snow

*Ferne Marie,
Kathy, Lynne
Smith and Brud,
Jan and Ron Smith*

*Allen, Ferne
and children
with Carroll's Packard*

*Brud,
Ferne Marie,
Kathy, Mike,
Jan and Morine*

Brud loading,
Ron Smith
driving

Brud, Ron Smith and Allen

Brud, Allen, Dick and Roany

Lynne Smith
and George Sherman

Brud on
shovel stilts

Stinky

goofy cows
Beauty

Pride

148

*Lucky
hunting day
Harry, Wedin,
Kathy and Brud*

Allen with Lisa in his arms

Help from the next generation

150

Drawing Sawdust and Laundry Day

*I*n the fall before the leaves on the trees changed to all their brilliant colors, Allen would start the project that he called drawing sawdust. Allen always kept a thick layer of fresh sawdust underneath the cows. He felt they needed a fresh layer of sawdust to keep them clean and give them a comfortable place to lay down. These goofy looking creatures seem to bawl loudly if they are not well fed and comfortable.

There was a huge empty space underneath the thick plank flooring where we were driven into the barn with a load of hay to be stowed away. Underneath the thick plank flooring, was an empty space about sixty feet long and twelve feet deep. This was where Allen stored his sawdust. He would put enough in there to last him for the entire year.

There were two local sawmills where Allen could get sawdust. One was located about a mile south of the farm. It was not far from the old Whipple Hollow Cemetery. The sawmill was operated by Jim Harrison. Jim also had a small farm and was a logger as well.

The other one was Smith's Sawmill, and it was located at the extreme south end of the Whipple Hollow Road on the right side of the road just across the railroad tracks. It was a much larger mill than Harrison's, so the availability of sawdust was much more consistent. At first, there was no market for sawdust and farmers could get it for free. As Allen had no truck, he would borrow Axel's large truck. It was a flat rack truck with six-foot side racks. Through a series of pipes, the saw mills would blow the sawdust into huge piles beside the mills. Allen would shovel the entire load onto the truck by hand and then unload it the same way back at the farm.

One day Allen had borrowed Axel's truck, and first he'd fill it up with gas in West Rutland. Brud, who was a young boy at the time, had gone with Allen for the ride. While they were in West Rutland, Allen bought Brud a chocolate ice cream cone. Allen worried that Brud would get ice cream all over Axel's truck since the boy was doing a fine job of getting it all over his face, hands, and nearly everything else was plastered with chocolate ice cream.

They stopped at Harrison's sawmill and Allen began loading the big truck. Brud was too small to shovel so he played around the truck while Allen loaded it. Harrisons had a white-tailed deer they kept as a pet. They had raised the fawn after its mother had been killed by an automobile. The little deer wandered into the yard where Allen was loading the truck with the sawdust. He stopped shoveling for a moment to watch as the deer went to work, cleaning up Brud by licking his hands and face. The deer cleaned all the chocolate off Brud so Allen no longer worried about Brud making a mess of Axel's truck.

When Allen got the load of sawdust back to the farm, he would back the truck up to the barn floor, remove some of the thick wooden planks in the floor and shovel the load down into the large cavern below the floor. It took many truck loads to fill this large space.

By the time Allen got his own truck, Brud was big enough to help load and unload the truck. Allen and Brud would stop at the house for a drink and snack before going after another load and Jan who was still quite little would ride along to supervise the sawdust project.

* * * * * * * * * * * * * * * * *

Laundry day was quite a big job in those days and was an all-day project. Ferne, Kathy and Ferne Marie washed and hung on the clothes line, the many loads of laundry that a large family produced. Ferne and the girls would first pull the wringer washing machine in from the back porch, fill it with water, add detergent, then add the dirty clothes and start the washer. If they needed to use hot water, the water had to be heated on the wood stove first. Then they'd drag in the two set-tubs for the rinsing process. Both before the laundry was rinsed and after, it had to be run through the wringer. This wringer was a contraption consisting of two rollers on top of the washing machine that squeezed most of the water out of the laundry as it was passed through them. Kathy soon learned that you had to run the rubber pants of the foster children, (who I'll tell you more about in a little while), through the wringer from crotch to top or risk blowing out the sides of the rubber pants as they ran through the wringer.

Brud was fascinated by the wringing process and thought that the clothes that came out so stiff and flat could be used to build something with if it wasn't for their irregular shapes. As Brud played with the handle that activated the wringers, Allen warned him not to monkey with the thing or he might injure himself or break something. Ferne said that if he was so interested in house work, she would find some for him to do. That remark took immediate effect. Monkeying around with stuff was one thing Brud loved to do. But the threat of house work, turned his attention back to his father who was ready to go after another load of sawdust.

Jim Harrison sold his farm to a family whose name was Birmingham and they did not run the saw mill. For this reason, Allen could only get sawdust from Smith's which was, now, the only local saw mill. As sawdust became more in demand, Smith's Lumber Company began charging for the sawdust. The sawdust could be loaded with their bucket loader which sped up the job quite a bit. A little later, Smith's built a storage building where the sawdust was blown into directly from the saw mill. It was a large building on stilts, so a truck could be backed in underneath the building. There was also a sliding trap door in the floor of the building. Sometimes, the door could be slid open, causing the sawdust to pour into the truck and fill it up quickly. Most of the time, however, Brud would have to climb a ladder on the outside of the building, enter a small window in the top and climb down in and shovel the sawdust down into the truck. Although it was extremely hot in the building, it wasn't too bad if the blower wasn't running. With the blower running, it was necessary to wear goggles as the sawdust blew everywhere. Brud would begin to sweat from the exertion of shoveling and the heat inside the building. The sawdust would stick to his sweaty body, making him very uncomfortable and I know Brud was really happy when they finally had enough sawdust.

Foster Children

Ronald Mott
Dennis Curtis
Donnie Marlette
Mark Pike
Kendra Pike
Debbie Kenyon
Gail Kenyon
Bobby Kowalski
Mickey Kowalski

*U*nfortunately, there are children who, for various reasons, do not have a home. Several of them came to our farm and I would see these children arrive and always wondered why some of these children seemed so sad, with a kind of faded look about them, though they were all beautiful children. What could have happened to make them look this way? There were some that reminded me of wilting flowers; just needing some care, some sunshine, and a good place to grow.

When the children were brought to my pasture, at first, I thought that they had no necks; they pulled their heads down into their shoulders, as if they were trying to hide within their bodies. I had to search to see their downcast eyes.

When I could see them, their eyes were dull, sad, and hollow. In some, I could see fear, and even anger. The children, their hair and clothing looked unkempt and in poor condition. They reminded me of that sad old horse that had arrived suddenly, out of nowhere, with the old man and the surrey. The children looked as though no one cared at all or even noticed them. Some of them also had black and blue bruises and two of them even had odd, little round burn marks on their skin.

Worst of all they didn't seem to know what it felt like to be loved. I knew they would feel that here. It was wonderful to see the transformation in these children that happened in whatever amount of time they had to stay in this magical valley. Just like any seed that was ever planted or even the tiny acorn which landed on the earth, took root, grew, became strong and healthy, and turned into this mighty oak tree that I stand under. These children will have a better chance to become all that they can be; their lives and paths forever changed by their experiences, adventures and friendships here.

What they will learn in our Valley:

From Ferne - *They learn to forget hunger. Ferne's delicious food; her love and affection, nourished them, body and soul. She listened to them and tended their wounds. From her they all knew, maybe for the first time, what it feels like to have a mom. To be loved.*

From Allen – *They learn that a man can have strong, work-roughened hands and still have a kind and gentle touch. I'm sure that they also learned persistence from him: to see a project through and to not give up on something just because it's challenging. And... that a man really can be as big as the shadow he casts.*

From Ferne Marie – *They learn to seek knowledge: and to learn all that they can. From her they will also learn how to have patience with your siblings, "nincom-poops" or not.*

From Kathy – *They learn to nurture, to love, and to help each other. And, of course, to stop and smell the roses, or in her case, to stop and pick some wildflowers.*

156

From Brud – *They learn about imagination and curiosity. They learn, by watching, that you can become completely distracted by nature, any time, if you look and listen. They also learn to love all animals, and to be wary of bats.*

From Jan – *They learn to laugh, dance, skip and play. She helps them to remember to have fun and enjoy life. They also learn how to supervise on a job that they're too young to help with. Her sense of humor, fun, and adventure, helped them to be less fearful and sad.*

Some lessons from the animals:

Chickens – *Always stay busy*

Tippy – *Be proud and brave, even if you happen to be a small dog with only three legs.*

Kittens – Be *kind and gentle to those who are smaller and weaker than you.*

Us, horses – *Keep your body strong and willing to work. With us, the children were able to get to know a type of being that many, if not all of them had never been around to get to know. And they learned to giggle at the tickle of our long whiskers, the softness of our velvety muzzles and the warm breath on their tiny hands.*

From the Farm, Itself – *The knowledge that there are peaceful places where plants, animals and children have plenty of nourishment; a place to just enjoy being a child, without fear and abuse; and to experience what loving and being loved really is like.*

I really enjoyed getting to know these children. And I know that both we and these children are better for having them here in the Valley. On this very special farm, in this beautiful valley, we all learn gratitude.

A special message from me:
horses don't speak human, but we do understand.
So, here's some words about words, from me

A Word- *The world's sharpest sword*

A Word- T*he most healing balm*

A Word- *Be careful how you use them. Especially with children.*

Back to School
and
Friends in the Valley

*T*he fall season is coming to the valley. Some of the leaves are already turning colors and by this time all the children are back in school. Even little Jan is going to school now. I feel better now seeing them leave as they now have a large yellow school bus with many windows.

The children would come running out of the house as soon as the bus drove into the yard. Ferne insisted that they would all be out and ready so the bus driver, Earl Rider, would not have to wait for them.

The girls, especially Ferne Marie and Kathy, would be loaded down with books and papers, along with their lunch pails. Jan, who had just started school, would come out, skipping and hopping with her pigtails bouncing, and carrying her lunch pail. Brud would come out of the house carrying one book and his lunch pail. He never carried more than one book; neither myself nor anyone else knew how he got such good grades in school as it looked like the books were rarely opened.

Brud carried an old, battered black workman's lunch pail that had been discarded by Lawrence Champine when he no longer felt it was suitable to carry his own lunch. Allen had fashioned a rawhide strap to use as a handle. Ferne had to use this old battered lunch pail to pack Brud's lunch in after she had purchased two nice, green student lunch-pails for

Brud. It seemed that, on two separate occasions, the school bus had somehow run over the green lunch pails. Most likely, due to the fact, that Brud had left them on the ground. I am sure that Ferne loved him with all her heart, but she must have thought: this boy was going to need a great deal of the luck of his Irish heritage to get him through life. I could tell she was frustrated by the situation, but good for Brud to have admitted his carelessness. Honesty is important and Ferne and Allen had taught the children to tell the truth. You can always work with the truth.

* * * * * * * * * * * * * * * *

I always had mixed feelings as the children all headed off for school. I really wanted them to stay in this beautiful, peaceful valley. It seemed that all that anyone really needed and wanted could be provided or found in the protection of this unique, pristine valley. I could see, however, from all the things and people coming and going into this valley, that there was a much bigger place out there than our farm, perhaps even bigger than the Whipple Hollow Valley itself, and that the children would have to learn all they could about it and how to relate to the people they would meet. School was a place where they could learn this. I grew more excited for the children as they told me all of what they had learned at school and about the people they had met. They formed friendships with the kids at school, many if not all, came from farm families themselves.

Brud would head off to school, looking forward to seeing his best friend, Sonny Poremski. They had become friends before Sonny was old enough to go to school. It was inevitable that the two boys would become friends. They both loved horses, adventure. The boys liked jokes (and pranks, I've heard it said). At five and six years old, they were real cowboys.

Brud and Sonny were playing at Sonny's house one afternoon and the two boys were walking down the road to the farm where Sonny's grandfather lived. They were going to ride the Poremski's pony; whose name was Rusty. Sonny said that if they were going to be cowboys, they would need to find Rusty's saddle first. Sonny said Dziadzio; (pronounced "jah-joo") was the word for grandfather, in Polish. (Sonny's dziadzio, was from Poland) and that he would know where the saddle was kept.

Brud and Jan had talked to me about Sonny's grandfather, who they called "Pop" Poremski. They were somewhat frightened of Pop. Allen and Jan had gone to his place one day, and upon seeing the little girl with her shiny, black hair, he turned to Allen and said, "I want the little black one". Pop's voice was a gruff sounding and his English had a heavy Polish accent. His huge drooping mustache hid his friendly smile and rosy dimpled cheeks which made it hard to notice his twinkling blue eyes.

Sonny had told Brud about how his grandfather was an excellent horseman and teamster and that by the gently coaxing of his voice, he could back his work team and wagon out of the barn and down the steep open ramp which was in back of the barn. Sonny also told Brud that when Sonny's grandfather had lived in Poland, he had been a chauffeur for a wealthy land owner and had driven a fancy coach pulled by four horses.

After not finding the saddle in the shed where it should have been, Sonny said, "Ja is in the barn, we'll ask him". Pop was clipping cows when they asked him about the saddle. Pop turned to Brud and said, "Come here, I'll clip um up". This remark sent Brud running with fear, and out of the barn. Sonny came out of the barn and said that Ja had told him that the saddle was at Red's. Red was Sonny's uncle, who owned the next farm down the road from Pop's farm. The two little boys started down the road for Red's, looking for the saddle. When they arrived at Red's, he told them that he thought the saddle was at another nearby farm. So off Brud and Sonny went, in quest of the saddle.

When the two little boys arrived at the neighbor's farm they asked a woman there, about the saddle. Mary was her name. Her only reply was to tell them she thought they were much too little to be roaming around the neighborhood. She called Ferne and told her about the little boys' escapades. Allen was way out in the flat meadow working, so Ferne, who had no driver's license, went after the boys in the blue Plymouth. Even though Brud had expressed his objections about riding with someone who doesn't have a driver's license, Ferne told him to" be quiet and get into the car." Ferne told Sonny that she would give him a ride home too. But Brud had likely told him how serious it was to drive a car without a license. Sonny started running back to his house as fast as he could. Ferne simply followed along to make sure the boy got home safely. Sonny, who could always run extremely fast, was soon back home.

The school bus would arrive at Florence School more than an hour before school started and would not pick the children up after school until more than an hour after school was over for the day. This gave Brud and Sonny plenty of time to explore every nook and cranny of the Florence School; making mischief wherever they went. The teachers, by and large, were not amused.

Florence School had a large playground. It was bordered by woods at the back and south ends of the school yard. Although, it was forbidden to leave the playground, the woods were an irresistible attraction for Brud and Sonny, who probably enjoyed being in the woods more than most any place else.

They built secret huts, set rabbit snares on the game trails, commandeered a row boat and floated around the pond which was located in back of the school. Sonny and Brud often made trips through the woods to end up at McLaughlin's store and explore the old abandoned Florence Marble Mill. There was one time when Brud had to pull Sonny out of the brook. Sonny fell through the ice when they were breaking ice on the beaver dam. These pre- and post-school adventures always ended the same way, with a mad dash to catch the bus for a ride home or to get into school before they were late. Sometimes, they would sneak through the basement of the school if they were late and wanted to slink into the classroom unnoticed and if they were, could always say they were in the bathroom which was located in the basement.

Jan's special friends were Carol Mullis and Lucille Zelazny. Carol was full of fun and laughter and that is what Jan is all about. Jan went to Lucille's family farm often and she thought it was unusual that they were not allowed in the barn. For Jan, being in and knowing about the barn was just part of what is was to be a farm kid.

Kathy's friends were Louise Poremski and Diane Davis. Louise is usually quite serious and works very hard at any task or her classroom studies. Diane brings laughter to the friendship. She also brings music as she can make music from a piano or it seems any instrument she picks up.

Ferne Marie's friends were Ronnie Davis, Bernie Poremski and Kathryn Parrow. Ronnie was the clown of the classroom. He went to any length to make everyone laugh. When Grace Gronnell, their teacher, left the classroom, (probably for a cigarette break in the teacher's room) Ronnie would put on her sweater and wrap himself up in it just like she did, then he would add the teacher's large, fur coat and hat and go parading around the classroom to roars of laughter.

Bernie seems to require a great deal of Ferne Marie's attention to get him through his classroom work. If not for her help everyone was certain that he would never finish school. Bernie had many interests, but school wasn't really one of them. He bought a fancy car that Sonny and Brud said must have only two gears: reverse, and fast.

Ferne Marie and Kathryn Parrow's friendship revolved around friendly competition. Ferne Marie rooted for the New York Yankees baseball team while Kathryn favored the Boston Red Sox. Kathryn's favorite cowboy was Gene Autry, while Ferne Marie's was Roy Rogers. The girls' common ground, at least in part, was that they played cowboys and wild horses, right up until high school, while many girls their age preferred dolls and lace.

Brud got to learn what having a girl for a friend was like. He started school in the first grade with sweet little Mary Fran Kurant and graduated high school at Otter Valley

Union High School with her. I know he will always cherish her sweet smile and friendly greeting wherever and whenever they meet.

The bus ride to school was long and went over some rough country roads. It gathered up the bouquet of blond-haired flowers like Rosemary Poremski and her cousin Barbara Poremski; filling the bouquet at the end with Charlene Cecot.

One of the children's friends was Val Sherman. Val, with her cute little dimpled cheeks, was just like Jan, and was always tagging along by her father's side. Constantly being around George might have been the reason that Val learned and used his full vocabulary of curse words. The tiny, little girl would drawl out "Gaawd" (as well as other choice phrases) the same way as George did.

Our farm and the Sherman farm often traded work and equipment, so Val spent a great deal of time with us on the farm. Val was younger than Jan, but they became good friends. Jan thought she would try out some of Val's curse words. Although, Val was even younger than Jan, she never got in trouble for using them. Ferne, however, got very upset when Jan used some of those words. She said these were bad, dirty words and the only way to clean these words from a person's mouth was to wash the mouth out with soap. Not all that surprising to me, as Brud, with his typical curiosity, had to make his own experiment with the curse words, but he had gone up to my pasture to try them out, well out of his mother's hearing. He said that these words had no taste at all, not dirty or anything else. It seemed that only one application of soap was all that was needed to rid the children of these words. I saw it work with Jan and Ferne Marie who needed the same procedure.

* * * * * * * * * * * * * * * *

Farm families were friendly with each other and helped each other. Allen and Norm Champine helped Red Poremski when he got the first Baler that was used in the area.

It was a huge machine that he dragged behind his tractor. It looked like a dinosaur as it chewed up the windrows of hay and smashed it inside the machine and spit out bales of hay from its backend. Allen and Norm helped Red pick up the bales and put them into his barn. Several local farmers borrowed Allen's tractor and saw rig.

The telephone, which seemed to be both a blessing and a curse helped to keep the farm families connected. Our telephone was used primarily, only by Ferne. Allen would speak on it after Ferne made the call, but only if he needed to explain something to a machinery dealer or the veterinarian. The telephones were connected by an eight-party line which meant that eight families all used the same line, just on different phones. Phone time had to be shared. Some people used the telephone for just chatting, but it was mostly used for business or to pass a message. Here, there was no chatting on the phone for the children, only rarely to ask a friend over for a visit. Sometimes people spent time listening to their neighbor's conversations, but I suppose this keeps neighbors connected and careful of what they say about each other. It reduced privacy to none at all, but I suppose these shared lines kept neighbors informed about who might need some help.

Allen explained neighborliness to Brud when he asked why Allen let the Markowski family get milk out of his bulk tank. Allen explained that even though the Markowski's did not pay him what he could get from the milk company, they were neighbors and they had a large family and that was their way of helping a neighbor. It was what you did.

Ferne helped Theresa Bathalon when she was ill and when she had the last of her children. Allen milked cows for George Sherman while he recovered from an operation and Allen milked for Al Poremski while he recovered from a knee injury. Neighbors cared for each other and would help if they could. It was that simple. Farms, for obvious reasons, are in rural areas and in some places very remote. Stores and doctors are not close by, so the farm families helped take care of one another.

A Time
of Sadness
and Loss

*T*here came a great time of sadness in the family when Allen's beautiful Irish mother, Kate passed away. I did not know Kate well as I very rarely saw her at the farm. I knew it was not easy for her to travel, even the relatively short distance between our farm and theirs. She had some trouble with her legs or her feet, it seemed, for she always walked with a cane. Kate was a large woman and couldn't climb up into Harley's buggy. So, I never got a chance to get to know her. I do know that everyone loved her and was very sad at her passing.

I remember one day that Allen and Harley were unloading wood by Harley's wood shed. Dolly stood beside me, napping. Kate came out of the house, wearing her ever-present apron, and walking with her cane. Kate's beautiful white hair, as white as my mane but much softer, was always precisely braided and rolled on her head like a crown. As she stood talking to Allen, I could smell apples and flour on her hands as she stroked my muzzle. I thought that she must have been making pies in her summer kitchen. Kathy, who I think looks very much like Kate, spent a lot of time with her in her summer kitchen, helping and learning from her grandmother.

I remember Jan was curious about Kate's cane. Jan was up on Kate's bed trying to help Kate make her bed and

Kate was using her cane to tuck in the covers on the back side of the bed. Jan was quite young and wondered why Gramma Kate would carry that cane around all day just to make her bed.

I recall noticing the print of Kate's apron. Ferne Marie had one just like it. Kate had made her one and I'd seen Ferne Marie in an apron just the same as Kate's. Kate must have made them both, and she made one to give to Ferne Marie for her birthday. Ferne Marie looked so cute in that apron. Whenever I see her wearing it, I think of Kate, who was always very kind to me. Sometimes if the day is hot and the wagon is heavy, I think of Kate and the strength she had.

As I listened and watched Kate talking to Allen, I see her stoic, blue eyes and I think they are just like Allen's eyes. Kate's eyes hid the pain she had in her legs, and the pain of grief from the loss of three of her sons. Nelson died as an infant. Eddie died from appendicitis, and John was killed in a car accident when he was sixteen-years-old. His car was hit by a train.

Brud, who was too young, at the time to understand about funerals and the death of a person, stayed with his aunt, Gussie Smith. She tells him about Gramma Kate's passing. Living on a farm, Brud knew about the death of animals, but this was the first time he had experienced the passing of a person who he loved. The little boy stared out the window into the rain. He could see his Gramma Kate's face in every drop of rain in the puddles and wonders why animals and people that he loves so much have to die.

Allen was grieving the death of his dear mother, but the work of the farm still needed to be done. So, with his mother's stoic eyes and her inner strength, he reminds himself that life must go on; the animals have to be taken care of and there is always work to be done.

You probably think this is pretty heavy thinking for an old work horse but I'm a pretty heavy old work horse; probably just "full of corn" and just when you were thinking I had forgotten.

The Hole
in the Wall; and
Losing Pride

When Allen plowed the garden, Brud would collect earthworms that he found in the freshly-turned, moist earth. One day, after putting some of these earthworms into a can he brought them into the house and began to carefully stuff them into a hole in the wall where a knot in the wood had come loose and had fallen off. It was in a trim board between the kitchen and the dining room.

Ferne came into the kitchen and caught Brud stuffing one of the last worms down the hole. "What in the world are you doing?", she shrieked. Brud always had a tender heart for animals and all living creatures, well, not bats I've heard. Brud replied, "I'm only trying to save them because Daddy unburied them from the dirt and I've saved other things in there but only if they fit into the hole". Ferne brought Brud and the few remaining worms in his hand out to the garden and told him to release them there, where he had found them, in the garden. She explained that the worms could find their own way back into the dirt and he need not feel he must save them. The garden was where they lived, and where they belonged. Brud learned something that day and so had Ferne. That very day she patched the hole and painted over it. I do not know what else, if anything, Ferne found while making the necessary repairs.

* * * * * * * * * * * * * * * *

New calves were constantly being born on the farm and Brud wanted to raise them all. He told Allen that they would fill the whole valley with cattle if they raised and kept every calf. Allen explained that it was not good to keep more animals than you could feed and shelter; that you would need a barn big enough to house your entire herd, during the winter. Brud asked why they raised heifer calves from only certain cows and why they never raised a bull calf. Allen explained that a farmer had to be constantly watching his herd; looking at how much milk each cow gave and watching to see which cows had good, strong, healthy bodies. It was important to keep track of which cows stayed healthy and productive. Keeping the heifer calves from those cows helped to make sure the herd would continue to be productive and healthy. The bull calves could not be kept because, in a very short time, their herd would be inbred. The cows would become runty and unhealthy and not very productive.

Allen told Brud that if he wanted to understand this better, then he should think about Raymond Casey's cattle that he kept at the bottom of the hill which leads to our valley. Mr. Casey let his cattle all run together: cows, calves and bulls. He had done this for several years, and over time they interbred and were a strange looking herd of cattle indeed. They were oddly-shaped, runty, and strange looking.

Brud asked his father what happened to the cows and calves that were sold to the cattle dealer. Allen said that the calves are sold for veal and the cows go for beef. Brud thinks, "Veal?! Beef?! No more questions! These cows have names! Freckles, Speckles, Star, Stinky and Sam! I better go see Dick".

Not long after having acquired this information, Brud came into the horse barn. He was crying, tears just streaming down his freckled cheeks. He hid his head under my long mane and I felt his wet cheeks on my neck. Allen had just told Brud that a cattle dealer would be coming to the farm and that Allen must sell Pride. Pride was a big Holstein cow. She'd had a rough start. As a calf, Pride got sick and required a lot of medicine to get her through. Brud sat with the calf, hoping she would get better, as he stroked her head. From then on,

Brud and the calf seemed to have a special relationship that so often happens between animals and the people who take care of and love them.

Pride's mother was one of Allen's best cows. After she had had her first calf, Pride gave a great amount of milk at each milking. At the end of her first cycle, Allen found out that Pride could not have any more calves. So, Allen told Brud that Pride would have to be sold and Pride would have to be sold for beef.

There was nothing I could do for the sad little boy except make him feel that I understood. It is always hard to lose a friend, no matter the circumstances. After a while, Brud left my horse barn and went to the house. I knew Ferne could help him with his sadness. Brud told her that Allen was going to sell Pride, and that she is being sold for beef! She said that she already knew, and that it made both her and Allen sad. Brud tearfully argued her case. Pride was special, why couldn't they make an exception. Ferne told Brud that each life is a cycle. The cycle was birth and growth, work and purpose, and then a time of slowing down, and passing on, and that this happens with all plants, animals and even people. The end of a cycle was a beginning; of new plants, animals and people. That is how things were meant to be. Ferne told him that farming would teach him this difficult lesson many more times, but also that everything would be all right. Ferne also told Brud that loss is a part of life and the pain that losing a person, or an animal caused should not make him afraid to make new relationships. Whether it lasts for a day or for many years, you should just enjoy your relationships for whatever time you have.

I did see this lesson taught many more times, to Brud, and I could also see that the boy doesn't have Kate or Allen's stoic, blue eyes.

Thistle Whacking, Mullen Dipping and Sweet Apples

O ut near the south pasture gate in the gravel pit pasture, grew a Sweet- apple tree. In the early fall, the children would make many trips to this tree. From my oak tree, I would see them coming back with their pockets full, and with apples in each hand; munching as they walked. I would meet them at the gate because I knew they would share an apple or two with me. The apples had a very pale-yellow skin with streaks of pinkish red throughout. They were the sweetest apples that grew anywhere on the farm. They were small, in size but what they lacked in size they made up for in their sweetness.

The gravel pit pasture had a huge area where gravel was taken out to be used on both ends of the Whipple Hollow Road by the towns of Pittsford and West Rutland. The soil was thin in the gravel pit pasture which allowed many thistles to grow. The trips to the sweet apple tree would usually begin with one of the strange games that the children often played. It was called Thistle Whacking. First, they had to find a good sturdy stick, preferably with a slight crook at the heavy end, similar to a golf club. Thistle Whacking was an exciting, and sometimes painful game, as the object of the game was to whack the thistle blossom with the stick and send it flying at your target. Being hit with a thistle blossom could be quite painful, so dodging the flying blossoms was an essential skill. When Ron Smith was around, the game was especially exciting. He thoroughly enjoyed both Thistle Whacking and Thistle Dodging. Happy to be on either end of the game. As I watched Jan play, I thought this girl could later become an excellent golfer as she had such a powerful, accurate drive, which sent the blossom flying, hard and true, at her target.

Another game was called Mullen Dipping. Sort of sounds like an herbal snack but quite the contrary. Mullen dipping or Mullen Flicking was more like a nasty trick than a game, with the emphasis on NASTY. Mullen dipping required selecting the best Mullen stalk which grew in abundance along the path that led out to the Sweet apple tree. Ferne Marie invented this game and with much practice, developed it into an art form before introducing the game to the other children. After the proper Mullen stalk was found, about three feet long and with a slight limpness at the heavily blossomed end, the blossomed end was dipped into the freshest plop of cow manure that Ferne Marie could find. She would then flick the manure off the stalk in a throwing motion at an unsuspecting target, most often the back of her brother. The Nin-com-Poop, one of the names she often called him, along with Numb Skull and Thimble Brain. But Nin-com-Poop seemed the favorite. He was such a wonderful target and would fall for most any trick she devised.

He even fell for the Rag-Weed Horse Trick once. For this trick, she would select two rag weed stalks with long seedy spires. She told Brud that if he were a horse, he'd have to be bitted. So, instructed, he eagerly took both stalks into his mouth between his teeth leaving the seedy spires dangling from each side of his mouth. Ferne Marie would than take the other ends of the stalks and pull them through the sides of his mouth filling his mouth with rag weed seeds. She laughed hysterically, leaving Brud spitting out rag weed seeds.

172

Kathryn Parrow was visiting Ferne Marie one day. The girls' competition over who the best cowboy was had come to the point of a showdown. Roy Rogers was Ferne Marie's favorite while Gene Autry was Kathryn's. Ferne Marie suggested they meet at high noon at the OK Corral (more accurately, my barnyard) and settle the dispute the cowboy way: with a competition at Mullen Dipping. If this seems a little unfair with Ferne Marie's well-practiced proficiency at Mullen Dipping against Kathryn who had no knowledge of the game at all, it was. Ferne Marie's opinion was that she was simply using a competitive advantage, as any gunfighter or Mullen Dipper would.

As they selected their Mullen stalks, Ferne Marie quickly found a good one about three feet long with a sturdy stalk and a heavy blossomed end. Ferne Marie neglected to tell Kathryn that the one she was choosing was much too long and the stalk was too thin. Roy (Ferne Marie) and Gene (Kathryn) faced each other, about twelve feet apart, with the noon heat raising swirls of dust in the corral. Both girls had a fresh cow pie in front of them. Kathryn nervously dipped her Mullen stalk, while Ferne Marie gave hers just a little twist, securing an extra heavy load of the gooey mess on the blossom.

Ferne Marie stood calmly and with great confidence. Kathryn raised her loaded Mullen stalk, (much too high, Ferne thought) and some of the load fell, hitting Kathryn on her shoulder. Then, with all her strength, Kathryn brought the Mullen stalk forward, causing the slim stalk to break in two places, making it quite useless, as the manure dropped harmlessly at her own feet. Ferne Marie, pressing her advantage, took one step closer to Kathryn. She knew Kathryn was left-handed and therefore, she would likely dodge in that direction.

Ferne Marie raised the Mullen stalk just forward of her right shoulder, and, having calculated her opponent's movement, gave an expert flick of the stalk. The manure hit Kathryn just above the right pocket of her red and white checkered blouse. With Kathryn's stalk broken and useless, Gene had lost, and Roy had won, making Roy the better cowboy. Ferne Marie considered the matter settled, but Kathryn, after cleaning off her blouse, leaving a green stain, her green badge of courage, said "But Gene Autry still sings better than Roy Rogers".

While I may have destroyed the myth of Ferne Marie always being serious and studious, I must say: I love her with all my Horsey Heart and she is the one that brings me the best sweet apples.

Nancy, Pal, and Sonny Jim

Brud and Sonny both loved riding horses so when Brud got his saddle-horse, Pal, they could ride together. Sonny would ride Nancy, who was a black mare that Sonny's grandfather had raised. She may have been of mixed breeding; Draft horse and Saddle horse. Nancy had not been trained to ride however, in fact, she had not been worked in harness or had someone try to ride her for many years. It soon became evident to the boys that this was just the way she liked it, and this was the way she meant to continue.

The boys were certain, that with all of their riding skills (which pretty much consisted of climbing on a horse and then hanging on because it hurt to fall off; I guess you'd call this seat-of-the-pants-riding), that they could make a Saddle horse out of Nancy. She clearly had no intention of cooperating. When the boys could get on her back she would stand, stubbornly still, not moving an inch, no matter how much they urged her to move. She would squeal, crow- hop, and sometimes pass gas, but that was about the most action they could get out of Nancy.

One day, the boys were making another attempt to train Nancy to be a Saddle horse. This time Sonny was on Pal and Brud was on Nancy. She was being her usual uncooperative self. Pop came out of the barn. He was carrying a rubber milking hose. It was the air line from the milking machine, and about six feet long. Pop, wearing his tall boots, clumped up behind Nancy and said, "I'll get um up". He gave Nancy a good whack on the rump with the rubber hose. All it really takes, if you must use this forceful method, is a slap on the rump with just your hand. Nancy gave a little crow-hop and squealed with pain. Not about to give in, she settled back into her stubborn, defiant stance again. Brud told me that Pop gave Nancy another whack, speaking gruffly to her in Polish. Brud said he didn't know if the words Pop used had been curse words, but it was said in the same tone of voice that Allen would use with his curse words. In any case, Nancy seemed to understand Polish better than English for she immediately took off, down the road at her fastest trot. She didn't stop until she got all the way to Red's corner barn on the Fire Hill Road.

Soon afterwards, Sonny bought a handsome, arrogant, shiny red chestnut, Morgan/Arabian stallion. He was truly an admirable little fellow, and he knew it. His name was Sonny Jim and even though he was smaller than Pal, he could run equally as fast.

One day, Sonny and Brud wanted to go riding. Brud would ride Pal and Sonny's dad, Al, had saddled Sonny Jim for Sonny to ride. Sonny Jim had a habit of puffing his belly out when the cinch was tightened, so a potential rider would check to make sure the cinch and saddle were on properly and securely. By puffing his belly out at cinching, Sonny Jim's saddle would not be stable.

The boys made a mistake they would likely not make again. They forgot to check the cinch on Sonny Jim, after they had walked the horses a little while. As they went around the corner and headed into the big meadow on the left, the boys put the horses into a full gallop. As the horses' speed increased, Sonny Jim's saddle rolled over. Sonny grabbed the horse's mane. With his foot caught in the off-side stirrup, Sonny clung desperately to the horse's mane. With both horses at a full gallop, Brud rode Pal up close to the side of Sonny Jim. He reached over and put his arm under Sonny's arm, raised him up and freed him from the saddle. Then, Brud slowed Pal down and was able to get Sonny safely to the ground.

They rode horses quite a bit together. Once they rode down to the Florence Catholic Church, then all the way up around Fire Hill and past the Plezga farm. As they rode by the farm, Sonny's handsome little stallion sent Theresa Plezga's mares into such a frenzy that Theresa had to ask the boys not to ride by her farm anymore.

It is likely that their mutual appreciation for horses brought the two boys together. Shared experiences, a love of adventure and mischief, and triumphs and calamities large and small, began a friendship that would last. I imagine that when the boys grew up, the memories and stories remained, to be talked over and re-lived.

Fresh Air Child:
Michael James Joseph Horan

Michael James Joseph Horan. That is a lot of names for such a small boy. We just called him Mike. I know I have mentioned Mike before, but I remember him quite well. As all the other Fresh-Air and foster children were, Mike was immediately welcomed and accepted. This little fellow became a member of the family.

Mike had first arrived on the farm with a girl named Maureen Cannon. Maureen stayed two weeks and then went back to the city, but Mike asked to stay longer. So, with his parent's approval, Mike spent the entire summer on our farm. Mike was only five years old when he came to our farm. Normally, the boy would have had to wait another year to come but because his mom had suffered a heart attack and he was part of a large family; he was allowed to come a year earlier than was normal. He had nine brothers and sisters and they all lived together in a place called the Bronx; in New York City. Mike's father was a city bus driver.

Upon his arrival, the sight of such a large area of open land would cause the boy to just start running. Mike would run until he was tired and then flop down in the grass to rest awhile and then run again, just enjoying all that open land. He enjoyed all of us animals, but Mike was most interested in the cats. He was constantly either carrying a cat or petting one, if he could.

Perhaps it was because he was from a large family and he was used to and understood sharing and the disciplines of family life, he fit in our farm family just as if he had actually been born into it.

Mike enjoyed seeing all the different wild animals that appeared on the farm as well. One day, Mike found a nest of mice, and he called Brud's attention to it. There were four baby mice and the mother. Mike squatted down to watch the mice; thoroughly absorbed and focused. Brud suddenly told Mike, "Grab it!" Perhaps it was the urgent tone in Brud's instruction, or just Mike's love of animals. Mike grabbed up the mother mouse. The mouse, objecting to her capture, bit right through the tip of Mike's finger. Mike hopped around with the mouse dangling from his finger. When the mother mouse finally let go of his finger, Mike asked Brud, "Why did you tell me to 'grab it'?" Brud laughing, replied, "Why did you actually do it?"

With Brud's natural curiosity combined with Mike's wanting to explore the natural world. The farm was a remarkable place that was so different to the concrete and steel world that Mike came from. The boys often, and sometimes painfully, got into trouble with the bees and other critters who objected to their explorations.

Allen immediately became Mike's hero from the moment they met. He would often call Allen, "Dad," just as naturally as the other children did. Due to Ferne's loving and caring nature, it went without saying that Mike called her "Mom."

Mike was fascinated by the size and strength of us horses. At five years old, Mike would climb up onto the buck stick next to Allen who was holding the reins. I can remember Mike saying to Allen, "Daddy, can I say the WOIDS?" So, with his tongue behind his front teeth and his mouth open, he would suck in air causing us horses to move forward. (Try it yourself. Put your tongue behind your front teeth and with your mouth open suck in air as if you were drinking. There it is and away we go!) Can you imagine what an awesome experience that must have been for a five-year old boy from New York City?

When Mike turned sixteen and could no longer go to the farm through the Fresh Air Fund, Allen and Ferne sent him money for a bus ticket. Mike came and stayed all that summer.

Mike had a difficult time learning his lessons in school, so at the end of that summer, and because he was sixteen, he asked Allen and Ferne if he could quit school and work on the farm. They told him that he could if his parents approved. After getting his parent's permission, Allen told Mike that he could work for his wages along with earning his board. If Mike wanted to do this, he could not lay in bed in the morning the way he liked. He would have to get up when Allen did, every morning and work all day, just like Allen did. Allen advised Mike that, at the very least, high school was important in that it lead to better opportunities and maybe even easier work than a farm laborer. As always, Allen felt that a person should make their own choices.

I guess Allen thought that Mike could learn the most about being a farm laborer from the handle of a shovel, because that is what I saw him doing a great deal of the time. He fed the cows, cleaned out the barn and shoveled bedding. Winter gave still more opportunities to learn from that shovel, with the snows which fell often and deep.

Allen would wake Mike at 4:30 in the morning when he got up. He would remind Mike to move around quietly because everyone else would still be sleeping.

The one deciding factor about becoming a farm laborer may have come in the form of "thirteen blocks". These were not the usual city blocks that Mike was used to. These blocks were of stove-length wood that Allen had cut from a large Oak Tree which over hung the meadow and was a nuisance when the hay loader had to pass under it during haying season.

After Allen fell the huge Oak Tree, he cut thirteen blocks off the butt end of the tree. These blocks would make excellent fire wood for next winter, all they would need is for Mike to split each block, so the wood would dry and be of appropriate size to fit into the wood stove.

Allen cut the Oak tree in early January and Mike immediately started splitting the blocks of wood. Allen gave

Mike a splitting maul and four wedges. He told Mike that it was not as important how hard you hit the wedges as it was where you placed the wedge in the block and how accurately you hit it. Mike said, "But how do I know where to place it?" "Oh, you'll pick that up as you go," Allen replied, "Just be careful not to strike over and hit the maul handle on the wedge or you will break the handle". Allen would repair and replace many maul handles as Mike split the thirteen blocks. Allen would only say with a grin, "Struck over, didn't you?".

Splitting hard woods, Maple and Oak in particular, is difficult at its best; but in freezing temperatures, it is even more so. The sap and resin freeze inside the wood which makes even just starting the wedge a problem. Many times, even if the wedge is struck accurately and firmly, it will fly from the block of wood, and just as if the flying wedge had some heat-seeking capabilities, the wedge would always fly directly at the shin bone of the person splitting wood; striking the person just below the knee and just above the protection of the boot. Mike got quite skilled at hopping away from the flying wedges but not before being struck many times on the shin bone causing him to shout out some of Allen's curse words, which was a violation of his religious training.

By the end of that February, Mike decided he would go back to the city for a spring break. So, with still-bruised shins, he got on the bus and went back to his home in the city. He returned that summer with plans to go back to school and get his G.E.D. (the equivalent of a high school diploma) in the fall, and enlisted in the Air Force to satisfy his military obligation.

Fall Settles in the Valley; Unpleasant Work; and a Visit from Dr. Smokey

Fall has come to the Valley. The leaves change colors, creating a blanket of reds, oranges, yellows or so I hear. We horses see color differently than humans. We see mainly just hues of blue and green and can distinguish the color red not at all.

In the early morning darkness, I see Allen walking to the cow barn. Frost blankets the valley and Allen is wearing his customary grey sweatshirt to keep warm. I always feel sorry for humans when the temperature drops, and the cold weather arrives and stays. Humans must wear heavy clothing, layers of it, some days. They must wear hats, scarves, gloves and big heavy boots. All of which, make the relatively slow, awkward creatures even more so. Please do not take offense at this but there is judging and there is simple observation. We animals observe, maybe me more so than some.

We animals have coats of hair that grow thicker as the temperature begins to get colder, so that we stay warm and comfortable. When Brud comes into the horse barn to feed us, he likes to come in to my stall to visit and put his arms around my neck and feel my warmth. He will bury his small fingers into the thick hair on my back and marveling at the warmth he feels underneath despite the cold.

As the early morning mist rises from the valley and the sun starts up over the eastern rim, it makes the frost sparkle on the still-green grass and reveals the splendor of the fall foliage, making a crown of splendor around the valley.

The fall season's cool weather and with all the crops harvested and stored, was a time to do some of the more unpleasant tasks of being a farmer. Two of these tasks were butchering and dehorning the cattle. These two tasks were unsettling to me even though I had no part in it. It only added to the respect I have for Allen. No matter how unpleasant or dirty a job is, he can and will do it.

Allen didn't want horns on his cattle because they made it more difficult for a cow to get in and out of her stanchion. With horns the cows injured each other and the humans who worked with them. Dehorning was done in the fall when the days got cooler. Fly contamination was not a factor and infection less likely. Allen would have Ferne call Bill Phillipsen, the veterinarian, to come and do the dehorning. Every fall, any young cow, from about six months to a year old, would have their horns removed.

When Brud was nine years old, he told his father that he wanted to help with the dehorning. Allen told him that he would not like to watch the process and that he should stay in the house. Brud insisted that he should know about all things that went on at the farm, so he was allowed to watch.

Allen had six young heifers to be dehorned that year. Brud wondered why Dr. Phillipsen put on a long white coat over his clothing before he started. Dr. Phillipsen put a few small items in the pocket of the long coat. He took a tool out of the trunk of his car that looked to Brud like brush cutters. They had an anvil at the bottom with an enclosed shear which was driven by the small gears that pushed the shear past the anvil as the handles were brought together. Brud stood close by as Allen held the young animal's head. Dr. Phillipsen placed the shear over the young heifer's horn and pulled the handles together. The horn was quickly sheared off the animal's head. Blood squirted from the stub, hitting Allen on the sleeve of his shirt and the front of Dr. Phillipsen's long white coat. Dr. Phillipsen quickly stopped the bleeding and sealed the wound, but by this time Brud had run off. He hid behind a large post in the barn. As the other horn was sheared off, the young animal bellowed, and Brud said, "Daddy, I'm going to the house". Brud never asked to help with the dehorning after that day.

Allen and Ferne felt that as farmers, they could grow, raise, and harvest, from the forests and fields, all that they needed to sustain their family. As for my horse sense, I think that because of their close connection and dependence on the land, us animals, nature and its changes; they took nothing about life for granted and passed these ideals on to their children.

Allen and Ferne raised pigs and cattle for meat, and chickens for eggs and meat. Allen and Ferne did the butchering of the animals themselves, as well as the preparation of the meat. Allen butchered the animals and both he and Ferne, along with the children, cut up and wrapped the meat to be frozen for later consumption. This was another of the unpleasant jobs of farming, but one that had to be done.

On one cool, fall, Saturday morning, with the children off from school, Allen tells the family that after morning chores that it would be a good day to take care of the job of butchering some chickens and preparing the meat for storage. While Allen and the children are finishing up the barn chores, Ferne goes down to the house and starts heating a huge pot of water on the wood stove. Allen and the children come into the house and Allen asks if the water is hot yet. Ferne says that it is just starting to boil. Allen goes to the shop and gets his double-bitted axe. Before laying it on the chopping block next to the wood shed, he wets his thumb with his tongue and tests it by running his thumb along the edge to make sure it is sharp.

The whole family goes to the chicken coop where Allen catches a chicken for each of them to hold. With Allen helping Jan to carry her chicken, they all head for the chopping block. When they arrive, Allen asks Jan if she will be able to hold the chicken by herself, this year, while he slaughters the chicken. "Sure! I can hold him" Jan replied bravely.

After Allen has killed all the chickens, the chickens are set aside to bleed out. Allen and Ferne bring out the boiling water and put it into a five gallon pail. Allen dips each chicken into the hot water "scalding them", he calls it. The chickens are then handed back to each member of the family. With the chickens' feathers hot and drippy with water, everyone begins the distasteful job of plucking chickens; removing their feathers. No one, regardless of their skill, brags about this job, but being able to stick with it must certainly have felt like an accomplishment. The feathers are hot, and it seems like a nasty, smelly job. Ferne Marie and Kathy particularly dislike chicken plucking.

Allen finishes his bird first and helps Jan because she was the littlest and had the least amount of experience. Brud finishes his quite quickly. Too quickly maybe because Allen says, "Go back and get all the pin feathers". As Brud goes back to finish his chicken, Kathy brings her neatly plucked chicken into the house where Allen and Ferne are cutting them up.

Kathy watches the entire process intently and helps with wrapping by cutting tape for Ferne as she wraps up the packages of cut-up chicken. Ferne Marie, mumbling curses that end with the word "chickens," has finished plucking her chicken and has made up her mind that she is done with the process. I think that if she could find enough berries, she would probably never eat chicken.

Allen was able to slaughter farm animals and kill wild animals for meat. He also tended the wounds of the children. Most people had no idea that he had an extreme dislike for the sight of blood. The sight of his own blood actually causes him to pass out. He cut his hand once, while sharpening a scythe. His knees buckled, and he fell against the wagon rack, so he was unable to reach for the handkerchief he always carried for this very purpose. One time he passed out twice before he made it into the house after getting his thumb caught in the lift mechanism of the mowing machine.

Allen's dislike of the sight of blood never kept him away from a job he needed to do. He was able to bandage up someone else but seeing his own blood would make him pass out. One day, while running through the corn field, Brud had fallen and injured his stomach on the sharp stump of a corn stalk. The wound was bleeding severely. Allen took that handkerchief I mentioned and made a pad for the wound. He took out his jack knife and cut two strips of cloth from the t-shirt he was wearing to hold the pad in place.

Ferne had received some training as a nurse, so she took care of most of the wounds, and had plenty of opportunities to keep her nursing skills fresh. In those times, particularly in the rural areas, having a neighbor who had medical experience was, surely in some cases, life-saving.

Well, I've wandered off the path a bit.... Oh, I was telling you about plucking chickens. After the mess was cleaned up and everything taken care of, Allen told the children that, as a treat for finishing the necessary but rather grim and nasty job, he and Ferne would take them to the movies at the Joy Theater in West Rutland after supper.

Brud was really excited when the family arrived at the Joy Theater as he had never been to the movies before. Ferne Marie and Kathy had told him about movies. Grampa Waven and Gramma Jessie had taken them to the movies at the theater in Brandon.

Kathy told Brud about how she had been frightened when Ferne took her to see the movies in Rutland. It was a movie called "Treasure Island". As she settled in to watch the movie, the first character to appear was missing one leg and walked on a stick attached to his upper leg. He had a patch over one eye and a bird rode on his shoulder. He was dressed all in black with a sinister-looking hook protruding from one sleeve of his coat where his hand should be. His other hand, brandished a terrible, fearsome-looking sword. When Kathy saw this "Captain Hook", she got up and ran out of the theater. It seemed that she wasn't able calm down until Ferne took her to Perkin's Diner for ice cream.

What a place the Joy Theater was! Allen bought tickets and the family entered a room called a Lobby where a man named Billy Valch, (Margaret Spaulding's younger brother), gave each of the children a bag of popcorn. Brud was fascinated with the popcorn machine. He watched as the popped corn came boiling out of the top of the machine and cascaded to the bottom where Billy scooped it out and filled the bags with popcorn.

Brud had seen Grampa Waven make popcorn, of course. To make popcorn, Grampa Waven would start by making a fire in the kitchen stove, using small sticks of wood, which would make a quick, hot, fire. When the stove was good and hot, he put some corn kernels into a basket-like container and would shake the basket until it filled with popped corn.

The family took their sacks of popcorn into another room which was quite large and had many seats which all faced a huge, white wall. As they sat eating popcorn, the lights in the theater dimmed to dark and pictures appeared on the white wall. The pictures moved as though the story was happening right in front of you. This particular "movie," told the story of Lassie, a very special Collie dog.

The only experience so far that was like going to the movies, was when the teachers at the Florence School sent the entire school home early so that they could watch the coronation of a woman called Elizabeth on television. The Mills family did not have a television, so they went to Red Poremski's house to watch it. It was here, after the coronation that Brud got his first kiss from one of the pretty little blonde-haired girls in the area, Rosemary Poremski. He was six-years-old, and Rosemary was seven. At the time Brud didn't understand why the coronation was so important to everyone and he was too young to get why this kiss was so special, but I think he will figure it all out as he gets older; at least about the kiss.

As I've said, the farm families in particular helped each other. They shared work and equipment, phone lines, and in the case of the coronation, television sets. One fall, George

Sherman had to have an operation, so Allen milked George's cows while George was recovering. Every morning and every evening Allen went to George's farm to milk his cows after milking his own.

Al Poremski injured his knee once and Allen milked his cows, too. There may have been times when Allen had to have someone milk his cows, but in all the time I worked with him, I don't ever remember a day when Allen was too sick or too badly injured to milk his cows or do his field work. He injured his knee once and it was very stiff. He braced it and just worked with it.

* * * * * * * * * * * * * * * * *

In the fall we did a lot of plowing. Allen would watch his field and when the grass started to weaken and go back to the finer, more wild grasses such as June Grass, Allen would plow the field and spread manure on it until he covered the entire piece. In the spring, he would harrow the manure into the fields, loosen the soil and then plant it. Allen planted corn on a field for two years in a row. After two years, Allen planted oats and grass seed, a mixture of Clover and Timothy grass there. The Oats would provide a crop of hay the first season and then the next year the Clover and Timothy would come in and provide a good quality hay crop for several years. Allen did not grow Alfalfa on his fields because he felt that, on this land, it would require too much fertilizing. Also, because of the less dense soil in the valley, Alfalfa was more likely to winter-kill.

After Allen had done the morning milking, had his breakfast, finished the morning chores and spread the manure, he would hitch us to the plow and plow the field until lunch time. Lunch time was a welcome break after turning green soil, or better known as green sod, all morning. Green Sod is the first plowing when the ground is turned from grass land to crop land. After Allen had finished his lunch and maybe read the newspaper, he would hitch us to the plow

188

again and with the reins looped behind his neck, we would go back and forth plowing all afternoon until time for him to do afternoon chores in the cow barn.

I remember one day when Allen was plowing a section of meadow below the house next to the woods. It was an unusually cold, fall day with a strong north wind blowing steadily. Allen was plowing in a north-south direction making many trips up and down the long strip of meadow. As he plowed in the south direction, his head would often be turned, putting one side of his face directly into the cold north wind. He would be watching as the coulter split the sod and the shares turned the long neat furrows. He finished the piece in the late afternoon and was feeling an extreme chill in his entire body as he put the tractor and plow away.

There was no time for Allen to think or worry about that though. He had to do afternoon chores and get ready for and do the evening milking. After Allen finished the milking and had eaten his supper, he sat, relaxing, with his farm journal magazine. The house was warm and cozy, with the heat from the pot belly stove, but he was still chilled from working in the cold north winds.

The next morning when Allen got up, he knew right off that something was wrong, but even though he was not feeling well, the animals still had to be fed and the cows milked. I was the first one in the family to see Allen that morning, and I was shocked and concerned at his appearance when he came into the horse barn to feed us, after milking the cows. Allen's usually handsome face looked as though it was totally paralyzed on one side. On one side of his face, his eye, and that side of his mouth, drooped down. I felt sad and worried as I watched Allen carrying the pail of milk that he was bringing down to the house for the family.

he usual bustle of activity, as the family prepared for the day's work and school, suddenly stopped when Allen entered the house. Just as I had been, upon first sight of Allen that morning, they were all shocked and very worried about him. All kinds of questions ran through our heads. Will he get better? What could be wrong and what can we do? Would the alteration of his appearance be permanent with this dependably strong man? Would it get better, or worse?

I heard them using the word "stroke"; the children only knew that it was serious, and all I knew about that word was associated with being petted, like the way the children stroked my mane. There was uncertainty, worry, and sadness everywhere on the farm that day. It was as if a pall of gloom had descended on us all and normality came to a standstill. On top of being very sad and concerned for Allen, and despite the fact that (with exceptions), we animals live in the moment and get a sense of comfort from routine but that, it seemed, had come to an end. Allen and Ferne both said, however, that there was no sense in sitting around with worry and that everyone needed to get ready for school so that they wouldn't miss the school bus.

So, the children all headed off to school with the knowledge that Ferne had gotten a hold of Dr. Smokey and he would be coming out to take a look at Allen, but all of them were still worried about Allen. The children had told me about seeing Dr. Smokey. He looked into your ears and your mouth, putting a stick in your mouth so he could look down your throat. Then, the doctor took the instrument that he always carried around his neck. It had tubes that he put in his ears, a small cup attached to another hose and with this he would listen to your lungs and then listen to hear your heart beat. Brud thought that this last was quite strange. With what little medical knowledge he had, he knew that if your heart wasn't beating you weren't alive anyway. He pushed this thought away, feeling sure that Dr. Smokey could fix whatever had gone wrong with his father.

Dr. Smokey was the family doctor. His real name was Dr. Smolinski. He was short and kind of round, the opposite of the vet, Dr. Philipsen, who was tall and thin. Dr. Smokey was as good with people as the vet, Dr. Philipsen, was with us.

Some of the things that Dr. Smokey brought with him were an assortment of needles of various sizes. Once he decided what kind of medicine you needed, he would fill one of the needles with the medicine and then stab you in your arm or in your buttocks and soon you were feeling better. Ferne Marie had told Brud many times that he was a "pain in the butt." I never found him to be that, but I too have had shots in the rump, so I understand what she means.

When the children got home from school, Allen was, as usual, already in the barn doing chores and had started milking. Ferne told them what Dr. Smokey had said and they all went to the barn even before changing out of their school clothes to see him. His face was still partially paralyzed, but everyone seemed to feel better because he had seen Dr. Smokey.

Jan scurried into the horse barn, still with some dampness of sadness and now joy on her cheeks. She told me that Dr. Smokey said that Allen had not had a stroke. A cold had settled in the fifth nerve of his face and because he had spent so much time with that side of his face taking on the cold north wind, he had a condition called Bell's Palsy. Dr. Smokey advised massage for that side of Allen's face, and said that over time the condition would probably go away.

Anytime Allen was sitting still, Ferne would spend several minutes, an hour, or however long he could sit still. The doctor's advice had given Ferne a way to help Allen, so she was determined to do her part. I knew that with the magic balm of love in her touch, she would soon make the palsy disappear, as life returned to the nerves and muscles of his face. As it turned out both I and Dr. Smokey were right and soon Allen was back to himself again.

I am quite certain that Allen healed faster because of Ferne's diligence with bringing life back into his face through the massaging that Dr. Smokey advised. All animals can feel a human's (or another animal's) energy, and I can feel her love as she pets my face. The magic in her hands is pure love. For instance, if Allen asks her to move us along with the wagon, she rolls herself onto the wagon on her stomach, rising quickly to her feet. She steps up onto the buck stick, her tongue folded between her teeth, and move us along. I can feel the energy of her hands all the way through the long leather reins. With the fall splendor fading, the leaves on the trees fall to

191

the earth, becoming dry and brittle. The grass and plants dry, and their seeds drop to the earth. Nature is readying for winter, and I think about the cycles of life: nourishment, sprouting, growing, gaining strength, reproduction, aging and then passing. It all has a purpose and yes, this old work horse does believe that there is a Higher Power.

At times, I feel sorry for people, in part because they feel they must argue and fight the over which religious beliefs are the "right" ones. Or when they attempt to explain it all with science, despite its limitations. I feel that these poor creatures, in their quest to acquire more and better things, they are beginning to lose touch with their feelings and their connections to both the natural world, and each other.

Allen and Ferne have strong religious beliefs and they share their beliefs with the children. They taught largely by example. The way they appreciated and took care of what they had. Their work ethic. The family worked hard and did what they could to live in harmony with nature. When farming is done with respect and gratitude for the land, the plants and the animals; you have a productive, sustainable, way of life, and it is a great teacher of the miracle of life.

The family, attended the Florence Congregational Church. The children got their religious education there. Several families in the Florence community attended that church.

One of the ministers at the church was an elderly man named Bowen Shattuck. He led the religious services at the church. He had a strong, yet soft and gentle voice. He stopped to visit many of the local families, so he could learn more about the people who were going to his church. I heard him talking with Allen one day when Shattuck had arrived just as we were about to go out for another wagon load of hay.

Shattuck ended up moving to another church, so the religious services were led by David Pearsons and Norman Champine. Norman was a cousin of the Mills children. Both young men were in college at the time and thinking about becoming ministers. Alice Champine, Norman's mother and Allen's sister, played the organ during the church services. There were two young women of about college age who taught religious lessons to the children. Their names were Elsie Holden and Ruth Earnst. They were great examples of young adults for the children. Ferne also taught Sunday School for a while. Brud said that she explained the meaning of Christianity; which she said was to live your life, Christ-Like. Being human, you would fail that lesson, now and then, but that you should never stop trying.

Harry and Harley; and Dandelion Wine

Harry Wedin was a great, old fellow. He was a calm, gentle man who could work all day at a slow but steady pace that would allow him to accomplish a great deal of work in one day. He loved all the children and treated them as if they were his own. With his calm, confident, kind-but-firm, easy-going manner, I and the other horses enjoyed working with Harry. He was very good at guiding us, too.

Harry lived in the house with our family for quite a while before he moved in with Harley after Kate passed away. Harry was a great deal of help to Allen. Harry enjoyed drinking alcoholic beverages though, but when he was drinking, it was very difficult for him to be of much help. Both Harry and Harley had times when they just couldn't control their drinking. This was why Harry decided that he would not have a family of his own. He knew his drinking would cause trouble, and that it would not be fair to them.

Harry would get so involved in his work that he would forget everything that was happening around him. One day, we were down in the north meadow where Harry had been cutting wood nearby, at the southwest edge of the meadow. Allen and Brud were loading wood onto the wagon. Harry was burning brush a short distance away. I watched as Harry poked at the burning brush pile. This caused sparks to rise into the air and then come down all around Harry. Harry wore the same type of blousy, denim hat that Allen did. I grew very nervous when I saw several small spots on Harry's hat begin to smolder. Not being able to yell "Help!" or "Fire!", I began to fidget nervously, hoping to catch someone's attention.

Suddenly a gust of wind swooped by causing Harry's hat to burst into flames. Brud noticed the fire burning on Harry's head and finally got Allen's attention. Harry yelped and grabbed his flaming hat, throwing it into the air. He quickly patted out his still smoldering hair. He suffered no real injury from the burning hat, but there was now a big section of singed hair and a few tender places on his scalp. Brud was able to retrieve Harry's hat, but unfortunately, it was a total loss. The only parts left were the hat band and the visor. Harry took the hat, and shook the remaining black ash from it, clamped it on his head and went back to work.

After Harry had finished working that day, I saw him walking back over to Harley's house with the burned cap still on his head. That slow and steady pace of his, finally got him back over the hill to Harley's place. When he got there, he found Harley on his stomach caught under the heavy hatch door to the cellar. The door was made of heavy planks, covered with tin roofing.

Harley, you see, had gotten to thinking about the Dandelion Wine that he and Harry had made and had put down in the cellar to age. Harley felt that the wine had aged long enough. To insure quality, Harley tested it, tossing back a goodish amount.

The hatchway door was too heavy for Harley to lift, but he was able to move it up enough so that he could prop it up with a board which would give him just enough room to crawl in and get the wine. So far, so good. Harley was on his way back out, when he dislodged the prop, causing the hatchway door to pin him securely between it and the ground. At least he wouldn't be thirsty while he figured out how to solve this problem, or until Harry returned. Harley was able to reach the jug of wine and had a good sample. With the first sip, he noticed the "Kick," as he called it. His sample had shown him that the aging process was indeed complete. Being stuck halfway in and half way out of his cellar door, was certainly not the ideal setting to enjoy the homemade wine, but there may be some time waiting before help arrived and it was beginning to look like thirsty work, this waiting, so he thought, maybe just another sip or "a few".

When Harry got home, he found Harley, still stuck between the cellar ground and the heavy door. Harley had made all attempts to" keep himself "hydrated". So, by now he was quite intoxicated, with the partially empty jug of wine next to him. Harry and Harley had previously agreed that they would test the wine together. Harley assured Harry that it was the predicament with the door along with his gathering thirst that caused him to break the agreement. After Harry freed Harley from the door, he had a sip or "a few" from the jug himself. Soon, Harry's burnt hat and singed hair were soon in the past, and since there had been no tragedy, possibly chuckled over, on such a great day.

Halloween
and
Deer Hunting

Fall also brought a strange holiday that the children participated in. It was called Halloween. They would dress up in costumes pretending to be someone different than who they were. Ferne would help them with homemade costumes such as ghosts, cowboys, pirates or hobos. Brud made a great Hobo as it was easy for him to get dirty anyway, and Jan, with her pigtails and freckles was going as an "Indian Princess". They had Halloween parties at school and would go to Pittsford to trick or treat Waven and Jessie Spaulding.

There was one Halloween when Waven, who was always ready to raise a ruckus and make noise and have fun, organized the First and Only Plains Road and Furnace Road Halloween Parade. Every parade needs a band to lead with some kind of music, so he borrowed Jessie's big galvanized wash tub attached by ropes to the handles and hung it over his neck. So, with two sticks to beat his drum, in the early evening darkness, the parade began. Waven made perfect time with this drum and the children noisily marched behind. The first stop was at Bob and Gussie Smith's house, where they received treats and were also eagerly joined in the parade by Ron and Lynne. The next stop was Harry and Jessie Smith's house. Jessie gave them donuts, candied apples and popcorn balls. They traveled up towards Furnace Brook gathering more treats and more children all being led by Waven and his drum and then back down the Furnace Brook Road, all the way to Carrara's. Waven led the best Halloween Parade the Furnace Road had ever seen.

The early part of November is the start of Deer Hunting Season. I always knew when it was about to start, because the chores were done extra early in the morning. Allen, who was a great hunter and an excellent shot with his rifle, would have the milking done, his breakfast eaten, and be on top of the West Mountain overlooking Hubbardton by daylight. He would bring a sandwich, an apple and a candy bar, with him, and return with the meal still uneaten by 7:30 on the first morning dragging a buck deer.

Brud got very lucky as a hunter. He got his first buck at age twelve and got one nearly every year after that. Brud felt that, because Allen and he had hunted the woods from the house to the top of the West Mountain that they could, after separating at the house, meet up at anyplace in the woods that they wanted to. All land features would have names, some only known to them. Sometimes a particular rock, tree or place where they have previously gotten a buck would pinpoint the meeting place exactly.

Often times, the whole family would be involved in hunting. On one particular morning during deer hunting season, Allen was spreading manure and we were there, hitched to the manure wagon. Allen had just finished when a large buck crossed the meadow right in front of us. Roany and I could feel Allen's excitement as the magnificent animal ran by, only a few yards from where we stood. It would have been an easy shot for Allen if he had his rifle, but he only had his manure fork and shovel; a rifle shot might have spooked us horses; which can be very dangerous with us all hooked up as we were. Allen, Roany and I stood together, watching as the deer disappeared into the woods, heading for Nub's Peak.

When we got back to the farm, we were quickly put in the barn. Allen was planning on how to hunt the buck. Allen would go north at the edge of the swamp where he figured the buck would go after Brud had chased him off from Nub's Peak. Allen would place Ferne and the girls at various spots around the north meadow and surrounding spots where he thought the buck might also go.

Ferne Marie, a somewhat reluctant hunter, headed off, armed to the teeth, with all the supplies necessary for a successful hunt. She carried a book, a huge bag of brownies, and the 22 single-shot rifle, the lightest rifle Allen owned.

Brud started the buck off the ridge and it headed in Ferne Marie's direction. As it emerged from the woods and started through the scrubby brush of the pasture, the deer slowed his pace to a walk. Probably curious at the strange, sweet, chocolatey aroma of Ferne Marie's brownies. Ferne Marie sat quietly munching the brownies, the only noise she made was the slight rustle of the pages when she turned a page. She stopped reading with a feeling that someone was watching her. She looked up and saw two brown eyes of the large buck watching her. Ferne Marie was able to stuff the last of her brownie into her mouth, put down the book and get her rifle up while the buck stood, just watching her. She took careful aim and pulled the trigger. The buck though, had heard the light click her gun made (her gun was not loaded), and had already spotted his would-be assassin. The buck ran off, in Kathy's direction.

Kathy was laying down on the ledge overlooking the North Meadow when she saw the deer and his big antlers. She took careful aim with Brud's 25 rim fire and pulled the trigger. She hit the deer with her first shot but hadn't killed him. Shaking with buck-fever, Kathy watched as the deer ran, toward Ferne now, who, with Jan at her side, shot the buck. Everyone ran toward the downed buck. Allen field-dressed the buck while Brud went after the little grey tractor, with a trailer, to haul the deer back.

I was amazed that so many people wanted to hunt. Most any day of hunting season there would be eight or ten cars parked in the yard. Frank Kurant, and at least two Mc-

Cullough's, Lloyd and Bill, were always there. Bill's son Billy, often came with his father and Georgie ("Dubber") Sherman was a regular. In the early afternoon, Billy and Dubber would usually come down to the house to play with the children instead of hunting. The game was quite often "Hide-and-Seek". Brud or Jan were always "it". Kathy, Georgie, Billy, and Ferne Marie went off in pairs to hide. I'm not sure but, seeing them pair off to find their hiding places, I think Jan and Brud were the only ones playing the game of Hide-and-Seek and I would watch as they would disappear in pairs out of sight.

During hunting season, the house was as much a Deer Camp as any other. Ferne made many batches of what everyone called her "Deer Hunting Cookies". She baked pies and always had a huge pot of "Refrigerator Soup" kept warm on her stove. The hunters all stopped for some of Ferne's delicious food and to tell stories of the day's hunt. If a hunter had missed the buck, Ferne would get out her shears to cut off a piece of their shirt tail and hang it up on a beam in her kitchen.

Allen was in favor of game laws. He obeyed them and expected everyone else to do the same. For certain they would, on his land. I was in my pasture one night, it was just after the evening milking time, and I was standing under my oak tree. Allen was just coming out of the barn. It was well after dark, and the late fall had hushed the valley, particularly at night. We heard a shot in the upper corner of my pasture by the apple trees. Allen ran the milk he was carrying into the house and came back outside and into my pasture. Waiting and listening. I have a keen sense of smell and of hearing. I knew someone was coming down through my pasture. I gave a slight whinny to alert Allen.

Two men were carrying a deer they had shot. Only it was well after dark, the time when deer-hunting becomes deer-poaching, which is illegal. One of the men was a new neighbor of ours. He was a known deer poacher and had no regard for any game laws. He and his brother were carrying the illegal doe, her front and back legs tied over a long pole. Being as there was about two inches of snow on the ground, they figured by carrying the deer, they wouldn't leave tell-tale drag marks.

Allen approached the men. He had noticed that the pole they'd tied the doe to was in fact, one of the bars that closed Allen's gateway onto the hill. He told them to take the pole back where they found it. He told them to carry the deer back on the hill, replace the pole and then carry the deer off his property making sure that they didn't leave any drag marks and that they had better hurry; because Ferne would probably call the Game Warden and they were not to come on his property again.

A Birth in November

We're going to go back a little. I want to tell you a story that is, in part, a story of how nature gives us challenges in the winter. There had been a couple of small snow storms so there was a light coating of snow on the ground.

Allen had gotten his deer, early in the hunting season as he usually did. He had the advantage of being a great shot and spent time watching the deer herds; where they slept and ate. Ferne brought Kathy and Brud, each carrying table knives up into the pasture to meet Allen and help him as he came down dragging his deer. Brud wanted Ferne to hurry and he couldn't understand why his mother seemed to walk so slow and uncomfortably, certainly not with her usual hustling pace.

There is a growing excitement in the family this year. Ferne has announced that Brud is no longer going to be the youngest in the family and that she is going to get a baby. She told the children that she would have to go to the hospital to get it. Brud knew that anything you couldn't grow or get on the farm you had to get at the store. He had talked with his mother about the baby and had told her since he already had two sisters that this time she should get a boy baby and then he would have a brother. She told him she would see what she could do about it. He felt that if Ferne had to go to the "hospital store" to get the baby, she surely would pick out a boy.

Ferne Marie was going to school in Pittsford at the Furnace School and stayed with Grandpa Waven and Grandma

202

Jessie during the school week. The school bus would not go all the way out to the farm to pick her up. While Ferne was at the hospital store getting what Brud assumed would be a baby brother, Brud would have to stay with Ferne Marie and their grandparents. It was difficult for Brud during this time, especially since he would have to stay in the "City of Pittsford'. Ferne had packed all the things that Brud would need, including plenty of extra clothes to wear, but she forgot his pillow: "Three Feathers," and the quilt that Grandma Kate had made for him. Without those two things, how would he ever be able to sleep? Brud thought. He began to fuss and complain; worrying. As always, Ferne Marie was there to say something kind and reassuring to him. Something like, "Ok, you little Nin-com-poop, lay down and go to sleep!" This worked best because Brud always had to listen to his big sister and do what Ferne Marie said.

Ferne knew that even though Kathy was only four and a half years old, she was already a very responsible and helpful little girl. She would be a big help to Allen and stayed with him. They put a pot roast on the stove before they went to do the chores and evening milking. The wood cooking stove must have been too hot for when they returned to the house the pot roast was quite blackened in the pot. Allen got out the ketchup and said with a lot of ketchup that the pot roast was pretty good.

The day that Ferne brought the baby home, Kathy went with Allen to the hospital store to get Ferne and the baby. Brud was using the toilet in his grandparent's house which was a strange thing for Brud as the toilet was upstairs and actually in the house and when you finished you pushed a little handle and everything in the toilet was gone. It appeared that it went down a large black pipe that went down from the toilet through the next room below and down into the cellar. Brud never wanted to go down there.

Gramma Jessie told Brud that his mother and father would soon be there and that they would have the new baby with them and that her name was Janice Linda Mills. Her! And Janice! A "Girl!" What a disappointment! All that time at the hospital store and his mother had picked out a "Girl". He began to cry, "I didn't want a baby sister. I wanted a baby brother!"

When his parents arrived with the baby, Kathy seeing how disappointed Brud was with the baby girl, said that they should name the baby, Linda Jane Smith and give her to Aunt Gussie who only had two children. But they finally decided that they would now be the big sister and big brother and keep her and see what she turned out to be.

Winter on the Farm

*T*here was another light snow fall last night. There is about eight inches of snow on the ground and as I walk in the barn yard I can hear the crunch of the frozen earth beneath my shoes. The hair all over my body has grown in long and thick.

Yesterday afternoon when Brud was in the horse barn to give us hay and grain, he stood in my stall next to me, watching as I ate my grain. He took his mittens off and was trying to work his fingers into the thick hair on my back. When he was finally able to touch my skin with the tips of his fingers, he thought that it must be like having a thick carpet all over your body.

Allen hitches us to the high-sided wagon to draw out the manure and spread it on the fields. I noticed he has already gotten the heavy work sleds out of the barn to be ready as soon as he needs them this winter. The children have gotten out their runner sleds and I enjoy hearing them laugh and squeal as they go sliding down the hill, in back of the barn where Allen keeps his motor car and the grey tractor.

Waven was very skilled at making things out of wood, and he likes to see the children having fun as much as I do. Whatever the season, he often shows up with something he has made from wood for the children to play with. During the summer, he showed up with several pairs of stilts that he had made out of wood. This winter day, he is here with a contraption he has made that he calls a Jack Jump. He said that some of these are made with only one runner but this one has two. The Jack Jump had a seat above the two runners. He handed it to Brud, probably thinking that his sisters had more sense that to try the experiment.

Brud took the Jack Jump up on a hill. He had no instructions regarding its use, but it's construction made it clear that the bold and or the foolish were to sit on the seat and just let it go, like a sled. After several, short, unsuccessful attempts; with each attempt ending with Brud sprawled in the snow where the Jack Jump had thrown him, he believed he'd discovered the way to have a successful ride. First, balance is very important, you needed to have really good balance to stay on the Jack Jump. Secondly, there is no way to have a successful Jack Jump ride. Waven, who is laughing, probably already knew that! Another thing Brud discovers is that the Jack Jump has no mechanism for steering. Because there was no method for steering the Jack Jump, if it was heading for danger like a fence or tree, that left the rider with two things to do – first was to yell, "AAAAAAAAH!" And the next was to bail off quickly.

When winter came to the valley, it also meant that all the cattle needed to be kept in the barn and feeding and cleaning up after them was a constant job. The whole family was involved in the care of the animals and keeping the barn clean to Allen's satisfaction. The gutters would be full every morning. Allen would clean the gutters daily, leaving not a speck of manure in the gutters. He did it all with a shovel and a wheel barrow which he filled, requiring many trips out to the manure chute and dumping the wheel barrow load into the wagon or sleds.

After Allen cleaned the gutters in the cow barn, he would come to the horse barn and clean out our stalls. He would load our manure, which was quite dry and absorbent into his wheelbarrow, bring it into the cow barn and spread a thin coating into the gutters to absorb the moisture from the cows. He had no mechanical gutter cleaner as many farmers did, probably thinking it was an unnecessary expense and that it would not do a good enough job anyway.

Allen hauled and stored tons of sawdust which he used for bedding under the cattle to keep them comfortable and clean. The sawdust was kept in an area underneath the hay barn floor. There was single access door at one end and one single light bulb to give only minimal light to the interior of the area. Allen referred to this area as the DARK HOLE! The name itself gave a sense of eeriness and the children, whose job it was to get the sawdust and spread it for bedding and then leave piles of sawdust along the interior walls of the stable to be used later, could feel the eeriness every time they entered the DARK HOLE! The whole interior of the place seemed to be shrouded with long dusty spider webs which seemed to be constantly moving, eager to reach out and grab whoever passed by with a basket of sawdust. The shadows cast by the dim light bulb, from the movement of the webs and sometimes the shadows of the children, themselves as they loaded their basket full of sawdust, gave the imaginative minds of the children a feeling that weird creatures were lurking in the dark places and spiders the size of the barn cats were clinging in the webs poised to attack. They wished that Allen had named this place something different than the DARK HOLE!

It seemed that there was an almost constant job of throwing hay from the mows into the hay chutes to be ready for the next feeding. The hay had to be pulled from the chute and dragged to the other end of the barn and fed to the cows. Then, there was the daily job of climbing up and into the silo to throw down enough silage to feed the entire herd. In the coldest part of the winter, the first two inches of the corn silage would freeze making it necessary to loosen the first layer and throw it down the chute where in the warmth of the barn, it would thaw and then be fed to the cows. It took another four inches of loose unfrozen silage to make enough for all the cattle.

One day as Ferne Marie and Brud were up in the silo throwing down silage, Brud was trying to loosen the frozen silage and managed to drive his silage fork right through his rubber boot and into his foot behind his toes. When they finished throwing down the silage, Brud went down to the house to see how badly he was injured. Ferne bandaged the foot but told him he would need to go down and see Dr. Smokey for a tetanus shot to prevent lock jaw. LOCK JAW would probably mean that you couldn't open your mouth. He started to worry that if he got LOCK JAW, how long would it take before he starved to death. When they got to Dr. Smokey's office, Brud felt better when Dr. Smokey opened the drawer where he kept his magic needles and gave him a tetanus shot in the arm. Although the shot in his arm did seem a long way from his foot injury, it probably would do the trick.

After Allen finished cleaning out the barn, he would put our harnesses on us and hitch us to either the wagon or sled and we would take the manure out to the field and Allen would spread it on the field. I never remember a day when it was too cold or snowing so hard that Allen did not spread the manure. Even after Allen got the manure spreader when the snow got too deep for the little grey tractor, Allen would draw out and spread the manure by hand with the sled pulled by us horses.

The snow did get so deep that the little grey tractor even with chains around its big back tires could no longer go and it would bog down and get stuck. But I never saw a day when Roany and I couldn't pull whatever load we were hitched to through the snow no matter how deep it got.

At the barn, while Allen was spreading manure, the children would bring out the sawdust and pile it against the inside walls of the barn. Ferne Marie could fill the big metal basket with rope handles and carry it out to the piles. Brud, in amazement and frustration, would use this as a gauge to measure the strength of his sister. He would be amazed that Ferne Marie could fill the basket and then lift it and carry it off and he would be frustrated in that he couldn't even lift it. Kathy and Brud would use smaller baskets to carry sawdust and Jan used a small metal bucket.

After the sawdust was spread and piled, the grain cart had to be filled. There was a huge tank that held three tons of feed for the cows. It was a mixture of ground grains, such as oats, corn and barley. It was bought from Brown's Grain Company in Castleton and delivered in bulk by a truck with an auger system that filled the tank in the barn. The tank was located on the second floor above where the cows were kept. The cart was filled by pulling the grain cart under a chute with doors that could be opened to fill the cart.

As stupid as the cows seemed to me to be, they seemed to be able to learn where their own particular stanchion was located and when they were put back into the barn they would trail into the barn one after the other and take the same stanchion every time and wait to be locked in.

While Allen was spreading manure and the children were finishing the barn chores, Ferne was in the Milk House washing the milking machines, pails and bulk milk tank. She would use gallons of hot water and she would be enveloped in thick clouds of a strong sanitizing solution containing Iodine.

After the morning chores were done and the cows were back in the barn, Brud said that it actually smelled pleasant with the aroma of the fresh sawdust and the good quality hay that the cows were eating and the smell of the cattle and the warmth of their bodies. Even in the coldest weather, the heat from their bodies kept it warm enough in the barn so the people only needed a sweater or sweat shirt to keep warm while they were working in the barn.

Quite often after the chores are done and the children are going back to the house, a snowball fight will break out. Then they will usually put on another layer of winter clothes and head out for sliding before lunch time. It also seemed that from the first snowfall to the last of it melted in the spring, there was a constant job of shoveling snow. Shoveling snow for Brud seemed to be an endless and unsatisfying job, as in just a short few hours the job could be all undone and you would have to start all over again. When Allen got his bulk milk tank, he found he needed to have much more area cleared of snow to allow for the truck that came to the farm and room to turn around and get to the milk house. He was able to purchase a snow plow that attached under the little grey tractor and with cables and pulleys could be raised and lowered by the tractor's rear hydraulic lift arms. This helped greatly lessening the amount of shoveling that had to be done.

Christmas in the Valley

*T*he early winter has come to stay, and I knew that soon there would be a special celebration. The word "Christmas" is making the rounds and I knew that the special day was fast approaching. There are many preparations for this winter celebration. Sometimes, I wonder if humans give themselves so much to do to get ready for the big day so that all that running around will keep them warmer.

On a weekday morning a few days before the big day, Waven Spaulding would come driving into the yard in his Buick. He needed Brud's help to get spruce branches with cones on them. Allen would have previously scouted out several large spruce trees growing in the woods on the farm. So, he knew just where to send Waven and Brud to get the best branches. They would head out with a hand saw and a runner sled.

When they had selected one of the spruce trees, Waven would have Brud climb the tree with the hand saw and Waven would point out the branches he wanted cut down. He wanted only branches with new cones that had developed that year. Since they were fresher, newer, they would stay on the branches better, even after being cut away from the tree. Brud would toss them down to Waven, who would catch them, tie them into bundles and put them on the runner sled. When they had gathered enough branches, they would drag the sled out to the edge of the meadow where we would meet them with the work sleds. Once the branches and the runner sled were loaded, and Waven and Brud had climbed back on the wagon, Allen would start us out at a trot back to the farm. I could smell the spruce branches, hear our trace chains jingling, and then, in his big, husky voice, Waven would start singing, "Jingle Bells".

Waven would take the branches home and decorate them. He called these decorations, Sprays, and gave them to friends and relatives, and to people who were confined to their homes, putting the decorations up on their doors. There was one day when Waven and Jessie took Brud with them to deliver the sprays, along with some cookies that Jessie had made. I believe Waven took Brud along not just for his company. He wanted to show Brud what he did with the sprays. Waven, Jessie and Brud travelled to Whitehall, New York for one of their Christmas time visits. Waven parked the car and they took Jessie's cookies and the spray into the house. Sitting in a rocking chair near the one sunny window of the otherwise quite dark house, was the oldest woman that Brud had ever seen. Her name was Nellie Hoy. She was wrapped in a heavy, green, shawl. Brud had heard that some people lived to be one hundred years old and Brud thought that she must be at least one hundred maybe two hundred. She seemed to be all by herself in the house. When she saw Waven and Jessie, the spray and cookies that they gave to her, her face lit up with a big smile and she seemed so happy that tears rolled down her cheeks. Brud went outside while Waven hung the spray on her door and Brud stayed outside, sitting on the steps and thought how happy the little old woman had been with the kindness of his grandparents.

At this time before Christmas, Allen would fill a bushel basket with the butternuts that the family had collected in the fall. He would take them down into the cellar of the house and crack the hard shells of the nuts with a hammer. Ferne and the children would dig the nut meats out of the cracked shells. Ferne would put a huge amount of chocolate, sugar, butter, milk and of course butternut meats, which would be added later, into the pot on her woodstove. The contents of the pot would turn into a sweet molten chocolate giving a sweet chocolatey aroma that permeated the whole house drawing the children to the kitchen. The children would eagerly help with the constant stirring of the pot until the molten chocolate fudge got to the perfect consistency to add the butternuts and would be poured into the pans to be set on the back porch to cool.

Allen would have to crack several bushels of butternuts and Ferne would have to make many batches of fudge to have enough for the Christmas Season. She knew that some of the fudge would mysteriously disappear from the pans where it was cooling on the porch. Ferne Marie, who could not resist chocolate, would swipe fudge out of the pans as she went out of the house to play or do barn chores. She would also get fudge for whoever was with her, so they would be obligated to keep her secret. Ferne knew she had to allow for the pilferage factor into her fudge making because she expected Allen was probably also guilty for some of the missing fudge.

At this time of year, the family would go into the woods and cut down a spruce tree and bring it back to the farm house. Allen would stand it up in the house and the family would decorate it. One year, the children head out across the meadow and they are going to where Allen told them they could find a nice Christmas tree. They trudge out through the snow and Ferne Marie is carrying Allen's handsaw. Somehow, they manage to cross the Gulley and get to the spruce trees. After looking at all the trees, Ferne Marie decides that the biggest one was the best. The children had to take turns sawing in order to get all the way through the huge trunk of the tree. After the tree finally fell, the children tried dragging the large tree. With all of them pulling, they could hardly move the big tree. Brud said, "So how are we going to get it across the Gulley? It's too big!" Ferne Marie said, "It's perfect! Shut up and start pulling." Jan is dragging the handsaw as the other children struggle with the tree. Kathy says, "I can hear the horses coming!" As Allen drives Roany and me, hitched to the work sleds, with our winter shoes crushing the ice that has formed on the edges of the Gulley at the shallow crossing place, we reach the struggling children with our nostrils blowing clouds of steam. Brud thinks, "There is nothing that can stop Dick and Roany!" Allen helps the children load the tree which takes much of the entire length of the bed of the sleds. After the children all climb onto the sleds, we head back to the farm with the snow flying from our hooves and our trace chains jingling. We are thinking Christmas really is getting close. When they get back to the farm with the tree, Allen has to cut several feet off the bottom of the tree and several feet off the top to be able to stand the tree up in the house, but as Ferne Marie said, it was perfect.

One day as the children arrive home from school, it is snowing heavily and keeps snowing through milking and the family's supper time. The children have a Christmas program at school this evening and they have doubts that they will be able to get there as the snow plow won't be through until morning. Allen goes out and puts chains on this red Dodge pickup truck. It has high wooden racks and an extra-long bed. He attaches his big canvas over the top of the rack to make a roof. With the chains clacking, they head for the Florence School with Ferne Marie, Kathy and Brud in the back and Allen driving with Ferne and Jan in the cab. They stop at the neighbors houses along the way. Mary Davis rode in the front with Ferne and Jan, now on Ferne's lap. Some of the Davis children climbed in the back with my children. As they traveled along the Whipple Hollow Road, it got warmer in the back when Louise, Barbara and Sonny Poremski got in, then the Rider children and after that cute little Mary Fran Kurant and finally at the end of the Hollow Janette and Steve Lizewski squeezed in as well. They finally arrived at the school where "the show must go on".

The next morning was Saturday and the children were off from school. The only tracks visible were the two wheel tracks up the road that had been made by the pickup from the night before. The family was just finishing breakfast, when the big red road grader came around the turn and was plowing the snow out of the road. Two of Ferne's cousins were in the cab of the grader. Bud Parker was driving and operating the front plow while his brother, Bob, worked the wing plow attached to the side. They turned the big machine around by the barn and started back down the road. By then Ferne was out in the yard and stopped them and told them to come into the house and have a piece of pie and a cup of coffee. They left the grader idling in the yard as the diesel exhaust from the machine spewed into the Valley. Bob and Bud were both kind of short stocky men and both men seemed to smell of diesel fumes. Bud always had the same kind of stick that he sucked on and blew foul smelling smoke out of his mouth that the cattle dealers had in their mouths although I don't think he was a cattle dealer.

Bud and Bob would visit with Allen and Ferne while they drank coffee and ate a piece of pie or most often two pieces of pie. Ferne gave them a plate of fudge and they continued on their way. There was hardly anyone who came to the farm who left without something to eat.

As it got closer to Christmas, Allen cracked several more bushels of butternuts. The children helped Ferne pick out the nut meats and many more batches of fudge were made. Ferne and the girls made pies and cookies; much more than the family could possible eat. Anyone who came to the farm as given something. The Veterinarian, the man who worked for the Artificial Breeding Service for the cattle, the bulk milk tank truck driver, and even the cattle dealers with their smelly old cigars left with something delicious.

A few days before Christmas and usually when the children were in school, Allen and Ferne would fill boxes with some of the things that Ferne and the girls had made. After the boxes were packed with pies, cookies and fudge, they would deliver them to people who otherwise probably would be alone and wouldn't get any treats at Christmas time.

Harry Wedin was one of the people who received the Christmas boxes. After Carroll Mills, who was Harley's brother, retired from the Army and moved in with Harley, Harry Wedin decided he would move out of Harley's house. Allen and Ferne asked him to move back to the farm but Harry felt it would be better if he lived by himself in a small one room cabin that he had built in the woods near the house where Harry's brother lived. Harry's cabin had no running water but was located near a brook which supplied his water. It was heated with wood and the lighting was supplied by kerosene lamps. When Allen and Ferne went to Harry's cabin, Ferne carried the box of treats. Allen had a box of western novels as he knew a passion of Harry's was reading Westerns. They stayed and visited with Harry for some time in his small cabin. As they left, Harry would get one of Ferne's special hugs and it was then that she noticed the tears in the usually tough old Swedish gentleman's eyes.

Another place where Ferne and Allen stopped was at the small farm of an elderly couple by the name of Carey. They ran the farm with much help from an adult learning-disabled woman. When Allen and Ferne would arrive with the Christmas box, the couple's and the girl's faces would seem to light up with joy because of the gifts and the visit from Ferne and Allen. It usually took a few days to deliver the boxes as people seemed to enjoy their visits more than the delicious gifts.

Marco Rosato was another person who got one of the Christmas boxes. Allen would usually deliver the box to Marco by himself. Sometimes Brud would go along with Allen. Marco ran a small farm all by himself at the northern end of Whipple Hollow. His family all lived in Connecticut, so Marco lived alone. Marco had curly grey hair connected to a grey beard which appeared that he trimmed himself whenever he felt it necessary. His barn, house, clothing and his person were not kept very clean, but I suppose it was because it just was not a personal priority. It was probably because Ferne had such an extreme difference in her priority of cleanliness that she did not visit there. Brud spoke of how he actually enjoyed going to Marco's because even though everything seemed to be unclean, he seemed to have everything he needed or wanted and just had unusual ways of using them and keeping them. In the house, herbs and dried hot peppers hung from various places. There was always the strong smell of garlic and an ever-present jug of red wine that he had made sitting on the table. There were many books and papers around the house. Brud felt that because of Marco's soft speaking voice, the opinions he expressed on many things and the topics he spoke to Allen about that under the unkempt condition of Marco's appearance was a man of great knowledge and wisdom. Marco showed much gratitude and appreciation for the Christmas box and sent a large woven willow basket, that he had made, home with Allen to give to Ferne.

Pop Poremski had plenty of family in the area but Ferne would make up a plate of her butternut chocolate fudge for him.

Finally, after all the anticipation and preparations: It's Christmas Eve! The children hang their stockings in the afternoon. Ferne has sent a request to Santa Claus that if he could, it would be best if he came during the evening milking on Christmas Eve. The family always goes to Pittsford to celebrate with Waven and Jessie and the entire Spaulding family on Christmas Day. Because of milking and all the morning chores, it would be impossible to get to Waven and Jessie's by noon on Christmas Day and that is why Santa always came during milking time on Christmas Eve.

Allen has finished milking and the children are doing some of the final chores with just an occasional curious peak out the barn windows. Suddenly, from outside the barn comes the sound of sleigh bells. The children run and hide behind the grain box to be sure they are not seen by Santa.

While the children are hiding, Brud has a chance to really think about the prospects of being left something by Santa. He thinks Ferne Marie and Kathy would surely get something, with Jan, he was a little uncertain, but as for himself, unless Santa was only considering the last couple of days when he had really been trying, it was extremely doubtful if he would receive anything. When they got back into the house, they found that Santa had left presents for "everyone". There was even a brand, new Lightning Glider Sled for Ferne Marie.

Christmas morning meant everyone would be up early. The milking had to be done and after breakfast, all the usual morning chores needed to be done as well. We were usually visited by most everyone in the family on Christmas morning along with our morning feeding, there was extra petting and everyone who visited would give us an extra handful of sweet grain.

After the morning chores were done, the family would all pile into Allen's blue Plymouth. Everyone would be loaded down with gifts to exchange with Waven and Jessie and all the rest of the Spaulding family or food that Ferne had made for the celebration. They return home in the late afternoon, all were still full of the huge Christmas meal and all the Christmas treats. The children are all tired from running and playing with all the cousins. But, before they relax and rest, first they must do the evening chores and Allen must do the milking.

After Christmas, the snow keeps getting deeper and it gets much colder. Roany and I enjoy being hitched to the sleds every day. Before we start out with the sleds heavily loaded with manure, Allen never forgets to loosen the runners as they freeze solid in the ice and we would probably break harness straps if he were to forget. He uses an iron bar to pry each one of the four runners loose. Once the sleds are broken loose, we move the sleds quite easily through the snow. What an awesome sense of power I get with the sleds sliding through the snow, our nostrils sending our clouds of steam, our hooves spraying showers of snow and the sound of our winter shoes crunching the ice. Brud, when he is available, will ride along on the back of the sleds and help Allen spread the manure. He said the thrill of the ride was worth the work of spreading the manure

Farm Life
in Deep Winter

Allen would cut wood during the winter to be used for heating the house and cooking the meals. He would cut the wood in the winter so that it would have plenty of time to dry before being burned the next winter. After morning chores, Allen would load his wood cutting tools into the sleds and we would head out to the woods. He would use a double-bitted axe. I enjoy watching him swing the razor-sharp axe and watching the chips fly as he chops.

He also has a cross-cut saw which has a long blade with many teeth and a handle at both ends. Harry Wedin helps him with that tool. He uses this saw as it is faster than the axe for cutting the large part of the tree. Just as a team of horses working together to move a heavy load, it also takes two people working as a team to effectively use a cross-cut saw. Brud, who is still struggling with his boyish awkwardness, has not developed much skill with the cross-cut saw to be able to do the work required yet. I hear Allen keep reminding Brud not to push the saw, just to pull if back and let the saw do the work. Allen says, as he often does, "You are handier than a cub bear wearing boxing gloves", but after they finish a job that they are working on together, he will also say, "That's a good stroke of work."

One day while Allen was talking to Red Poremski about cutting wood, Red tells Allen to borrow his two-man chainsaw. The chainsaw has a heavy motor with handles and controls to work the saw on one end. It has a long chain with sharp teeth attached which travels around the long bar. The saw has a single handle on the other end of the bar for another person to help control the saw. While the saw was quite heavy, it would cut quickly through the butt of a large tree. Allen used this saw a couple of times with Harry's help. He would not let Brud help with the saw as he felt it was too dangerous for a young boy. Allen finally purchased a big Homelite one-man chainsaw which made the wood cutting job much easier.

It is late afternoon just before evening chores, Allen is in the house and the children are not home from school yet. It is snowing heavily and as I stand under the Oak tree, I can, actually, hear the flakes of snow as they settle to the ground and pile up one on top of the other. When the air is perfectly calm, and it is snowing heavily, is the only time you can experience this amazing gift of nature.

The deepening snow will mean that after milking in the morning, Allen will have to delay breakfast until he can get the driveway plowed so that the milk truck can pick up his milk.

When the children get home from school, they find that the fresh snow is perfect for making snowballs. While Allen is milking, the children build a large snow fort near the path between the house and the barn. After the fort is finished, they make a big supply of snowballs to throw at Allen when he leaves the barn. When they hear the milking machine motor shut down, they know Allen will soon be leaving the barn. Jan leaves the fort and goes into the barn and warns Allen of the planned attack. She always wants to be on Allen's side which she also feels is the winning side. As Allen and Jan come out of the barn door, the snowballs begin to fly from the fort. Jan is busy making snowballs for Allen as he quickly and accurately returns fire. Ferne Marie, Kathy and Brud decide the best and bravest thing to do is to abandon the fort and throw snowballs as they run. The snowball fight ends when Allen and Jan escape into the house.

The next morning, Allen has just finished milking and is getting ready to plow the driveway. The children are up and getting ready for school. Brud is hoping the bus won't be able to make it up the hill with all the snow that has fallen. Just then around the corner comes the big blue dump truck with the snowplow attached to the front. It has huge wheels that make it sit high above the ground. It has chains on all four wheels and is spraying snow way out in the meadow as it tears up the road.

The plow is driven by John Keith. He is the Road Commissioner for the town of Pittsford. He is a short, extremely husky man, which makes you wonder how he gets up into the cab of the truck that is so high above the ground.

Allen knows John doesn't hear very well and thinks that is why he travels so fast so that he can hear the roar of his engine. Allen thinks that John cannot see much better either as he has knocked down many mailboxes throughout the town with his plow and knows that John had hit the stone wall at the turn before coming into the meadow. Allen is standing outside by the back porch when John comes roaring into the driveway. He is hoping John turns quickly before he hits the concrete foundation of the silo and, of course, he does not. The impact brings the truck to a sudden stop. The back wheels of the truck lift up off the ground and are set down several feet sideways. A part of the plow comes flying from the truck and lands in the snow. John is raised up from the seat and his head slams into the roof of the truck. After John settles down from the impact, he turns the truck around and goes roaring back down the road with one side of the plow digging into the ground more than the other as the part that broke off from the plow was one of its shoes. No luck for Brud though as the school bus will now be able to make it up the hill. No snow day for him!

Allen was able to plow enough snow, so the milk truck could get to the milk house and pick up the milk but as he was plowing snow between the house and the barn, he got over the bank too far and the little grey tractor was stuck. Even with chains on both wheels, it still could not churn itself out.

Allen left the tractor right where it was stuck fast in the snow and after he had done the chores and spread the manure with Roany and me, he drove us over to where the tractor was stuck. Ferne came out of the milk house where she had been washing the bulk tank. Allen hooked a chain to the tractor and then he hooked the other end of the chain to our eveners. Ferne climbed on the tractor and as Allen spoke to us, we slowly started to pull. I could feel the caulks on my winter shoes grip the frozen ground and I could feel the tractor begin to move as we pulled steadily. We got the tractor on level ground where it could move on its own. As we are unhitched from the tractor, I can't help but give a little snort as I think, the tractor is a great little machine but if you truly want some real horse power, get Dick and Roany.

It is late Saturday afternoon and Brud is feeding us our hay and grain. One of the cats is in the horse barn hoping to catch a mouse trying to steal our grain. Brud is excited and he tells me that after supper, the Smiths are coming to visit. I can't help but get excited too and wish I could come down to the house, just to hear Lynne laugh. She has such a joyous laugh, it makes me want to laugh too.

After the family had finished supper, the Smiths arrive. The children play games in the living room while Allen, Ferne, Gussie and Bob gather around the dining room table to play a card game that they call Canasta. The card game goes on late into the evening with a pause for Ferne to help Ferne Marie make popcorn on the wood stove by shaking the basket back and forth while the corn pops. Gussie and Bob have brought orange soda for a special treat.

While the canasta game goes on, it becomes necessary for Ron's parents to speak to him as it is almost impossible for Ron to keep his mischievous pestering in check for that long a period of time. The card game goes on until Allen must call a halt to it as his day will begin again at 4:30 in the morning. By this time, the children are asleep in the living room. Sometimes, the Smith children are loaded into the car still asleep and sometimes they are allowed to stay and wake up at the farm the next morning.

223

It is the next morning and the children are just getting up. Allen has finished milking and Ferne has mixed up a huge bowl of pancake batter. Ron Smith has stayed overnight, and he is the reason for all the pancake batter. Ron loves pancakes! Ferne has a big oval-shaped cast iron griddle. She heats it up on her wood cook stove. By sprinkling water from her fingers, she can tell that the griddle is hot enough, so she starts frying pancakes. Ferne is amazed at how many pancakes Ron can eat. She thinks, how could such a thin young boy eat so many, but she knows that as soon as he slides out of the chair and his feet hit the floor, he will be running as that's the only way he travels and only stops to make mischief.

It seemed that during the winter was when Allen wanted to raise most of the calves for replacements to the herd. The cows would be kept during their years of high milk productivity and then it would be necessary to sell them as their years of high productivity started to decline. Allen had to be constantly studying his herd and deciding what characteristics he recognized in the cows that he like or didn't like when he choose a calf to raise as a replacement for a particular cow in the herd.

Brud wanted to raise all the heifer calves and Allen had to explain that the farm and the barn could only support a certain number of cows and that replacements had to be chosen with certain desirable characteristics in mind such as: disposition, breeding problems and ease of milking. Therefore, he wanted to raise the calves only from his best cows. When a calf was chosen to be raised, they were not allowed to nurse from the cow only a very few times after they were born. It seemed the whole family would be involved in choosing a name for the calf; often taking turns in the actual choice of the name.

The cow's records would be kept by the name she was given as a calf throughout her years on the farm. Only one cow acquired a new name which was late in her time on the farm. She was a cow that produced a large amount of milk and instead of her given name of Duffy, she was call Old Sway Bag. I guess, you can figure that one out.

In the winter, when the children were not out sliding in the snow, they would be in the barn helping Allen with chores while he was milking the cows. The children would often be the ones who would teach the young calves how to drink out of a pail. Allen would not use a pail with an artificial teat on the side of it to feed the young calves. He felt that teaching them to drink out of the pail was much better and they would forget the nursing habit much more quickly.

To teach a calf to drink, the children had to hold the pail in front of the calf and with one hand over the calf's nose allow the calf to take a finger into its mouth as the calf began to suck the finger, they had to lower its head into the pail of milk and then slowly withdraw the finger from the calf's mouth. The calf would keep sucking as it tasted the milk in the pail. After several of those session, the calf would put its head in the pail and drink on its own. Brud told me that often the little creatures will bunt the pail and slosh themselves and the person feeding them with milk. When Abel Brown gave Jan a little calf that she named Bambi and she was teaching her to drink both Jan and the little calf got severely sloshed several times. It was at times like this that Brud would try out some of Allen's curse words but only, so the calf could hear him and no one else. I suppose it was a satisfying thing to finally teach the stupid little critters how to drink. I can't imagine this ever happening with a horse.

As the winter wore on, the levels of the hay mows would gradually get lower. All of the hay was brought out to feed the cows from a door in each end of the two rows of hay mows. There was a hay chute in front of each door. The hay had to be taken out of the mows in layers and sections, just as it had been put in. It was almost impossible to get the hay out of the mow if you tried to take it out any other way.

As each section of the mows were taken out to feed the cattle, it created different levels from one mow to the other which made an irresistible lure to the children for jumping in the hay. Jumping in the hay mows seemed to be a practice that was mildly disapproved of by Allen and Ferne. I think it was more for safety reasons than anything else. The children did not play in the cow barn very much as there was no running allowed as Allen felt that it would make the cows nervous.

The big hay barn is a great place to play and I enjoy having the children come into the horse barn to visit with us horses. They had a game they called, "Hide and Seek" and the big barn is a terrific place for that game. It is also a wonderful place to play Cowboys and Indians. These games get really loud and wild when Ron Smith comes over to play.

In the winter, the cows' hair gets longer and thicker, so Allen clips their hair with electric clippers. He does this to keep them cleaner as unlike us horses they don't seem to have much self-pride and will get themselves quite nasty if they are allowed to.

I don't think Allen likes the job of clipping very much as he passed it on to Brud as soon as he was big enough to do it. Brud did a good job of clipping cows except he would sometimes leave his initials clipped into the long hair on the side of the cow and he would sometimes write the cow's name on her side, but Allen would tell him to remove these when he saw them. The cow's tail would be shaved, and the switch left at the end. Brud thought that because the cow would often get the switch wet and it would sting when she slapped him across the face with it that he would just shave the switch off on a couple of the cows and see if that might be better. This practice just left them with a stiff boney club which hurt worse when they hit him with it and again met with the disapproval of Allen. When Tippy, the dog, was in the barn while Brud was clipping cows, he considered clipping him to look like a lion but gave up on the idea as he knew Ferne would probably be angry if he did it. He tried to clip the old tom cat but gave that up quickly when the cat objected fiercely with his claws.

It is a cold winter day with snow and an icy wind blowing from the south. We are in the meadow south of the barn, facing into the wind as Allen has his back turned to us spreading manure. The ear lappers of his hat are down, and his collar is pulled up to protect him from the blowing snow. I can see Brud's saddle horse, Pal, trotting happily down through the barn yard and out into the meadow where we are standing. A good work team like Roany and I are trained to stop and stand until we are asked to move forward again. Pal is standing on Roany's off side and suddenly reaches and gets her rein just below her bridle. He gives a sharp tug on Roany's rein causing her to step forward and of course I had to step with her. As the sleds lurch forward Allen pitches forward catching himself before he steps into the manure. By the time Allen can catch his balance and turn around Pal has already let go of the rein and is standing innocently by Roany's side.

There are three stages of Allen's rising anger and we now fall victim to the first as he shouts, "Hey! Hey! Hey! You two, what's the matter with you? Stand Still!" He turns his back and starts spreading again. Pal reaches and gives Roany's rein another yank, causing Allen to pitch forward again. This puts Allen into his second phase of anger as he turns around to us and begins with the usual curse words. Now I will take some liberties here because this is serious. Allen says loudly, "God Damn It! I said, Stand Still!" Allen turns back around and begins spreading manure again. Pal gets Roany's bridle again and gives it another pull, this time causing Allen to step forward into the soft manure. By this time Allen is already at level three and as he turns and says, "Jeeesus! Kerr-ist!" I am now very nervous as I know that no man or beast has taken Allen beyond level three and I fear that at this point he is very close. I know there are skeptics out there who will say that horses don't think this way, but I can tell that Pal is stifling a big horse laugh. I think as Allen cleans off his boot, "What can I do to stop this before it gets worse". After Allen turns around, I have an idea and I give out a loud snort just as Pal reaches for Roany's rein. Allen catches Pal with Roany's rein in his mouth. "Oh, so that's it!" he says. Allen jumps down from the sleds and grabs Pal's lead rope which he is trailing. Allen stomps through the snow leading Pal and puts him in the barn yard with a sound slap on Pal's rump with his heavy leather mittened hand and closes the gate behind him. Allen comes back to our sleds and peacefully finishes spreading the manure.

When Brud get home from school, Allen tells him what happened and that he has to tie Pal in a way so that Pal cannot untie the lead rope.

It is late in January and the temperature has risen throughout the day. They call it a January Thaw. It stays warm during the night and starts to rain. I hear a loud rumble as the snow slides off the south side of the barn roof. This puts a huge pile of snow nearly five feet deep in front of the door from the barn that leads out to the barn yard. Because it is raining hard, the water which is coming off the barn roof is being damned up by the pile of snow and running under the door and into the stable. When Allen comes to the barn to do the milking, two of the gutters are filled with water and it is running all over the floor. Allen goes down to the house to wake Brud as he knows he needs help to clean up this mess. The first place to start is in the barn yard to clear the door way of snow. They start shoveling the hard-packed snow in the darkness of the early morning and it is still raining. They must remove all of the snow, so the water will run away from the door and if they don't get the snow away from the doorway, it will freeze, and the cows could not be let out of the barn.

By the time Allen finishes milking, Brud has made much progress in getting the water out of the barn. They will stop for a quick breakfast and then get back to cleaning up the mess. At least it has stopped raining when they come back to the barn. The manure is extra sloppy and there is a lot of wet sawdust to get rid of as well. I am glad we have sharp caulks on our shoes as I know there is ice everywhere in the barnyard and there will be for many days to come. Because of all the wet sawdust, there is a large load of manure to draw and for Allen to spread. Because of the extra clean-up, it is lunch time when they finally finish the morning chores.

After lunch, Allen says that they need to shovel out the big barn doors where the hay is stored and all the doors on the other barn before the snow freezes and makes them inaccessible. At least the little grey tractor with its plow will be able to help some with that job.

As they finish shoveling, it is raining lightly and is turning much colder. They notice four deer have come down to the apple trees to get the last remaining apples which have fallen from the trees. Allen and Brud are going up to the barn to start milking. The temperature is now well below freezing and the snow has a sheen of glassy ice on the surface. The four deer are heading back to the woods and they find that their hooves will not pierce the glassy crust. As they try to climb the hill, they slip and fall and go sliding back down to the stone wall. Several times the lead deer will fall and come sliding down the bank and just like bowling pins knock down the rest of the deer and they all end up in a pile by the stone wall. Brud says that maybe they should try to help them to more level ground and maybe bring them some hay. Allen explains that it would not be good as at this time of year, the deer are eating browse and the hay probably wouldn't be good for them if they did eat it. He said that trying to help them would only panic them and would do more harm than good. He explained that they will get tired and rest by the stone wall and when the footing gets better, they will leave on their own. The next morning, the deer were gone with no trace of any more trouble.

I am remembering a time when the snow was deep, and a light crust formed on top. The crust would not support the weight of a deer, but domestic dogs could run on top of the crust. There was a pack of five domestic dogs that, for sport, were chasing deer. When Allen finished milking one morning, he saw a deer struggling desperately in the deep snow. The deer fell and laid still in the meadow. Allen walked out to where the deer was and discovered that it had been attacked by domestic dogs and was bleeding severely from the neck. He went back to the house and asked Ferne to call the Fish and Game Warden. In about an hour, a deputy warden came to the farm. Allen took him out to where the deer still alive, laid in the snow. The deputy warden took out his pistol and from just a few feet away, took careful aim, fired and missed the deer. He fired this pistol several more times, missing the deer each time. Allen with his dry sense of humor said, "With the last shot, you are getting closer; you just put a hole through its ear." The deputy warden stated, "I will have to make the next one count as it is my last bullet". Allen suggested that the deputy warden put the barrel on the deer's head as the deer surely wasn't going anywhere.

Because the snow was so deep, the traveling conditions were exhausting for the deer that winter. It was easy for dogs to catch the deer as were weak from starvation as well. The warden had shown Allen the marrow of one of the exposed bones on the deer that he had shot. The warden broke the bone and the marrow ran out of the bone in a pink liquid form instead of being semi-solid as was usually the case and this was a sign of starvation.

From where Allen and the warden were, they could see another deer dead on the meadow and then they followed a bloody trail to another. After the warden left, Allen found another trail where the deer was not bleeding but was having extreme difficulty traveling through the deep snow and breaking through the crust at every step.

He followed the deer trail for a short distance and found a young doe laying in the snow. She appeared to be uninjured but was totally exhausted and was unable to move other than her extreme shivering. Allen could not leave the deer to just die there where it laid. He went back to the farm and got one of the children's sleds. It was a round saucer type sled. He gently lifted the deer and put her on the sled. She had no to energy to resist but Allen could feel her spasms of shivering as he held her in his arms.

When Allen got back to the barn with the deer, he carried her into one of the empty hay mows and laid her there and he covered her with a blanket. Allen carefully gave the deer small amounts of tepid water which the deer drank enthusiastically and seemed to stop its shivering. Allen did not know what he should feed the deer but felt she could eat some hay if she wanted to. He found that the deer loved carrots and would eat them from his hand when he offered them to her.

For reasons that I may be able to understand better than people, the deer seemed to accept Allen's presence and what he had to offer her but would become nervous and frightful when anyone else approached her. Allen would allow people to observe her but not to get too close as he seemed to understand her and what she was feeling. He knew the hearts of his children also and didn't want them to get attached to her and make a pet out of her as deer can be a real nuisance if they are turned into a pet. He thought it was better to just let her rest and get her strength back, so she could return to the wild where she belonged. I think she could sense his strength and confidence and that he only wanted to take care of her and that he could and would without harming her.

I don't know when the deer left or actually what happened to her, but I suspect that when the traveling condition for her improved and she had her strength back, he brought her to the door and let her choose to go back to the wild. I still like to think now, when I see a set of deer tracks passing through the farm yard, that it is her checking on that very special man who helped her.

Fun in the
Winter Time

*I*t is well after Christmas, Ferne Marie and Gussie Smith have had their birthdays and so have Allen and Brud. It seems that because of the long cold winter and with so much snow, Allen and Ferne have been confined to the interior of the caverns of snow banks around the yard for an awfully long time. With all the children off in school, it seems they have done little else all winter other than doing chores, feeding the family and cleaning the snow out of the yard continually all winter long.

Allen notices as we are out with the sleds that even us horses only sink into the hard surface of the snow just a little bit.

The snow has frozen solid from the bottom to the top. As we start back with the now empty sleds, I notice Ferne climbing over the snow bank and then she seems to be enjoying walking where ever she wants to on the open meadow. After Allen parks our sleds and takes our harnesses off, he lets us out to enjoy the winter day. I, then, see him walking out on the meadow to greet Ferne.

They return to the house but soon I see them climbing back over the snow bank. Ferne is pulling Kathy's long old runner sled and Allen has the new Lightening Glider that Ferne Marie got for Christmas. It now has a permanent bend in the front where Brud ran it into a tree after he borrowed it. Allen straightened it so that it would still steer but Ferne Marie has still not forgiven her brother for damaging it.

I can hear Allen's laughter and Ferne's scream of joy as they head down the hill in back of the barn on the sleds. They gather enough speed sliding down the hill to take them all the way across the meadow. They are having so much fun, it makes me wish Roany and I could take the big sleds up the hill and try a ride down but how would we steer those big sleds. Allen and Ferne take several more rides and get back to the house at lunch time.

While they are having their lunch, Allen mentions that the paper it says that the weather will remain cold for several more days. That gives Ferne an idea and she says, "Let's have a neighborhood sliding party!" Even before the children are home from school, she starts making cookies for the party. Ferne tells the children about her idea and of course, they are excited, and the phone lines get busy inviting the neighborhood children.

The next day was Saturday and the valley farm seemed to fill up with fun and laughter. There was Georgie and Val Sherman, Bernie and Rosemary Poremski, Louise, Barbara and Sonny Poremski and some of the Kurant children. The children were sliding on everything from runner sleds to pieces of cardboard. Allen showed them how to ride a scoop shovel. The only problem with riding a piece of cardboard was that there was no way to steer it. Brud started down the hill on a slick waxed piece of cardboard and as he sped down the hill, he was headed right for Kathy who had no time to get out of the way. When he hit Kathy, she flew into the air and came down on top of Brud, squashing his face into the crusty snow. Brud's face was skinned up a bit and as he got up, he blamed Kathy for jumping on his head on purpose which of course, she didn't. The sliding party ended with hot chocolate and Ferne's cookies.

A few days later, Brud and Jan are headed up through the pasture, dragging runner sleds with them. They take the sleds all the way up to the Peak bar way. As they head up the wood road, Brud notices that in places the road is solid ice. He warns Jan to keep the sled to the right when she comes back down through the gateway or she might hit the big solid locust gate post. When they reach the Peak bars, the highest point in the pasture, Jan hops on her sled and starts down first. As Brud hops on his sled, he can't believe how fast Jan is already going as she passes the big butternut trees. As Brud speeds by the big oak tree, Jan is out of sight and he thinks Jan is too little to control the sled and he fears she will hit the gate post. When he pitches over the next hill, he breathes a sigh of relief when he sees that Jan is already through the gateway unharmed. But he soon finds himself skidding on the ice and misses the gate post by only a few inches. They ride down by the house and across the meadow all the way to the turn where the road comes into the valley. When they finally come to a stop, Brud says, "Wow! That was a great ride!" Jan replies, "Yeh! Let's do it again!" Brud convinces her that they had better quit for the day.

Normally, while Allen was reading his newspaper in the evening, it was practically impossible to distract him. Often times, he could be asked a question, while he was reading and somehow never looking up, he would file the question away in his mind and maybe fifteen or twenty minutes later after he was done reading the article, answer the question as if it had just been asked.

One evening as he was reading the paper, with Jan sitting on the arm of his chair, she had a shoe string around the arm of the chair and was pretending to be the famous cowboy, "Sam Shoestring", a name Ferne Marie had given her. Brud was pretending to be "Lash Lareau" and was flicking a small piece of rope at Sam Shoestring. In an attempt to get away from the terrible stinging whip of Lash Lareau, Sam Shoestring was spurring her armchair steed. After jiggling the newspaper and several bumps to Allen's side from her heels, Allen was provoked to his first level of anger as he grabbed Jan by the knee and said, "Hey! Hey! Hey! Settle down there!" He, then, went back to reading his paper. Lash Lareau could not resist one more flick of his whip which unfortunately struck Allen's paper knocking it from his hand. This sent Allen right to level three. "Jee-sus! Ker-rist!" But wait a minute, what happened to level two? But as Allen was gathering up his paper while staring over the top of this reading glasses, Brud decided that maybe he shouldn't ask about level two.

During the winter when it was just too cold to work outside, it gave Allen a chance to go over his records and access how the herd and farm were doing. Part of it was necessary because income taxes were due in the early spring and in typical Allen fashion everything must be done early as there was no sense in wasting time in good weather with things that could be done in cold weather.

Allen would plan fields to be tilled, pasture usage and other projects to be done. One of the projects that was done, as winter was getting over, was cutting white pines in the pasture above the spring. Allen and Harry Wedin were cutting pines and Francis Pelkey, a cousin, and Brud were going up to help but first they were sharpening their hatchets on the grinding stone. Brud turned the wheel as Francis put a very sharp edge on the hatchets. Francis had helped his father sharpen tools and he was three years older than Brud, so he was very good at sharpening with a grind stone. Before they started out for the pasture, Ferne stopped them and examined the hatchets. She decided that the hatchets were much too sharp to be used by young boys. She took the hatchets over to the stone wall and immediately took the edge off by whacking them on the stones. When she was through, warm butter couldn't be cut with the hatchets and certainly not white pines, but she felt that at least the boys wouldn't get hurt with them unless it was from blunt instrument trauma.

Maple Sugaring Time

Winter seems to be releasing its icy grip on the valley. Although the nights are still cold, it warms up a little during the day. I notice that the snow is starting to melt away from the roots of the Maple trees in my pasture.

It is Saturday morning after milking and morning chores when Waven Spaulding arrives. After we have spread the manure, Allen stops Roany and me in the driveway. Waven and Harry Wedin help Allen stack sap buckets and a basket of spouts on the sleds. They also load the new boiling pan that Allen just bought onto the sled. With Brud peeking over the buck stick of the sleds, they all head out to the sugar woods.

Brud tries to scamper along as they tap the trees, but his legs are too short to actually be of much help. After tapping all the trees by the sugar house, we go into the other pasture where there are maple trees growing up by the spring and tap those trees.

Allen had felt he was too busy to do the Sugaring this year, but Waven encouraged him to do it. Maybe, the reason Allen didn't want to do sugaring is because he really doesn't like Maple Syrup anyway. The only way he will eat it is when Ferne makes a cake with maple frosting and butternut meats in it. He loves pancakes but will only eat them with Log Cabin, Mrs. Butterworth's or plain Karo Syrup. He has been known to even use Sorghum Syrup which Brud has said should not be eaten but only used to attract insects or mixed with peanut butter to bait mice.

One of Allen's concerns, I believe, was that Waven and Harry Wedin would be sharing the job of boiling the sap into syrup. They both seemed to enjoy drinking alcoholic beverages and when the two of them got together, it often led to them drinking too much. I can remember the strange affect it seemed to have on them. There was the time, when they borrowed the children's skis and decided they would ride down the hill on the skis. I watched from my pasture, as the two men struggled up the hill with the skis. First, Waven would fall down and then Harry would. The alcoholic beverages seemed to give them a false sense of courage in that if they were having trouble walking, how did they think they would be able to ski? Harry would get on the skis and only get a few feet down the hill before falling into the deep snow and then Waven would try and end up the same way as Harry had. The skiing ended when they lost both skis down the hill.

The sugaring season was going well as the sap ran good for many days and the new pan was working out nicely. They didn't have an evaporator, so they used two flat pans on their arch to boil the sap. When the sap reached a certain point in the boiling process in the larger front pan, the sap was taken out and transferred to the smaller new back pan to finish boiling. Because of this, it required close attention to the boiling process and keeping the fire burning just right under both pans.

Harry Wedin started boiling right after morning chores as there still was a good amount of sap left from the day before and the sap was already running fast on that morning. After Allen had eaten his lunch, he brought Harry some lunch to eat. Allen gathered all the sap from the buckets in the sugar woods. He would gather the sap from the upper Maples by the spring later in the afternoon. After Allen left the Sugar House, he met Waven walking out to the Sugar House. Waven was going to help Harry boil the sap.

When Allen got back to the barn, he took his opportunity to throw some hay out of the back bay of the barn. This took a considerable effort in that the loose hay had to be first pitched out of the back-hay bay and then dragged across the scaffold and then thrown down the front bay. He knew with Waven to do the boiling, Harry would be back to help with afternoon chores and to help him gather sap from the upper Maples.

Allen thought it was unusual when Harry did not show up for afternoon chores. While he hitched us up to the sleds so that he could gather the sap from the upper Maples, he grew even more concerned and curious. As we were gathering sap especially because of my superior sense of smell, I sensed the usual sweet odor of Maple coming from the Sugar House which was a considerable distance from where we were, but I could also sense a strange burnt smell. When we finally arrived at the Sugar House, there was not the usual steam coming from the Sugar House but instead a sickly, sweet smoke. Harry and Waven sat outside the Sugar House. They smelled strongly of the alcoholic beverage and an almost empty bottle was sitting between them on the ground.

When Allen entered the Sugar House, he was furious though he spoke not a word. Both pans were scorched and totally ruined. The fire had pretty much burned down underneath the pans. I think this was the final culmination of all the disappointment that people who could not control the drinking of alcoholic beverages had caused him.
He poured the remaining sap in the Sugar House into the pans. I could hear a loud hiss as the sap hit the hot pans, cooling them quickly. He, then, threw them outside and then dumped sap into the arch to finally kill the fire. Allen slammed the door to the Sugar House and left Waven and Harry sitting outside.

There would be no more sugaring on the farm for a very long time. Although, one year after Ferne Marie urged him, he tapped a few Maples close to the house. The children gather the sap and Ferne boiled it all on her stove in the house.

Changing Times

Kathy has just come into the barn with a message for Allen. She is petting my head and I can't help thinking, what a beautiful young girl she has become. It seems to me, she looks a lot like Allen's older sister, Alice. As she is petting me, I'm sure I can feel the same kind of energy that Ferne has. It is not something that they think about, it just is! As Kathy strokes my neck, I think how rapidly things are changing on the farm and how quickly my dear children are growing up.

Ferne Marie has finished high school and graduated top of her class, no surprise to me, of course. Ferne Marie is now in college and spends most of her time living out at the college in Castleton. The long periods away from the farm is very difficult for her but her college experience seems to be a banquet of learning and with her appetite for learning, I am sure she will gorge herself with knowledge and become a teacher as that is what she wants to become.

She has made many friends at college and many times on the weekends, Ferne Marie will come home with five or six of her friends with her. I have no idea where Ferne finds a place to sleep for all of them or how she feeds the Flash Flood of Females, but the sounds of laughter seem to fill up the house and spill out into the yard. I know that by the way that Ferne and Allen welcomes them that they know they are in a very special place.

Just what Brud needs, more girls to deal with! Although, I think, he enjoys the extra attention that he gets. Also, I think he has forgotten about my cautions when he got sawdust in his eyes when he was younger all because of a girl. It seems, all of a sudden, Brud has grown to man-size and he now works, with the strength of a man, beside Allen.

Jan is also growing up quickly. She escapes housework as much as she can so that she can be with Allen. She is such a friendly gal and seems to gather friends like a magnet. This is something she gets from Ferne, I think. She is always with a friend or has one at the farm and wherever she is, there is always laughter and fun.

Along with the children growing up, things seemed to be changing rapidly on the farm. Allen has already started using his Ford truck to draw hay into the barn. He had hitched the hay loader behind the truck and as Brud drove the truck, Allen would load the hay on the truck from the hay loader. Roany and I were only used on the hay wagon when they worked on the steep or small meadows where it was too steep or not practical to use the truck. By this time most all work teams had long before disappeared from the farms of Whipple Hollow and Florence.

Allen had purchased a new manure spreader, it was made by a company called New Idea. Allen took good care of it and it would last him through the rest of his farming career. I believe the single most determining factor of change on the farm happened when Roany passed away. I think as I stated before that her big beautiful heart stopped as she was leaving our horse barn and as I said I was devastated. Along with my grief, I knew the farm work had to go on, but how? I supposed I would have to get use to another team mate, but I knew it wasn't going to be easy as Roany had been a great one!

Roany's passing happened in the late fall after all the crops were in and most of the heavy work that work team was needed for was done. The decision of a new work team could be delayed for a while. The snow came early that year and it became apparent that something had to be done when the little grey tractor could no longer pull the new manure spreader through the deepening snow.

Allen would have to pile the manure until spring as there was now no way to move and spread it on the fields. I grew concerned as I saw an ever-increasing mountain of manure accumulating outside, at the southeast corner of the barn. All winter long the pile of manure grew, and I wondered how Allen was going to get rid of it. Spring finally came, and I saw Allen and Brud loading the new manure spreader by hand with their shovels and manure forks. At least, the spreader works great, and he can spread a load quickly with it.

I can't believe it, but in about a week, sometimes by himself and sometimes with Brud's help, Allen had cleaned up the entire pile. This feat was accomplished in addition to doing his milking, morning and night and regular chores as well.

Our Neighbor: George Sherman & Cooperation

*I*t is strange how things work out but sadly for George Sherman, his wife no longer wants to farm so she leaves George and the farm taking the children with her. Over the years, George and Allen have become really good friends. With Allen's loss of Roany, they decide that maybe they should do the field work together. George has two tractors and a large farm truck, as well as a hay baler. They thought that with by combining labor and equipment being pooled together, it would work out well for George and Allen would not have to replace Roany.

I can honestly say I was not sorry that Roany was not going to be replaced. I have worked hard for many years and there is still work for me to do when I am worked singly. I still do cultivating, and I rake scatterings.

It was great to see how well Allen and George worked together. The field work was done more quickly and efficiently, and I felt that because of this, it took some stress away from Allen. I also felt that, because George doesn't get to see his children very much, it is good for George as Ferne treats him as one of the family. With his friendly easy-going manner, he had become very close to the children as well. He spends a lot of time at the farm house as his only companion in his house is a strange-looking old bird, called a Parrot. The parrot can only say two phrases: one is "Hey, George!" and the other is "Goddamn you, George!" How much quality time can he have with a bird that just yells and curses at him?

Ferne invites George to take many of his meals with the family. When he is asked, he always replies in the same way, "Well! Gawwd, I'm not very hungry!" At which point, he will load his plate full of a large amount of food and finish it all. He then goes into the living room, loosens the long laces of his work boots and stretches his long lanky frame with his belly bulging out on the couch and immediately falls asleep. The long laces dangling from George's boots are too much of a temptation for Kathy as she can't resist tying the laces together. George sleeps for fifteen or twenty minutes while Allen reads his newspaper. Then Gorge will wake up quickly from his nap saying, "Weeell, it's time to get going!" He never seems to notice that his boot laces are tied together until he goes stumbling across the floor or landing sprawled on the floor, sometimes both.

Waven Spaulding retired from the Vermont Marble Company and because he found he needed something to do, he went to working part-time for a carpenter in Pittsford, named Henry Alexander. Henry had built a new house and was selling his small farm. Because of this connection through Waven, Allen found out that Henry was also selling all his farm equipment. Because Waven knew Henry and told Allen that Henry maintained his equipment just the way that Allen did, he also thought Henry would give Allen a good deal on the machinery. Allen bought Henry's Case 200 Tractor which was big enough to run the power take-off driven baler that Allen also bought as well as a fairly new side-delivery rake. I was extremely excited the day that the equipment was delivered. The Case also had a front-mounted bucket loader and I knew this would certainly be a help when Allen had to move the huge manure pile in the spring. It also had a plow blade that would much improve the snow plowing job in the winter. I can now say, with no regrets, that the work team has been replaced. I think that although tractors and machinery have some limitations that horses don't have, I guess, they will work out all right.

With the new equipment added to the farm, it meant less need for equipment to be moved back and forth between Allen's and George's farms. Brud learned to operate the equipment really well and did most of the baling and George finally taught Brud how to double-clutch his old farm truck. He did this, probably, because he couldn't stand the sound of Brud grinding the gears.

By this time Ferne Marie and Kathy were working off the farm and as George and Brud were picking up hay and Allen was using his tractor to do another job, such as raking or mowing. Jan would be with Brud and George as they were picking up hay. George would often say to Jan, "You drive." Jan said, "But, I don't know how." So, George would shift the truck into first gear and hop out. Jan would say, "What do I do now!" George would say, "Weeell, Gawwd, just steer." So away she went steering the big awkward truck across the field.

One day as George was using his little tractor to pull the rake. The hay had dried nicely and Brud was already baling with George's big tractor. George had a strange habit of filling a little bowl full of tobacco. The bowl had a funny little stick attached to the bottom of the bowl and he would put the stick in his mouth and then light the tobacco on fire. Then, he would suck smoke through the stick and blow huge plumes of smoke into the air. He would suck on the stick until he burned all the tobacco, I guess.

On this particular day as George was raking, he was smoking his pipe as he called it. After he burned all the tobacco, George banged out his pipe on the side of his tractor and kept on raking. With a warm summer breeze on George's back, the sparks from the burned tobacco caught the windrow of hay on fire. Brud looked up from baling to notice the fire catching up with George as he raked. Brud shut down the baler and alerted George of the fire following along behind him. Brud helped George separate the burning windrow of hay from the rake and then the two of them stomped out the fire with their "Big Feet".

It was a good thing that Allen was able to get another tractor and equipment as George did not farm very long after his wife, Wilma, left. I feel, myself, that a farm really needs a family to make it work and probably a really good work horse, if I do say so myself. I imagine it was a big lonely old house with nothing but an ugly old parrot that squawked and cursed at George.

Wow! What a day, it has been! As soon as morning chores were done, Allen and Ferne have been hurrying to get the oats and grass seed in before it rains. I marvel at how the two of them work together. Allen's tractor is pulling the seeder to plant oats and grass seed. He is using the Case and Ferne is using the little grey tractor to boat in the oats. With her tongue folded between her teeth, she follows along behind Allen.

After all the chores have been finished and the milking has been done, the family has had supper. Dusk is just settling into the valley, causing lights to come on in the house. A light rain has started to fall, dampening the earth and seeping down to the new sown seeds. I am feeling tired as darkness settles in.

Till the Soil,
Plant a Seed
In Farming,
there is only
The Beginning.

In Spirit
From the Oak Tree

Allen has finished milking but there is no time for supper now. Allen has a piece of hay that is dry. It is definitely going to rain soon, but maybe, just maybe, with a little luck, they can beat the rain and get the hay in the barn before it got wet.

Ferne and Brud are just hitching the wagon to the little grey tractor as Brud's wife, Bobbie, and the two girls, Vanessa and Linnea, come into the yard. They climb on the wagon and head for the meadow south of the barn.

Allen is already baling. He now has a new Ford tractor and baler. He sold his Case tractor and baler, knowing he needed to upgrade.

When they get to the meadow, Ferne stays on the wagon, Bobbie drives the grey tractor and the girls ask, "But, what can we do?" Ferne says, "Well, you can make roads." Ferne shows them the line of bales that they can roll back so that Bobbie can drive through and the hay can be loaded from both sides of the wagon. They had just started loading when Kathy and her husband, Bob Smith, come into the yard. Their two children, Cindy and Lon, are with them and right after they arrive, here comes Ferne Marie and her husband, Steve Wright, and their children, Lisa, Vicki and Christie.

They all come running to the field. Ferne Marie is trailing along behind. She will not be able to handle bales as she is carrying Stephanie in her arms. Stephanie is only a little over five months old but Ferne Marie knows that she wants to be there with the rest of the family.

Ferne gets down off the wagon and Brud takes over the job of loading the wagon. With such a big crew to make roads and roll bales in toward the wagon, they will need Ferne to direct them.

Load after load, the field is quickly cleared and as Allen is covering the baler and putting his tractor in the garage, the last load is just coming to the barn. At this very moment another car comes into the farm yard. It is Jan and her husband, John Bork. They have driven up all the way from Virginia. She immediately takes her place by Allen's side as they walk up to the hay barn. Scampering by her side is the strangest little creature, I have ever seen. It sort of looks like a long-bodied woodchuck with long hair and long ears. It is actually a dog. His name is Tigger. It's a good thing he is a southern dog, it doesn't look like he could travel in the snow with those short legs. He probably even barks with a southern drawl.

As the men are unloading the last load of hay, Ferne is outside of the hay barn with all her grandchildren huddled around her. She has Stephanie in her arms and bends down and picks a four-leaf clover from the grassy lawn. She is always finding them and holds it up and seems to be staring and smiling at the Oak tree. One of the grandchildren asks, "What is it Grandma?" Ferne replies, "Oh! It's Dick! He was a big beautiful work horse. He is a member of the family. He is always there whenever you need him, especially when there is work to be done. If you look hard enough and think hard enough, you will see him.
Thank you, Dick!"

Acknowledgment

In my mind, I struggled with this part of the book for a long time as I thought I had no written sources to acknowledge. I thought how could this be? Where did it all come from? It occurred to me that it is all from memory; and those I must give credit to many of you.

First to a special valley farm, the likes of which you will probably never see. It is a place where a boy could grow up to be a young man and be allowed to explore his own odd curiosities.

Credit must be given to my parents whose teachings and examples are evident throughout Dick's story.

At this time, another word comes to me, a wonderful and awesome word that means so much to all of us: "Encouragement". It all started many years ago when I was in the fourth grade at Florence School. A special teacher, Stella Daily, said to me after I had written a story for her. She said, "Never stop writing, you have a special gift". I, with my natural curiosity; wondered what the gift she had for me was? I waited the rest of the year and no gift. So, after being patient for so long, "Mrs. Daily, please where is the gift?"

Thanks, and credit to my sisters for your encouragement. We made these memories together, I only put them to words. You inspire me always for the people that you are, and I love you for that. And yes, I do apologize for you girls not getting to do a lot of the outside fun stuff as I did, but I don't regret it.

Thank you and credit to my daughter, whose encouragement began this whole thing and who helped me throughout, from first word to last. And thank you to my other daughter, Vanessa, who has encouraged me and whose own gift of artistic talent is evident throughout.

Thanks to my grandsons whose evident curiosities and sense of adventure brought back memories of my own.

Credit to my wife, Bobbie, for patience, patience, patience as well as constant encouragement. Thanks for her ideas and help. She came up with the great title and thanks for putting up with my rambling mind and still boyish curiosities and who knows maybe someday I'll remember where the light switches are.

Thanks to all my friends and relatives who have heard about this book and encouraged me, especially Bob Snow, although he does not know it, who helped Bobbie with the title. I appreciate you all. Many of you will recognize yourselves and I hope you will be pleased with the result.

Thanks to Mrs. Miller, you know who you are, and still has a Yankee Rake!

Thanks also to Sonny; there is nothing quite like "Old Friends".

I must lastly acknowledge those of whom have contributed so much to this book and to my life. The animals: I struggle in my own feeble attempts to learn from you, wonderful creatures. I must really pay attention to you and listen with my heart?

Thanks to DICK, whose spirit still speaks to me!